Chetan Bhagat lives in Hong Kong and works in investment banking. He is marr *Night at the Call Centre* is a be to be published around the wo

Find out more on: www.che

One Night at the Call Centre

Chetan Bhagat

BLACK SWAN

ONE NIGHT AT THE CALL CENTRE
A BLACK SWAN BOOK : 9780552773867

First publication in Great Britain
First published by **Rupa . Co**, India, 2005

PRINTING HISTORY
Black Swan edition published 2007

3 5 7 9 10 8 6 4

Set in 12/15 pt Minion by
Falcon Oast Graphic Art Ltd.

Black Swan Books are published by Transworld Publishers,
61–63 Uxbridge Road, London W5 5SA,
a division of The Random House Group Ltd.

www.rbooks.co.uk

Addresses for companies within
The Random House Group Limited can be found at:
www.randomhouse.co.uk/offices.htm

The Random House Group Limited Reg. No. 954009

A CIP catalogue record for this book
is available from the British Library

The Random House Group Limited supports The Forest Stewardship
Council® (FSC®), the leading international forest-certification organisation.
Our books carrying the FSC label are printed on FSC®-certified paper.
FSC is the only forest-certification scheme supported by the leading
environmental organisations, including Greenpeace. Our
paper procurement policy can be found at
www.randomhouse.co.uk/environment

MIX
Paper from
responsible sources
FSC® C016897

Printed and bound in Great Britain by Clays Ltd, St Ives PLC

*To my twin baby boys
and the wonderful woman
who created them**

*with a little bit of help from me

Before you begin this book, I have a small request. Right here, note down three things that

    i) you fear
    ii) make you angry and
    iii) you don't like about yourself

Be honest, and say something meaningful to you.

Don't think too much about why I am asking you to do this. Just do it.

One thing I fear:

_____

One thing that makes me angry:

_____

One thing I do not like about myself:

_____

Okay, now forget about this exercise and enjoy the story.

Have you done it?

If you haven't, please do it. You will enjoy this book a lot more.

If you have, then thanks. And sorry I doubted you.

    Now, please forget about the exercise, or that I doubted you, and enjoy the story.

Prologue

THE NIGHT TRAIN FROM KANPUR TO DELHI *was the most memorable journey of my life. Firstly, it gave me the idea for my book. And second, it is not every day you sit in an empty compartment and a young, pretty girl walks in.*

Yes, you see it in the movies, you hear about it from friends' friends, but it never happens to you. When I was younger, I used to look at the names on the reservation chart stuck outside my train bogie to check out all the female passengers near my seat – F-17 to F-25 is what I'd look for most – yet it never happened. In most cases I shared my compartment with talkative aunties, snoring men and wailing infants.

But this night was different. Firstly, my compartment was empty: this new summer train had only just started running and nobody knew about it. Second, I was unable to sleep.

I had been to the Indian Institute of Technology in Kanpur to give a talk. Before leaving, I sat in the canteen chatting with the students and drank four cups of coffee, which no doubt led to my eight hours of insomnia alone in my compartment. I had no magazines or books to read and could hardly see anything out of the window in the darkness. I prepared myself for a dull and silent night.

She walked in five minutes after the train had left the station. She opened the curtains of my enclosure and looked around puzzled.

'Is this coach A4, seat 63E?' she asked.

The yellow light bulb in my compartment was a moody one. It flickered as I looked up at her.

'Huh?' I said. It was difficult to withdraw from the gaze of her eyes.

'Actually it is. My seat is right in front of you,' she answered her own question and heaved her heavy suitcase onto the upper berth. She sat down opposite me and heaved a sigh of relief.

'I got into the wrong coach. Luckily the bogies are connected,' she said, adjusting her countless ringlets. I looked at her from the corner of my eye. She was young, perhaps early to mid-twenties, and her waist-length hair had a life of its own: a strand kept falling onto her forehead. I couldn't yet see her face in the bad light, but I could tell one thing – she was pretty. And her eyes – once you looked into them, you couldn't turn away. I kept my gaze down.

She rearranged stuff in her handbag while I looked out of the window. It was completely dark.

'So, this is a pretty empty train,' she said after ten minutes.

'Yes,' I said. 'It's the new holiday special. They've just started it without really announcing it.'

'No wonder. Otherwise, trains are always full at this time.'

'It will fill up. Don't worry. Just give it a few days,' I said and leaned forward. 'Hi. I am Chetan, by the way, Chetan Bhagat.'

'Hi,' she said and looked at me for a few seconds. 'Chetan . . . your name sounds familiar.'

Now this was cool. It meant she had heard of my first book. I'm rarely recognized, and never by a girl on a night train.

'You might have heard of my book, Five Point Someone. I'm the author,' I said.

'Oh yes,' she said and paused. 'Oh yes, of course. I've read your book. About the three underperformers and the professor's daughter, right?' she said.

'Yes. So, did you like it?'

'It was all right.'

I was taken aback. I could have done with a little more of a compliment here.

'Just all right?' I said, fishing a bit too obviously.

'Well . . .' she said, and paused.

'Well what?' I said after ten seconds.

'Well, yeah, just all right. An OK-OK type of book,' she said.

I kept quiet. She noticed the expression of mild dis-appointment on my face.

'Anyway, nice to meet you, Chetan. Where are you coming from? IIT Kanpur?'

'Yes,' I said, my voice less friendly than a few moments before. 'I had to give a talk there.'

'Oh really? About what?'

'About my book – you know, the OK-OK type one. Some people do want to hear about it,' I said, using a sweet tone to coat my sarcasm.

'Interesting,' she said and went quiet again.

I was quiet too. I didn't want to speak to her any more. I wanted my empty compartment back.

The flickering yellow light above was irritating me. I wondered if I should just turn it off, but it was still not that late.

'What's the next station? Is it a non-stop train?' she asked after five minutes, obviously to make conversation.

'I don't know,' I said and turned to look out of the window again, even though I couldn't see anything in the darkness.

'Is everything OK?' she asked softly.

'Yes, why?' I said.

'Nothing. You're upset about what I said about your book, aren't you?'

'Not really,' I said.

She laughed. I looked at her. Her smile was as arresting as her eyes. I knew she was laughing at me, but I wanted her to keep smiling. I dragged my eyes away again.

'Listen. I know your book did well. You are a sort of youth writer and everything. But at one level . . .'

'What?' I said.

'At one level, you are hardly a youth writer.'

I looked at her for a few seconds. Her magnetic eyes had a soft but insistent gaze.

'I thought I wrote a book about college kids. Isn't that youth?' I said.

'Yeah, right. So you wrote a book on the Indian Institute of Technology, an elite place where few people get to go. You think that represents the youth?' she asked and took out a box of mints from her bag. She offered me one, but I declined.

'So what are you trying to say? I had to start somewhere, so I wrote about my college experiences. And the story isn't all about IIT. It could have happened anywhere. Is that why you're trashing my book?'

'I'm not trashing it. I'm just saying it hardly represents Indian youth,' she said and shut the box of mints.

'Oh really—' I began, but was interrupted by noise as the train passed over a long bridge.

We didn't speak for the next three minutes, until the train had got back onto a smoother track.

'So what represents youth exactly?' I said.

'I don't know. You're the writer. You figure it out,' she said, and brushed aside a few curls that had fallen over her forehead.

'That's not fair,' I said. I sounded like a five-year-old throwing a tantrum. She saw me grumbling to myself and smiled. A few seconds later, she spoke again.

'Are you going to write another book?' she said.

'I'll try to.'

'So what's it going to be about this time? The Indian Institute of Medicine?' she asked.

'No.'

'Why not?'

'Because it doesn't represent the country's youth.'

She started laughing.

'See, I am taking feedback. And now you're laughing at me,' I said.

'No, no,' she said. 'I'm not laughing at you. Can you stop being so over-sensitive?'

'I am not over-sensitive,' I said and turned my face away.

'Well, now, let me explain. The whole IIT thing is cool and everything, but what does it mean in the broader sense? What is it all about?' she said.

'Well, what is it about?'

'If you want to write about youth, shouldn't you talk about young people who face real challenges?'

'Like who?'

'Just look around you. Who are the biggest group of young people facing a challenge in modern India?'

'I don't know. Students?'

'No, Mr Writer. Get away from the student campus of your first book now. Anything else you see that you find strange and interesting? I mean, what is the subject of your second novel?'

I turned to look at her carefully for the first time. Maybe it was the time of night, but I kid you not, she was one of the most beautiful women I had ever seen. Everything about her was perfect. Her face was like a child's and she wore a little

14

bindi, which was hard to focus on because her eyes got in the way.

I tried to concentrate on her question.

'Second novel? I haven't thought of a subject yet,' I said.

'Really? Don't you have any ideas?'

'I do. But nothing certain.'

'Inte . . . resting,' she drawled. 'Well, just bask in the success of your first book, then.'

We kept quiet for the next half an hour. I took out the contents of my overnight bag and rearranged them for no particular reason. I wondered if it even made sense to change into night wear. I wasn't going to fall asleep. Another train noisily trundled past us in the opposite direction, leaving us behind in even greater silence.

'I might have a story idea for you,' she said, startling me.

'Huh?' I was wary of what she was going to say, for no matter what her idea was, I had to appear interested.

'What is it?'

'It's a story about a call centre.'

'Really?' I said. 'Call centres as in "business process outsourcing centres?"'

'Yes. Do you know anything about them?'

I thought about it. I did know about call centres, mostly from my cousins who worked in one.

'Yes, I know something,' I said. 'Some 300,000 people work in the industry. They help US and European companies in the sales, service and maintenance of their operations. Usually younger people work there in night shifts. Quite interesting, actually.'

'Just interesting? Have you ever thought of what they all have to face?' she asked, her voice turning firm again.

'Uh, not really,' I said.

'Why? Aren't they the youth? Don't you want to write about them?' she was almost scolding me.

'Listen, let's not start arguing again.'

'I'm not arguing. I told you that I have a call-centre story for you.'

I looked at my watch. It was 12.30 a.m. A story would not be such a bad idea to kill time.

'Let's hear it, then,' I said.

'I'll tell you, but I have a condition,' she said.

Condition? I was intrigued. 'What? That I don't tell it to anyone else?' I asked.

'No. Just the opposite, in fact. You have to promise me to use it for your second book.'

'What?' I said, almost falling off my seat. 'Are you kidding? I can't promise that.'

'It's up to you,' she said and turned silent.

I waited for ten seconds. She did not speak.

'Can't I decide after you've told me the story?' I asked. 'If it's interesting, I may do it. But how can I decide without hearing it first?'

'No. This is not about choice. If I tell you, you have to use it,' she said.

'For a whole book . . . ?' I asked again.

'Yes. As if it's your own story. I'll give you the contacts of the people in the story. You can meet them, do your research, whatever it takes, but make it your second book.'

'Well, then, I think it's better if you don't tell me,' I said.

'OK,' she said and turned quiet again. She got up to spread a bed sheet on her berth, and then arranged her pillow and blanket.

I checked my watch again. It was 1:00 a.m. and I was still wide awake. This was a non-stop train and there were no stations to look forward to until Delhi in the morning. She switched off the flickering yellow light. Now the only light in the compartment was an eerie blue one; I couldn't figure out where the bulb was. It felt strange, as though we were the only two people in the universe.

As she was sliding under her blanket, I asked, 'What is the story about? At least tell me a little bit more.'

'Will you do it then?'

I shrugged in the semi-darkness. 'Can't say. Don't tell me the story yet, just tell me what it's about.'

She nodded and sat up. Folding her legs beneath her, she began talking.

'All right,' she said, 'it's a story about six people in a call centre on one night.'

'Just one night? Like this one?' I interrupted.

'Yes, one night.'

'Are you sure that could fill a whole book? I mean, what's so special about this night?'

She heaved a sigh and took a sip from her bottle of mineral water.

'You see,' she said, 'it wasn't like any other night. It was the night of the phone call.'

'What?' I said and burst out laughing. 'So a call centre gets a phone call. That's the special part?'

She did not smile back. She waited for me to stop laughing and then continued as if I hadn't said anything. 'You see, it wasn't an ordinary phone call. It was the night . . . it was the night there was a phone call from God.'

Her words made me spring to attention.

'What?'

'You heard me. That night there was a phone call from God,' she said.

'What exactly are you talking about?'

'I'm not telling you any more. Now you know what it's about, if you want to hear the story, you know my condition.'

'It's a tough condition,' I said.

'I know. It's up to you,' she said and lifted her blanket again. She lay down and closed her eyes.

Six people. One night. Call centre. Call from God. The phrases kept repeating themselves in my head as another hour passed. At 2:00 a.m. she woke up to have a sip of water.

'Not sleeping?' she asked, her eyes only half open.

Maybe there was a voltage problem, but this time even the blue light in the compartment started flickering.

'No, I'm not sleepy at all,' I said.

'OK, goodnight anyway,' she said, and lay down again.

'Listen,' I said. 'Get up.'

'Huh?' she said, rubbing her eyes. 'Why?'

'Tell me the story,' I said.

'So you'll write it?'

'Yes,' I said, with a slight hesitation.

'Good,' she said, and sat up again. She was back in her cross-legged position.

For the rest of the night, she told me the story that begins on the next page. I chose to tell the story through Shyam's eyes because, after I met him, I realized he was the most similar to me as a person. The rest of the people, and what happened that night, well, I'll let Shyam tell you.

Chapter 1

8.31 p.m.

I WAS SPLASHING MY HANDS HELPLESSLY IN THE SEA. I can't even swim in a pond, let alone in the Indian Ocean. While I was in the water, my boss Bakshi was in a boat next to me. He was pushing my head down in the water. I saw Priyanka drifting away in a lifeboat. I screamed as Bakshi used both his hands to keep my head submerged. Salt water was filling my mouth and nostrils when I heard loud beeps in the distance.

My nightmare ended as my cellphone alarm rang hard in my left ear and I woke up to its 'Last Christmas' ring tone. The ring tone was a gift from Shefali, my new semi-girlfriend. I squinted through a half-shut eye to see 8:32 p.m. surrounded by little bells flashing on the screen.

'Damn,' I said and jumped out of bed.

I would have loved to analyse my dream and its significance in my insignificant life, but I had to get dressed for work.

'Man, the Qualis will be here in twenty minutes,' I thought, digging matter out of my eye. Qualis was the make of car that picked us all up individually and drove us together to the centre. I was still tired, but afraid of staying in bed any longer in case I was late. Besides, there was a serious risk of Bakshi making a comeback in my dreams.

By the way, I am Shyam Mehra, or Sam Marcy as they call me at my workplace, the Connexions call centre in Gurgaon. American tongues have trouble saying my real name and prefer Sam. If you want, you can give me another name, too. I really don't care.

Anyway, I'm a call-centre agent. There are hundreds of thousands, probably millions of agents like me. But this total pain-in-the neck author chose me, of all the agents in the country. He met me and told me to help him with his second book. In fact, he pretty much wanted me to write the book for him. I declined, saying I can't even write my own CV, so there was no way I could write a whole book. I explained to him how my promotion to the position of team leader had been postponed for one year because my manager Bakshi had told me I don't have the 'required skills set' yet. In my review, Bakshi wrote that I was 'not a go-getter'. I don't even know what 'go-getter' means, so I guess I'm definitely not one.

But this author said he didn't care. He had promised someone he'd write this story so I'd better cooperate or he would keep on pestering me. I tried my best to wriggle out of it, but he wouldn't let go. I finally relented and that's why I'm stuck with this assignment, while you are stuck with me.

I also want to give you one more warning. My English is not that great – actually, nothing about me is great. So, if you're looking for something sophisticated and highbrow, then I suggest you read another book with plenty of long words. I know only one big word: 'management'. But we'll get that later. I told the author about my limited English. However, he said big emotions don't come from big words, so I had no choice but to do the job. I hate authors.

Now let's get back to the story. If you remember, I had just woken up.

There was a noise in the living room. Some relatives were in town to attend a family wedding. My neighbour was getting married to his cousin ... er, sorry, I'm a bit groggy, my cousin was getting married to his neighbour. But I had to work, so I couldn't go to the wedding. It didn't matter, though, all marriages are the same, more or less.

I reached the bathroom still half-asleep. It was occupied.

The bathroom door was open. I saw five of my aunts scrambling to get a few square inches of the washbasin mirror. One aunt was cursing her daughter for leaving the matching bindis at home. Another aunt had lost the little screw of her gold earring and was flipping out.

'It's pure gold, where is it?' she screamed into my face.

'Has the maid stolen it?' Like the maid has nothing better to do than steal one tiny screw. Wouldn't she steal the whole set? I thought.

'Auntie, can I use the bathroom for five minutes? I need to get ready for the office,' I said.

'Oh hello, Shyam. Woke up finally?' my mother's sister said. 'Office? Aren't you coming to the wedding?'

'No, I have to work. Can I have the bath—'

'Look how big Shyam has become,' my maternal aunt said. 'We need to find a girl for him soon.'

Everyone burst into giggles. It was their biggest joke of the day.

'Can I please—' I said.

'Shyam, leave the ladies alone,' one of my older cousins interrupted. 'What are you doing here with the women? We are already late for the wedding.'

'But I have to go to work. I need to get dressed,' I protested, trying to elbow my way to the bathroom tap.

'You work in a call centre, don't you?' my cousin said.

'Yes.'

'Your work is all on the phone. Why do you need to dress up? Who's going to see you?'

I didn't answer.

'Use the kitchen sink,' an aunt suggested and handed me my toothbrush.

I gave them all a dirty look. Nobody noticed. I passed by the living room on my way to the kitchen. The uncles were outside, on their second whiskey and soda. One uncle said something about how it would be better if my father were still alive and around this evening.

I reached the kitchen. The floor was so cold I felt like I'd stepped on an ice tray. I realized I had forgotten the soap. I went back but the bathroom door was bolted. There was no hot water in the kitchen, so my face froze as I washed it with cold water. Winter in Delhi is a bitch. I brushed my teeth and used the steel plates as a mirror to comb my hair. Shyam had turned into Sam and Sam's day had just begun.

I was hungry, but there was nothing to eat in the house. They'd be getting food at the wedding, so my mother had felt there was no need to cook at home.

The Qualis horn screamed at 8:55 p.m.

As I was about to leave, I realized I had forgotten my ID. I went to my room, but couldn't find it. I tried to find my mother instead. She was in her bedroom, lost among aunties, saris and jewellery sets. She and my aunts were comparing whose set was heaviest. Usually the heaviest aunt had the heaviest set.

'Mum, have you seen my ID?' I said. Everyone ignored me. I went back to my room as the Qualis honked for the fourth time.

'Damn, there it is,' I said reaching under my bed. I pulled it out by its strap and strung it around my neck.

I waved a goodbye to everyone, but no one acknowledged me. It wasn't surprising. My cousins are all on their way to becoming doctors or engineers. You could say I am the black sheep of my family. In fact, the only reason people even talk to me is because I have a job and get a salary at the end of the month. You see, I used to work in the website department of an ad agency before this call-centre job. However, the ad agency paid really badly, and all the people there were pseudos, more interested in office politics than websites. I left and all hell broke loose at home. That's when I became the black sheep. I saved myself by joining Connexions. With money in your wallet the world gives you some respect and lets you breathe. Connexions was also the natural choice for me as Priyanka worked there. Of course, that reason was no longer relevant.

My aunt finally found the gold screw trapped in her fake-hair bun.

The Qualis's horn screamed again.

'I'm coming,' I shouted as I ran out of the house.

Chapter 2

9.05 p.m.

'WHAT, SAHIB. LATE AGAIN?' the driver said as I took the front seat.

'Sorry, sorry. Shall we go to Military Uncle's place first?' I panted to the driver.

'Yes,' he replied, looking at his watch.

'Can we get to the call centre by 10:00 p.m.? I have to meet someone before their shift ends,' I said.

'Depends if your colleagues are on time,' the driver replied laconically. 'Anyway, let's pick up the old man first.'

Military Uncle hates it if we are late. I prepared myself for some dirty looks. His tough manner comes from his days in the Army, from which he retired a few years ago. At fifty plus he is the oldest person in the call centre. I don't know him well, and I won't talk about him much, but I do know that he used to live with his son and daughter-in-law before he moved out – for which read thrown out – to be on his own. The pension was meagre, and he tried to supplement his income by working in the call centre. However, he hates to talk and is not a voice agent. He sits on the solitary online chat and email station. Even though he sits in our room, his desk is at a far corner near the fax machine. He rarely speaks more than three words at a time. Most of his interactions with us are limited to giving us condescending 'you young people' glances.

The Qualis stopped outside Uncle's house. He was waiting at the entrance.

'You're late,' Uncle said, looking at the driver.

Without answering, the driver got out to open the Qualis's back door. Uncle climbed in, ignored the middle seat and sat at the back. He probably wanted to sit as far away from me as possible.

Uncle gave me an it-must-be-your-fault look. I looked away. The driver took a U-turn to go to Radhika's house.

One of the unique features about my team is that we not only work together, we also share the same Qualis. Through a bit of route planning and recruitment of an agreeable driver, we ensured that my Western Appliances Strategic Group all came and left together. There are six of us: Military Uncle, Radhika, Esha, Vroom, Priyanka and me.

The Qualis moved on to Radhika Jha, or agent Regina Jones's house. As usual, Radhika was late.

'Radhika madam is too much,' the driver said, holding the horn down. I looked at my watch anxiously.

Six minutes later Radhika came running towards us, clutching the ends of her maroon shawl in her right hand.

'Sorry, sorry sorry . . .' she said a dozen times before we could say anything.

'What?' I asked her as the Qualis moved on again.

'Nothing. I was making almond milk for my mother-in-law and it took longer than I thought to crush the almonds,' she said, leaning back exhausted in her seat in the middle.

'Ask Mother-in-law to make her own milk,' I suggested.

'C'mon Shyam,' she said, 'she's so old, it's the least I can do, especially when her son isn't here.'

'Yeah, right,' I shrugged. 'Just that and cooking three meals a day and household chores and working all night and . . .'

'Shh,' she said, 'don't talk about it. Any news on the call centre? I'm nervous.'

'Nothing new from what Vroom told me. We have no new orders, call volumes are at an all-time low – Connexions is doomed. It's just a question of when,' I said.

'Really?' her eyes widened.

It was true. You might have heard of those swanky, new-age call centres where everything is hunky-dory, there are plenty of clients and agents get aromatherapy massages. Well, Connexions was not one of them. We are sustained by our one and only client, Western Computers and Appliances, and even their call flow had dwindled.

Rumours that the call centre would collapse floated around every day.

'You think Connexions will close down? Like, for ever?' Radhika asked.

Uncle raised an eyebrow to look at us, but soon went back to brooding by himself in the back seat. I sometimes wished he would say more, but I guess it's better for people to shut up rather than say something nasty.

'That or they'll make some major job cuts. Ask Vroom,' I said.

The Qualis moved painfully slowly. It was a heavy wedding day in Delhi and on every street there was a procession. We edged forward as the driver dodged several fat grooms on their over-burdened horses. I checked the time again. Shefali would do some serious sulking today.

'I need this job. Anuj and I need to save,' Radhika said, more to herself. Anuj was Radhika's husband. She married him three years ago after a whirlwind courtship in college and now lived in a joint family with Anuj's ultra-traditional parents. It was tough for daddy's only girl, but it's amazing what people do for love.

The driver drove to Esha Singh's (or agent Eliza Singer's) place next. She was already outside her house. The driver kept the Qualis's ignition on as he opened the back door.

As Esha got in the smell of expensive perfume filled the vehicle. She sat next to Radhika in the middle row and removed her suede jacket.

'Mmm, nice. What is it?' Radhika said.

'You noticed.' Esha was pleased. 'Escape by Calvin Klein.' She bent her knees and adjusted the tassels at the end of her long, dark brown skirt.

'Oooh. Have you been shopping?' Radhika said.

'Call it a momentary lapse of reason,' Esha said.

The driver finally reached a stretch of empty road and accelerated the Qualis.

I looked at Esha again. Her dress sense is impeccable. Esha dresses better on an average day than I have ever done. Her sleeveless coffee-coloured top contrasted perfectly with her skirt and she wore chunky brown earrings that looked edible and lipstick as thick as cocoa. She looked as if she'd just kissed a bowl of chocolate sauce. Her eyes had at least one of these things – mascara, eye-liner and/or eyeshadow. I can't tell, but Priyanka tells me they are all different things.

'The Lakme fashion week is in four months. My agent is trying to get me an assignment,' Esha said to Radhika.

Esha wants to become a model. She's hot, at least according to people at the call centre. Two months ago, some agents in the Western Computers bay conducted a stupid poll around the office. People vote for various titles, like who is hot, who is handsome and who is pretty. Esha won the title of the 'hottest chick at Connexions'. She was very dismissive of the poll results, but from that day on there's been just a tiny hint of vanity about her. Otherwise, though, she's fine. She moved to Delhi from Chandigarh a year ago, against her parents' wishes. The call-centre job gives her a regular income, but during the day she approaches agencies and tries to get modelling assignments. She's taken part in some low-key fashion shows in West Delhi, but apart from that and the hottest-chick-in-house title, nothing big has come her way so far. Priyanka once told me – making me swear that I'd keep it to myself – that she thought Esha would never make it as a real model. 'Esha is too short and too small-town to be a real model', is what she said exactly. But Priyanka doesn't know crap. Esha is five-five, only two inches shorter than me (and one inch taller in her heels). I think that's pretty tall for a girl. And the whole 'small-town' thing, that just went over my head. Esha is only twenty-two, give her a chance. And Chandigarh is not a small town, it's a union territory and the administrative capital of two states. But Priyanka's geography is crap as well. I think Priyanka is just jealous. All non-hot girls are jealous of the hot ones. Priyanka wasn't even considered for the hottest chick award. Priyanka is nice looking, and she did get a nomination for the 'call-centre cutie award', which I think is just because of her dimples and cute round face, but she didn't win. Some girl in HR won that.

We had to pick up Vroom next; his real name is Varun Malhotra (or agent Victor Mell), but everyone calls him Vroom because of his love for anything on wheels.

The Qualis turned into Vroom's road to find him sitting on his bike, waiting for us.

'What's the bike for?' I said, craning out of the window.

'I'm going on my own,' Vroom said, adjusting his leather gloves. He wore black jeans and trekking shoes that made his thin legs look extra long. His dark blue sweatshirt had the Ferrari horse logo on it.

'Are you crazy?' I said. 'It's so cold. Get in, we're late already.'

Dragging the bike he came and stood next to me.

'No, I feel stressed today. I need to get it out of my system with a fast ride.' He was standing right beside me and only I could hear him.

'What happened?'

'Nothing. Dad called. He argued with Mum for two hours. Why did they even separate? They can't live without screaming their guts out at each other.'

'It's OK, man. Not your problem,' I said.

Vroom's dad was a businessman who parted from his wife two years ago. He preferred shagging his secretary to being with his family, so Vroom and his mother now lived without him.

'I couldn't sleep at all. Just lay in bed all day and now I feel sick. I need to get some energy back,' Vroom said as he straddled his bike.

'But it's freezing . . .' I began.

'What's going on, Shyam sahib?' the driver asked. I turned around. The driver looked at me with a puzzled expression and I shrugged my shoulders.

'He's going on his bike,' I told everyone.

'Come with me,' Vroom said to me. 'I'll get us there in half the time.'

'No thanks,' I said, and folded my hands. I wasn't leaving the cosy Qualis to get on a bike.

33

Vroom bent over to greet the driver.

'Hello, driver sahib,' Vroom said.

'Vroom sahib, don't you like my Qualis?' the driver said.

'No, Driver *ji*, I'm in the mood for riding my motorbike,' Vroom said, and offered a pack of cigarettes to the driver. The driver took one and Vroom signalled for him to keep the pack.

'Drive the Qualis if you want,' the driver said and lifted his hands off the steering wheel.

'No. Maybe later. Right now I need to fly.'

'Hey, Vroom. Any news on Connexions? Anything happening?' Radhika asked, adjusting her hair.

Apart from the dark circles around her eyes, you could say Radhika was pretty. She has high cheekbones and her fair skin goes well with her wispy eyebrows and soot-black eyes. She wore a plain mustard sari, as saris were all she was allowed to wear in her in-laws' house. It was different apparel from the jeans and skirts Radhika preferred before her marriage.

'No updates. Will dig for stuff today but I think Bakshi will screw us all. Hey, Shyam, the website manual is all done by the way. I emailed it to the office,' Vroom said and started his bike.

'Cool, finally. Let's send it in today,' I said, perking up.

We left Vroom and moved to our last pickup at Priyanka's place. It was 9:30 p.m., still an hour away from our shift. However, I was worried as Shefali finished her shift and left by 10:20.

Fortunately, Priyanka was standing at her pick-up point when we reached her place.

'Hi,' Priyanka said as she entered the Qualis and sat next to Esha in the middle row of seats. She carried a large, white plastic bag as well as her usual giant handbag.

'Hi,' everyone replied except me.

'I said hi, Shyam,' Priyanka said.

I pretended not to hear. It's strange, but ever since we broke up, I've found it difficult to talk to her, even though I must think about her thirty times a day.

I looked at her. She adjusted her dupatta around her neck. The forest green salwar kameez she was wearing was new, I noticed. The colours suited her light brown skin. I looked at her nose and the nostrils that flared up every time she was upset. I swear tiny flames appeared in them when she got angry.

'Shyam, I said hi,' she said again.

'Hi,' I said. I wondered if Bakshi would finally promote me after he saw my website manual tonight.

'Where's Vroom?' Priyanka said. She had to know everything all the time.

'Vroom is riding . . . vroom,' Esha said, making a motorbike noise.

'Nice perfume, Esha. Shopping again, eh?' Priyanka said and sniffed, puckering up her tiny nose.

'Escape, Calvin Klein,' Esha announced and struck a pose.

'Wow! Someone is going designer,' Priyanka said and both of them laughed. This is something I will never understand about her. Priyanka has bitched fifty times about Esha to me, yet when they are together they behave like long-lost sisters.

'Esha, big date coming?' Radhika said.

'No dates. I'm still so single. Suitable guys are an endangered species,' Esha said and all the girls laughed. It wasn't that funny if you ask me. I wished Vroom was in the Qualis too. He was the only person in my team I could claim as a friend. At twenty-two he was four years younger than me but I still found it easiest to talk to him. Radhika's household talk was too alien for me, Esha's modelling trip was also beyond me and Priyanka had been a lot more than a friend until recently. Four months ago, we broke up (Priyanka's version) or she dumped me (my version).

So I was trying to do what she wanted us to do – 'move on' – which was why I hung out with Shefali.

Beep Beep. Beep Beep.

Two pairs of loud beeps from my shirt pocket startled everyone.

'Who's that?' Priyanka said.

'It's my text,' I said and opened the new message.

```
Where r u my eddy teddy?
Come soon — curly wurly
```

It was Shefali. She was into cheesy nicknames these days. I replied to the text:

```
Qualis stuck in traffic
Will b there soon
```

'Who's that?' Esha asked me.

'Nobody important,' I said.

'Shefali?' Radhika said.

'No,' I said and everybody looked at me.

'No,' I said again.

'Yes, it is. It's Shefali, isn't it?' Esha and Radhika said together and laughed.

'Why does Shefali always babytalk?' I heard Esha whisper to Radhika. More titters followed.

'Whatever,' I said and looked at my watch. The Qualis was still on the NH8 road, at the entrance to the concrete Delhi suburb of Gurgaon. We were ten minutes away from Connexions.

Cool, I'll meet Shefali by 10:10, I thought.

'Can we stop for a quick tea at Inderjeet? We'll still make it by 10:30,' Priyanka said. Inderjeet dhabha on NH8 was famous among truck drivers for its all-night tea and snacks.

'Won't we be late?' Radhika crinkled her forehead.

'Of course not. Driver *ji* saved us twenty minutes in the last stretch. Come, Driver *ji*, my treat,' Priyanka said.

'Good idea. It will keep me awake,' Esha said.

The driver slowed the Qualis near Inderjeet dhabha and parked it near the counter.

'Hey guys, do we have to stop? We're going to be late,' I protested against the chai chorus.

'We won't be late. Let's treat Driver *ji* for getting us here so fast,' Priyanka said and got out of the Qualis. She just has to do things I don't want to do.

'He wants to be with Shefali, dude,' Esha elbowed Radhika. They guffawed again. What's so damn funny, I wanted to ask.

'No, I just like to reach my shift a few minutes early,' I said and got out of the Qualis. Military Uncle and the driver followed us.

Inderjeet dhabha had *angithis* next to each table. I smelled hot paranthas, but did not order as it was so late. The driver arranged plastic chairs for us. Inderjeet's minions collected tea orders as per the various complicated rules laid down by the girls.

'No sugar in mine,' Esha said.

'Extra hot for me,' Radhika said.

'With cardamom for me,' Priyanka said.

When we were in college together, Priyanka used to make cardamom tea for me in her hostel room. Her taste in men might have changed, but obviously not her taste in beverages.

The tea arrived in three minutes.

'So what's the gossip?' Priyanka said as she cupped her hands around the glass for warmth. Apart from cardamom, Priyanka's favourite spice is gossip.

'No gossip. You tell us what's happening in *your* life,' Radhika said.

'I actually do have something to tell,' Priyanka said with a sly smile.

'What?' Radhika and Esha exclaimed together.

'I'll tell you when we get to the bay. It's big,' Priyanka said.

'Tell us now,' Esha said, poking Priyanka's shoulder.

'There's no time. Someone is in a desperate hurry,' Priyanka said, glancing meaningfully at me.

I turned away.

'OK, I have something to share too. But don't tell anyone,' Esha said.

'What?' Radhika said.

'See,' Esha said and stood up. She raised her top to expose a flat midriff, on which there was a newborn ring.

'Cool, check it out,' Priyanka said, 'someone's turning hip.'

Military Uncle stared as if in a state of shock. I suspect he was never young and was just born a straight forty-year-old.

'What's that? A navel ring?' Radhika asked.

Esha nodded and covered herself again.

'Did it hurt?' Radhika said.

'Oh yes,' Esha said. 'Imagine someone stapling your tummy hard.'

Esha's statement churned my stomach.

'Shall we go?' I said, gulping down my tea.

'Let's go, girls, or Mr Conscientious will get upset.' Priyanka suppressed a smirk. I hated her.

I went to the counter to pay the bill. Vroom was watching TV.

'Vroom?' I said.

'Hi. What are you guys doing here?' he said.

I told him about the girls' tea idea.

'I arrived twenty minutes ago, man,' Vroom said. He extinguished his cigarette and showed me the butt. 'This was my first.'

Vroom was trying to cut down to four cigarettes a night. However, with Bakshi in our life, it was impossible.

'Can you rush me to the call centre? Shefali will be leaving soon,' I said.

Vroom's eyes were transfixed by the TV set on Inderjeet dhabha's counter. The New Delhi news channel was on and Vroom is a sucker for it. He worked on a newspaper once and is generally into social and global issues and all that stuff. He thinks that just by watching the news you can change the world. That, by the way, is his trip.

'Let's go, man. Shefali will kill me.'

'Shefali. Oh, you mean Curly Wurly,' Vroom laughed.

'Shut up, man. She has to catch the Qualis after her shift. This is the only time I get with her.'

'Once you had Priyanka, and now you sink to Shefali levels,' Vroom said, and bent his elbow to rest his 6′ 2″ frame on the dhabha counter.

'What's wrong with Shefali?' I said, shuffling from one foot to the other.

'Nothing. It's just that it's nice to have a girlfriend with half a brain. Why are you wasting your time with her?'

'I'm weaning myself off Priyanka. I'm trying to move on,' I said and took a sweet from the candy jar at the counter.

'What happened to the re-proposal plan with Priyanka?' Vroom said.

'I've told you, not until I become team leader. Which should be soon – maybe tonight after we submit the website manual. Now can we please go?' I said.

'Yeah, right. Some hopes you live on,' Vroom said, but moved away from the counter.

I held on tight as Vroom zipped through NH8 at 120 km an hour. I closed my eyes and prayed Shefali wouldn't be angry, and that I would get there alive.

Beep Beep. Beep Beep. My mobile went off again.

```
Curly Wurly is sad
Eddy teddy is very bad
I leave in 10 min :(
```

I jumped off the bike as Vroom reached the call centre. The bike jerked forward and Vroom had to use both his legs to balance.

'Easy, man,' Vroom said in an irritated voice. 'Can you just let me park?'

'Sorry. I'm really late,' I said and ran inside.

Chapter 3

10.18 p.m.

'I'M NOT TALKING TO YOU,' Shefali said and started playing with one of her silver earrings. The ring-shaped earrings were so large they were almost bangles.

'Sorry, Shefali. My bay people held me up.' I stood next to her, leaning against her desk. She sat on her swivel chair and rotated it ninety degrees away from me to showcase her sulking. The dozens of workstations in her bay were empty as all the other agents had left.

'Whatever. I thought you were their team leader,' she said and pretended to work on her computer.

'I am not the team leader. I will be soon, but I'm not one yet,' I said.

'Why don't they make you team leader?' she turned to me and fluttered her eyeslashes. I hated this habit of hers.

'I don't know. Bakshi said he's trying, but I have to bring my leadership skills up to speed.'

'What is "up to speed"?' she said and opened her hand-bag.

'I don't know. Improve my skills, I guess.'

'So you guys don't have a team leader.'

'No. Bakshi says we have to manage without one. I help with supervisory stuff for now. But Bakshi told me I have strong future potential.'

'So why doesn't your team listen to you?'

'Who says they don't? Of course they do.'

'So why were you late?' she said, beginning her sentence with a 'so' for the third time.

'Shefali, come on, drop that,' I said, looking at my watch. 'How did your shift go?'

'It was OK. The team leader said call volumes have dropped for Western Computers. All customers are using the troubleshooting website now.'

'Cool. You do know who made that, don't you?'

'Yes, you and Vroom. But I don't think you should make a big deal out of it. The website has cost Connexions a lot of business.'

'But the website helps the customers, right?' I said.

'Shh. Don't talk about the website here. Some agents are very upset. Someone said they would cut people's jobs.'

'Really?'

'I don't know. Listen, why are you so unromantic? Is this how Eddy Teddy should talk to his Curly Wurly?'

I wanted to know more about what was going on at Connexions. Bakshi was super-secretive – all he said was that there were some confidential management priorities. I thought of asking Vroom to spy.

'Eddy Teddy?' Shefali repeated. I looked at her. If she stopped wearing Hello Kitty hairpins, she could be passably cute.

'Huh?'

'Are you listening to me?'

'Of course.'

'Did you like my gift?'

'What gift?'

'The ringtones. I gave you six ringtones. See, you don't even remember.'

'I do. See, I put "Last Christmas" as my tone,' I said and picked up my phone to play it. Vroom would probably have killed me if he'd heard it, but I had to for Shefali.

'So cute,' Shefali said and pinched my cheeks. 'So cute it sounds, my Eddy Teddy.'

'Shefali . . .'

'What?'

'Can you stop calling me that?'

'Why? Don't you like it?'

'Just call me Shyam.'

'Don't you like the name I gave you?' she said, her voice transcending from sad to tragic.

I kept quiet. You never tell women you don't like something they have done. However, they pick up on the silence.

'That means you don't like the ringtones either,' she said and her voice started to break.

44

'I do,' I said, fearing a round of crying. 'I love the ring tones.'

'And what about the name? You can choose another name if you want. I'm not like your other girlfriends,' she said and tiny tears appeared in her eyes. I looked at my watch. Three more minutes and time would heal everything, I thought. I took a deep breath. A hundred and eighty seconds and she would definitely have to leave. Sometimes counting seconds was a great way to kill time through a woman's tantrums.

'What kind of girlfriends?' I said.

'Like,' she sniffled, 'bossy girls who impose their way on you. Like you-know-who.'

'Who? What are you implying,' I said, my voice getting firmer. It was true; Priyanka could be bossy, but only if you didn't listen to her.

'Forget it. But will you give me a name if I stop crying?' Her sobs were at serious risk of transforming into a fully-fledged bawl.

'Yes,' I said. I'd rename the rest of her family if she stopped this drama.

'OK,' she said and became normal. 'Give me a name.'

I thought hard. Nothing came to mind.

'Sheffy? How about Sheffy?' I said finally.

'Nooo. I want something cuuuter,' she said. Shefali loves to drag out words.

'I can't think of anything cute right now. I have to work. Isn't your Qualis leaving soon, too?' I said.

She looked at her watch and stood up.

'Yes, I'd better leave now. Will you think of a name by tomorrow?' she said.

'I will, bye now.'

'Give me a kissie,' she said and tapped a finger on her cheek.

'What?'

'Kissie.'

'You mean a kiss? Yeah sure.' I gave her a peck on the cheek and turned around to return to my bay.

'Bye bye, Eddy Teddy,' her voice followed me.

Chapter 4

10.27 p.m.

THE OTHERS WERE ALREADY AT THE DESK when I got back from Shefali's bay.

Our bay's name is the Western Appliances Strategic Group or WASG. Unlike the other bay that troubleshoots for computer customers, we deal with customers of home appliances such as refrigerators, ovens and vacuum cleaners. Management calls us the strategic bay because we specialize in troublesome and painful customers. These 'strategic' customers call a lot and are too stupid to figure things out – actually the latter applies to a lot of callers.

We feel special, as we aren't part of the main computers bay. The main bay has over a thousand agents and handles the huge Western Computers account. While the calls are less weird there, they miss the privacy we enjoy in the WASG.

I took my seat at the long rectangular table. We have a

fixed seating arrangement: I sit next to Vroom, while Priyanka is opposite me; Esha is adjacent to Priyanka and Radhika sits next to Esha. The bay is open plan so we can all see each other and Military Uncle's chat station is at the corner of the room. At each of the other three corners there are, respectively, the restrooms, a conference room and a stationery supplies room.

However, no one apart from Uncle was at their seat when I sat down. Everyone had gathered around Priyanka.

'What's the news? Tell us now,' Esha was saying.

'OK, OK. But on one condition. It doesn't leave the WASG,' Priyanka said, sitting down. She pulled out a large plastic bag from under her seat.

'Guys,' I said, interrupting their banter.

Everyone turned to look at me.

I pointed at the desk and the unmanned phones. I looked at my watch. It was 10:29 p.m. The call system routine backup was about to finish and our calls would begin in one minute.

Everyone returned to their chairs and put on their headsets.

'Good evening, everyone. Please pay attention to this announcement,' a loud voice filled our bay. I looked up. The voice came from the fire-drill speaker.

'I hate these irritating announcements,' Priyanka said.

'This is the control room,' the speaker continued. 'This is to inform all agents of a fire drill next Friday at midnight. Please follow instructions during the fire drill to leave the call centre safely. Thank you. Have a nice shift.'

'Why do they keep doing this? Nobody is going to burn this place down,' Esha said.

'Government rules,' Vroom said.

Conversation stopped midway as two beeps on the computer screens signalled the start of our shift.

Calls began at 10:31 p.m. Numbers started flashing on our common switchboard as we picked up calls one after the other.

'Good afternoon, Western Appliances, Victor speaking, how may I help you?' Vroom said.

'Yes, according to my records I am speaking to Ms Smith, and you have the WAF200 dishwasher. Is that right?' Esha said.

Esha's memory impressed the caller. It was not a big deal, given that our automated system showed every caller's records. We knew their name, address, credit card details and past purchases from Western Appliances. We also had details on when they'd last called us. In fact, the reason why her call had come to our desk – the Western Appliances Strategic desk – was because she was a persistent caller. This way the main bay could continue to run smoothly.

Sometimes we had customers that were oddballs even by WASG standards. I won't go into all of them, but Vroom's 10:37 p.m. call went something like this:

'Yes, Ms Paulson, of course we remember you. Happy Thanksgiving, I hope you're roasting a big turkey in our WA100 model oven,' Vroom said, reading from a script that reminded us about the American festival of the day.

I couldn't hear the customer's side of the conversation, but Ms Paulson was obviously explaining her problem with the oven.

'No, Ms Paulson, you shouldn't have unscrewed the cover,' Vroom said, as politely as possible.

'No, really madam. An electrical appliance like the WA100 should only be serviced by trained professionals,' Vroom said, reading verbatim from the WA100 service manual.

Ms Paulson spoke for another minute. Our strategic bay hardly had a reputation for efficiency, but long calls like these could screw up Vroom's response times.

'You see madam, you need to explain to me why you opened the top cover. Then perhaps we'll understand why you got an electric shock . . . so tell me . . . yes . . . oh . . . really?' Vroom continued, taking deep breaths. Patience – the key to becoming a star agent – did not come naturally to him.

Radhika was helping someone defrost her fridge; Esha was assisting a customer in unpacking a dishwasher. Everyone was speaking with an American accent and sounded different from the way they normally spoke. I took a break from the calls to compile the call statistics of the previous day. I didn't particularly like doing this, but Bakshi had left me little choice.

'You see, madam,' Vroom was still with Ms Paulson, 'I understand your turkey didn't fit and you didn't want to cut it, but you should not have opened up the equipment ... But you see that's not the equipment's fault ... I can't really tell you what to do ... I understand your son is coming, madam ... Now if you had the WA150, that's a bigger size,' Vroom said, beginning to breathe faster.

Ms Paulson ranted on for a while longer.

'Ms Paulson, I suggest you take the oven to your dealer as soon as possible,' Vroom said firmly. 'And next time, get a smaller turkey ... and yes, a readymade turkey would be a good idea for tonight ... No, I don't have a dial-a-turkey number. Thank you for calling, Ms Paulson, bye.' Vroom ended the call.

He banged his fist on the table.

'Everything OK?' I said, not looking up from my papers.

'Yeah. Just a psycho customer,' he mumbled as another number started flashing on his screen.

I worked on my computer for the next ten minutes, compiling the call statistics of the previous day. Bakshi had also assigned me the responsibility of checking the other agents' etiquette. Every now and then I would listen in on somebody's call. At 10:47 p.m. I connected to Esha's line.

'Yes, sir. I sound like your daughter? Oh, thank you. So what is wrong with the vacuum cleaner?' she was saying.

'Your voice is so soothing,' the caller said.

'Thank you, sir. So, the vacuum cleaner ...?'

Esha's tone was perfect – just the right mix of polite-ness and firmness. Management monitored us on average call-handling times, or AHTs. As WASG got the trickier customers, our AHT benchmarks were higher at two-and-a-half minutes per call. I checked my files for everyone's AHT – all of us were within target.

'Beep!' The sound of the fax machine made me look up from my papers. I wondered who could be faxing us at this time. I went to the machine and checked the incoming fax. It was from Bakshi.

The fax machine took three minutes to churn out the seven pages he had sent. I tore the message sheet off the machine and held the first sheet up.

```
From: Subhash Bakshi
Subject: Training Initiatives


Dear Shyam,
Just FYI, I have recommended your name to
assist in accent training as they are short
of teachers. I am sure you can spare some
time for this. As always, I am trying to get
you more relevant and strategic exposure.
    Yours,
    Subhash Bakshi
    Manager, Connexions
```

I read the rest of the fax and gasped. Bakshi was sucking me into several hours outside my shift to teach new recruits. Apart from the extra work, I hate accent training. The American accent is so confusing. You might think the

Americans and their language are straightforward, but each letter can be pronounced several different ways.

I'll give you just one example: T. With this letter Americans have four different sounds. T can be silent, so 'internet' becomes 'innernet' and 'advantage' becomes 'advannage'. Another way is when T and N merge – 'written' becomes 'writn' and 'certain' is 'certn'. The third sound is when T falls in the middle. There, it sounds like a D – 'daughter' is 'daughder' and 'water' is 'wauder'. The last category, if you still care, is when Americans say T like a T. This happens, obviously, when T is at the beginning of the word like 'table' or 'stumble'. And this is just one consonant. The vowels are another story.

'What's up?' Vroom said, coming up to me.

I passed the fax to Vroom. He read it and smirked.

'Yeah, right. He sent you an FYI. Do you know what an FYI is?' Vroom said.

'What?'

'Fuck You Instead. It's a standard way to dump responsibility on someone else.'

'I hate accent training. You can't teach Delhi people to speak like Americans in a week.'

'Just as you can't train Americans to speak with a Punjabi accent,' Vroom said and chuckled. 'Anyway, go train-train, leave your brain.'

'What will I do?' I said, beginning to walk back towards our desk.

'Go train-train, leave your brain,' Vroom said and

laughed. He liked the rhyme, and repeated it several times as we walked back to the bay.

Back at my seat, Vroom's words – 'train-train' – echoed in my head. They were making me remember another kind of train altogether. It brought back memories of the Rail Museum, where I had a date with Priyanka a year ago.

Chapter 5

My Past Dates with Priyanka – I

Rail Museum, Chanakyapuri
One year earlier

SHE ARRIVED THIRTY MINUTES LATE. I had been round the whole museum twice, examined every little train model, stepped inside India's oldest coal engine, got to grips with the modern interactive siren system. I went to the canteen, which was on an island in the middle of an artificial pond. It was impressive landscaping for a museum. I thought of lighting a cigarette, but I caught sight of the sign: 'Only Steam Engines are Allowed to Smoke'. I was cradling a luke-warm Coke in the museum canteen when she finally arrived.

'OK. Don't say anything. Sorry, I'm late, I know, I know,' she said and sat down with a thump in front of me.

I didn't say anything. I looked at her tiny nose. I wondered how it allowed in enough oxygen.

'What? Say something,' she said after five seconds.

'I thought you told me to be quiet,' I said.

'My mother needs professional help,' Priyanka said. 'She really does.'

'What happened?' I swirled the straw in my Coke, making little fizzy drops implode.

'I'll tell you. First, how do you like this place? Cute, isn't it?'

'The Rail Museum?' I said, throwing my hands in the air. 'How old are we, twelve? Anyway, what happened with your mum? What was the fuel today?'

'We don't need fuel, just a spark is enough. Just as I was ready to leave to come here, she made a comment on my dress.'

'What did she say?' I asked, looking at her clothes. She wore a blue tiedye skirt, and a T-shirt with a peace sign on it. It was typical Priyanka stuff. She wore earrings with blue beads, which matched her necklace, and she had a hint of kohl around her eyes, which I was crazy about.

'I was almost at the door when she said, "Why don't you wear the gold necklace I gave you for your last birthday?"' Priyanka said.

'And then?' She obviously wasn't wearing a gold necklace as my gaze turned to the hollow of her neck, which I felt like touching.

'And I was like, no Mum, it won't go with my dress.

Yellow metal is totally uncool, only aunties wear it. Boom, next thing we are having this big, long argument. That's what made me late. Sorry,' she said.

'You didn't have to argue. Just wear the chain in front of her and take it off later,' I said as the waiter came to take our order.

'But that's not the point. Anyway,' she said and turned to the waiter, 'get me a plate of samosas, I'm starving. Actually wait, they are too fattening. Do you have a salad?'

The waiter gave us a blank look.

'Where do you think you are?' I said. 'This is the Rail Museum canteen, not an Italian bistro. You get what you see.'

'OK, OK,' she said, eyeing the stalls. 'I'll have potato chips. No, I'll have popcorn. Popcorn is lighter, right?' She looked at the waiter as if he was a nutritionist.

'She'll have popcorn,' I said to the waiter.

'So, what else is happening? Have you met up with Vroom?' she said.

'I was supposed to, but he couldn't come. He had a date.'

'With who? A new girl?'

'Of course. He never sticks to one. I wonder what girls see in him, and they're all hot, too,' I said.

'I can't understand the deal with Vroom. He is the most materialistic and unemotional person I have met in my entire life,' Priyanka said as the popcorn arrived at our table.

'No he isn't,' I said, grabbing more popcorn than I could hold.

'Well, look at him, jeans, phones, pizzas and bikes. That's all he lives for. And this whole new girlfriend every three months thing, come on, at some point you've got to stop that, right?'

'Well, *I'm* happy to stick to the one I have,' I said, my mouth overflowing with popcorn.

'You are so cute,' Priyanka said. She blushed and smiled. She took some more popcorn and stuffed it into my mouth.

'Thanks,' I said as I munched. 'Vroom has changed. He wasn't like this when he first joined from his previous job.'

'The one at the newspaper?'

'Yeah, journalist trainee. He started in current affairs. Do you know what one of his famous pieces was called?'

'No, what? Oh crap,' Priyanka said, looking at someone behind me.

'What happened?'

'Nothing, just don't look back. Some relatives of mine are here with their kids. Oh no,' she said, looking down at our table.

Now when someone tells you not to look at something, you always feel an incredible urge to do just that. From the corner of my eye I saw a family with two kids in the corner of the room.

'Who else do you expect to come here but kids?'

I said. 'Anyway, they are far away.'

'Shut up and look down. Anyway, tell me about Vroom's piece,' she said.

'Oh yeah. It was called "Why Don't Politicians Ever Commit Suicide?"'

'What? Sounds morbid.'

'Well, the article said all kinds of people – students, housewives, businessmen, employees and even film stars – commit suicide. But politicians never do. That tells you something.'

'What?' she said, still keeping her eyes down.

'Well, Vroom's point was that suicide is a horrible thing and people do it only because they are really hurt. This means they feel something, but politicians don't. So, basically, this country is run by people who don't feel anything.'

'Wow! Can't imagine that going down well with his editor.'

'You bet it didn't. However, Vroom had sneaked it in. The editor only saw it after it was printed and all hell broke loose. Vroom somehow saved his job, but his bosses moved him to cover the society page, page three.'

'Our Vroom? Page three?'

'They told Vroom he was good looking so he would fit in. In addition, he'd done a photography course and could take the pictures himself.'

'Cover page three because you're good looking? Now that sounds ridiculous,' she said.

'It is ridiculous. But Vroom took his revenge there, too. He took unflattering pictures of the glitterati – faces stuffed with food, close-ups of cellulite on thighs, drunk people throwing up all showed up in the papers the next day.'

'Oh my god,' Priyanka laughed. 'He sounds like an activist. I can't understand his switching to the call centre for money.'

'Well, according to him, there is activism in chasing money too.'

'And how does that work?'

'Well, his point is that the only reason Americans have a say in this world is because they have cash. The day we have money, we can screw them. So, the first thing we have to do is earn the money.'

'Interesting,' Priyanka said and let out a sigh. 'Well, that is why we slog at night. I could have done my B.Ed right after college. But I wanted to save some money first. I can't open my dream nursery school without cash. So until then, it's two hundred calls a night, night after night.' Priyanka rested her chin on her elbows. I looked at her. I think she would make the cutest nursery school principal ever.

'Western Appliances, Sam speaking, how may I help you? *Please* let me help you? *Please* . . .' I said, imitating an American accent.

Priyanka laughed again.

'Priyanka dideeee,' a five-year-old boy's voice startled customers from their samosas.

The boy running towards Priyanka had a model train set and a glass of Coke precariously balanced in his hands. He ran without co-ordination: the excitement of seeing his didi was too much for him. He tripped near our table and I lunged to save him. I succeeded, but his Coke went all over my shirt.

'Oh no,' I said even as I saw a three-year-old girl with a huge lollipop in her mouth running towards us. I moved aside from the tornado to save another collision. She landed straight on Priyanka's lap. I went to the restroom to clean my shirt.

'Shyam,' Priyanka said when I returned, 'meet my cousin, Dr Anurag.' The entire family had shifted to our table. Priyanka introduced me to everyone. I forgot their names as soon as I heard them. Priyanka told her doctor cousin I worked at a call centre and I think he was less interested in talking to me after that. The kids ate half the popcorn and spilt the rest of it. The boy was running his model train set through popcorn fields on the table and screaming a mock siren with his sister.

'Sit, Shyam,' Priyanka said.

'No, actually I have an early shift today,' I said and got up to leave.

'But wait—' Priyanka said.

'No, I have to go,' I said and ran out of the museum. This was no longer a museum, it had turned into the chaos of a real railway station.

Chapter 6

10.50 p.m.

'OUCH!' ESHA'S SCREAM DURING HER CALL broke my train of reminiscence.

'What?' I said. I could hear loud static.

'It's a really bad line . . . Hello, yes, madam,' Esha said.

Radhika was knitting something with pink wool while she waited for a call. People were busy, but I could sense the call volume was lower than usual.

'Eew,' Priyanka said five seconds later.

'Freaking hell,' Vroom said as he pulled off his headset from his ears.

'What's going on?' I said.

'There's shrill static coming every few seconds now. Ask Bakshi to send someone,' Vroom said, rubbing his ear.

'I'll go to his office. You guys cover the calls,' I said and looked at the time. It was 10:51 p.m. The first break was in less than an hour.

I passed by the training room on my way to Bakshi's

office and peeked inside: fresh trainees were attending a session. Some students were snoozing; they were probably still getting used to working nights.

'35 = 10', the instructor wrote in big bold letters on the blackboard.

I remembered the 35 = 10 rule from my training days two years ago. It helped agents adjust to their callers.

'Remember,' the instructor said to the class, 'the brain and IQ of a thirty-five-year-old American is the same as the brain of a ten-year-old Indian. This will help you understand your clients. You need to be as patient with them as you are when dealing with a child. Americans are stupid, just accept it. I don't want anyone losing their cool during calls . . .'

I dreaded the day when I would have to teach such classes. My own Delhi accent was impossible to get rid of, and I must have come last in my accent class.

'I have to get out of this,' I said to myself as I went to Bakshi's cabin.

Bakshi was in his oversized office, staring at his computer with his mouth open. As I came in, he rapidly closed the windows. He was probably surfing the Internet for bikini babes or something.

'Good evening, sir,' I said.

'Oh hello, Sam. Please come in.' Bakshi liked to call us by our Western names.

I walked into his office slowly, to give him time to close his favourite websites.

'Come, come, Sam, don't worry. I believe in being an open-door manager,' Bakshi said.

I looked at his big square face, which was unusually large for his 5′ 6″ body. The oversized face resembled the face of the conquered Ravana at the festival of Dusshera. His face shone as usual. It was the first thing you noticed about Bakshi – the oilfields on his face. If you could immerse Bakshi's skin in our landscape, you'd solve India's oil problems for ever. Priyanka told me once that when she met Bakshi for the first time, she had an over-whelming urge to take a tissue and wipe it hard across his face. I don't think one tissue would be enough, though.

Bakshi was about thirty but looked forty and behaved as if he was fifty. He had worked in Connexions for the past three years. Before that, he did an MBA from some unpronounceable university in south India. He thought he was Michael Porter or something (Porter is a big management guru – I'd never heard of him, either, but Bakshi told me in an FYI once) and loved to talk in manager's language or Managese, which is another language like English and American.

'So, how are the resources doing?' Bakshi said, swivel-ling on his chair. He never referred to us as people; we were all 'resources'.

'Fine, sir. I actually wanted to discuss a problem. The phone lines aren't working properly – there's a lot of static during calls. Can you ask systems . . .'

'Sam,' Bakshi said, pointing a pen at me.

'Yes?'

'What did I tell you?'

'About what?'

'About how to approach problems.'

'What?'

'Think.'

I thought hard, but nothing came to mind.

'I don't remember, sir – Solve them?'

'No. I said "big picture". Always start with the big picture.'

I was puzzled. What was the big picture here? There was static coming through the phones and we had to ask systems to fix it. I could have called them myself, but Bakshi's intervention would get a faster response.

'Sir, it is a specific issue. Customers are hearing disturbance . . .'

'Sam,' Bakshi sighed and signalled me to sit down, 'what makes a good manager?'

'What?' I sat down in front of him and surreptitiously looked at my watch. It was 10:57 p.m. I hoped the call flow was moderate so the others wouldn't have a tough time when they were one down on the desk.

'Wait,' Bakshi said and took out a writing pad and pen. He placed the pad on the middle of the table and then drew a graph that looked like this:

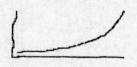

He finished the graph and turned the notebook 180 degrees so it faced me, then clicked his pen shut with a swagger, as proud as da Vinci finishing the *Mona Lisa*.

'Sir, systems?' I said, after staying silent for a few seconds.

'Wait. First, tell me. What is this?' Bakshi said and tapped his index finger on the diagram.

I tried to make sense of the chart and any possible connection to the static on the phone lines.

I shook my head.

'Tch-tch. See, let me tell you,' Bakshi said. 'This chart is your career. If you want to be more senior, you have to move up this curve.' He put a fat finger on the curve and traced it.

'Yes sir,' I said.

'And do you know how to do that?'

I shook my head. Vroom probably thought I was out smoking. I did feel some smoke coming out of my ears.

'Big Picture. I just told you, focus on the big picture. Learn to identify the strategic variables, Sam.'

Before I could speak, he had pulled out his pen again and was drawing another diagram.

'Maybe I can explain this to you with the help of a 2x2 matrix,' he said and bent down to write 'High' and 'Low' along the boxes.

'Sir, please,' I said, placing both my hands down to cover the sheet.

'What?' he said with irritation.

'Sir, this is really interesting, but right now my team is waiting and my shift is in progress.'

'So?' Bakshi said.

'The phones, sir. Please tell systems they should check the WASG bay urgently,' I said, without pausing to breathe.

'Huh?' Bakshi said.

'Just call systems, sir,' I said and stood up, 'using that.' I pointed at his telephone and rushed back to my bay.

Chapter 7

11. 00 p.m.

'NICE BREAK, EH?' VROOM SAID when I returned to our bay.

'C'mon, man, I just went to Bakshi's office about the static,' I said.

'Is he sending someone?' Vroom asked as he untangled his phone wires.

'He said I should identify the strategic variables first,' I said and sat down on my seat, resting my face on my hands.

'Strategic variables? What are they?' Vroom said, without looking at me.

'How the hell do I know?' I snorted. 'If I did, I'd be team leader. He also drew some diagrams.'

Radhika, Esha and Priyanka were busy on calls. Every few seconds, they would turn the phone away from their ears to avoid the loud static. I wished the systems guy would come by soon.

'What diagrams?' Vroom said as he took out some

chewing gum from his drawer and offered one to me.

'Some crap 2x2 matrix or something,' I said, declining Vroom's offer.

'Poor Bakshi, he's just a silly, harmless creature. Don't worry about him,' Vroom said.

'Where the hell is the systems guy?' I picked up the phone and called systems myself. They hadn't yet received a call from Bakshi. 'Can you please come now . . . yes, we have an emergency . . . yes, our manager knows about it.'

'Things are bad around here, my friend,' Vroom said. 'Bad news may be coming.'

'What do you mean? Are they cutting jobs?' I asked, now a little worried and anxious as well as frustrated. It's amazing how all these nasty emotions decide to visit me together.

'I'm trying to find out,' Vroom said, clicking open a window on his screen. 'The Western Computers account is really suffering. If we lose that account, the call centre will sink.'

'Crap. I heard something about it from Shefali. I think the website we made was too useful. People have stopped calling us,' I said.

A visitor in our bay interrupted our conversation. I knew he was the systems guy as he had three pagers on his belt and two memory cards around his neck.

Priyanka told him about the problem and made him listen to the static.

The systems guy asked us to disconnect our lines for ten minutes.

Everyone removed their headsets. I saw Esha adjusting her hair. She does it at least ten times a night. First she removes the rubber band that holds up her hair so it all falls loose, then she pulls it all together and ties it back again.

Her hair was light-coloured and intensely curly at the ends: the result of an expensive hairstyling job that cost as much as minor surgery. It didn't even look that nice if you asked me. Naturally curly hair is one thing, but processed curly hair looks like tangled telephone wires.

I saw Vroom stare at Esha. It's never easy for guys to work in an office with a hot girl. I mean, what are you supposed to do? Ignore their sexiness and stare at your computer?

Radhika took her pink wool out from her bag and started to knit frantically. Military Uncle's system was still working, so he stayed glued to his monitor.

'What are you knitting?' Esha turned to Radhika.

'A scarf for my mother-in-law. She's very sweet, she feels cold at night,' Radhika said.

'She is not sweet—' Vroom began to say but Radhika interrupted him.

'Shh, Vroom. She is fine, just traditional.'

'And that sucks, right?' Vroom said.

'Not at all. In fact, I like the cosy family feeling. They're only a little bit old-fashioned,' Radhika said and smiled. I didn't think her smile was genuine, but it was none of my business.

'Yeah, right. Only a little. As in always cover your head with your sari types,' Vroom said.

'They make you cover your head?' Esha asked, speaking through teeth clenched around her rubber hairband.

'They don't *make* me do anything, Esha. I am willing to follow their culture. All married women in their house do it,' Radhika said.

'Still, it is a bit weird,' Esha said doubtfully.

'Anyway, I look on it as a challenge. I love Anuj and he said he came as a package. But yeah, sometimes I miss wearing low-waisted jeans like you wore yesterday.'

I was amazed Radhika remembered what Esha had worn yesterday. Only women have this special area in the brain that keeps track of everything they and their friends have worn during the last fifty days.

'You like those jeans?' Esha said, her eyes lighting up.

'I love them. But I guess you need the right figure for them,' Radhika said. 'Anyway, sorry to change the topic, guys, but we're forgetting something here.'

'What? Systems?' I asked, as I looked under the table where the systems guy lurked within a jungle of tangled wires and told me he'd need ten more minutes.

I checked my watch. It was 11:20 p.m. I wondered if Bakshi would be coming for his daily rounds soon.

'I didn't mean the static,' Radhika said as she put her knitting aside. 'Miss Priyanka has some big news for us, remember?'

'Oh yes. C'mon, Priyanka, tell us!' Esha screamed. Military Uncle looked up from his screen for a second

71

and then went back to work. I wondered if he'd been this quiet when he lived with his son and daughter-in-law.

'OK, I do have something to tell you,' Priyanka said with a sheepish grin, making her two dimples even more prominent. She brought out a box of sweets from her large plastic bag.

'Whatever your news is, we do get to eat the sweets, right?' Vroom wanted to know.

'Of course,' Priyanka said, carefully opening the red cellophane wrapping on the box. I hate it when she's so methodical. Just rip the damn wrapping off, I thought. Anyway, it was none of my business. I looked under the table for a few seconds, as if to help the systems guy.

'So, what's up? Ooh milk cake, my favourite,' Radhika said, even as Vroom jumped to grab the first piece.

'I'll tell you, but you guys have to swear it won't leave WASG,' Priyanka said. She offered the box to Radhika and Esha. Radhika took two pieces, while Esha broke off the tiniest piece possible with human fingers. I guess the low-cut jeans figure comes at a price.

'Of course we won't tell anyone. I hardly have any friends outside the WASG. Now tell us, please,' Esha said and wiped her long fingers with a tissue.

'Well, let's just say my mum is the happiest person on earth today,' Priyanka said.

'No riddles. Just tell the story,' Vroom said.

'Well, you know my mum and her obsession for a match with an expat Indian for her rebellious daughter to take her away from India?'

'Uh-uh,' Radhika nodded as she ate her milk cake.

'So these family friends of ours brought a proposal for me. It came from one of their relatives in Seattle. I would have said no as I always do. But this time I saw the photos, which were cute. I spoke to the guy on the phone and he sounded decent. He works at Microsoft and his parents are in Delhi and I met them today. They are nice people,' Priyanka said and paused to break a piece of cake off for herself. She could have broken a smaller piece, I thought, but it wasn't really my business.

'And,' Esha said, her eyes opening wide and staring at Priyanka.

'I don't know, something just clicked,' Priyanka said, playing with her milk cake rather than eating it. 'They asked for my decision upfront and I said . . . yes.'

'Waaaoooow! Oh wow!' the girls screamed at the highest pitch possible. The systems guy trembled under the table. I told him everything was fine and asked him to continue. At least everything was fine outside. Inside I had a burning feeling, as if someone had tossed a hot coal in my stomach.

Radhika and Esha got up to hug Priyanka as if India had won the World Cup or something. People get married every day. Did these girls really have to create a scene? I wished the phones would start working again so I didn't have to listen to their nonsense.

I looked at my computer screen and saw that Microsoft Word was open. Angrily I closed all windows with the Microsoft logo on it.

'Congratulations, Priyanka,' Vroom said, 'that's big news.'

Even Military Uncle got up and came to shake hands with Priyanka. His generation like it when young people decide to get married. Of course, he was back at his desk within twenty seconds.

'This deserves more than milk cake. Where's our treat?' Esha asked. Girls like Esha hardly eat anything, but still jump around asking for treats.

'The treat is coming, guys,' Priyanka said, her smile taking up permanent residence on her face. 'I have only said yes. There've been no ceremonies yet.'

'You've met the guy?' Vroom asked.

'No, he's in Seattle. But we spoke for hours on the phone, and I've seen his picture. He's cute. Do you want to see the photo?' Priyanka said.

'No thanks,' I blurted out. Damn, I couldn't believe I'd said that. By sheer luck I hadn't said it loud enough for Priyanka to hear.

'Huh? You said something?' Priyanka asked, looking at me.

I shook my head and pointed under the table as if my only focus was to fix the phones.

'Do you want some milk cake?' Priyanka asked and shunted the box towards me.

'No, thanks,' I said and slid the box back.

'I thought milk cake was your favourite.'

'Not any more. My tastes have changed,' I said. 'And I'm trying to cut down.'

'Not even a small piece?' she asked and tilted her head.

At one stage in my life I used to find that head-tilt cute, but today I remained adamant.

I shook my head and our eyes locked. When you've shared a relationship with someone, the first change is in how you look into each other's eyes. The gaze becomes more fixed and it's hard to pull away from it.

'Aren't you going to say anything?' Priyanka said. When girls say that, it's not really a question. It means they *want* you to say something.

'About what? The phone lines? They'll be fixed in ten minutes,' I said.

'Not that. I'm getting married, Shyam.'

'Good,' I said and turned to my screen.

'Show us the picture!' Esha screamed, as if Priyanka was going to show her Brad Pitt naked or something. Priyanka took out a photograph from her handbag and passed it around. I saw it from a distance: he looked like a regular software geek, similar to the guy under our table but with better clothes. He stood straight with his stomach pulled in – an old trick any guy with a paunch applies when he gets his picture taken. He wore glasses and had a super-neat hairstyle as if his mum clutched his cheeks and combed his hair every morning. Actually, she just might have for this arranged-marriage picture. He was standing with the Statue of Liberty in the background and his forced smile made him look like a total loser if you'd asked me, like the kind of guy who never spoke to a girl in college. However, now he was hot, and girls with dimples were ready to marry him without even meeting him.

'He's so cute, like a little teddy bear,' Esha said and passed the picture to Radhika.

When girls call a guy 'teddy bear', they just mean he's a nice guy but they'd never be attracted to him. Girls may say they like such guys, but teddy bears never get to sleep with anyone. Unless of course their mums hunt the neighbourhood for them.

'Are you OK?' Priyanka said to me. The others were analysing the picture.

'Yeah. Why?'

'I just expected a little more reaction. We've known each other for four years, more than anybody else on the desk.'

Radhika, Esha and Vroom turned their heads away from the picture to look at us.

'Reaction?' I said, 'I thought I said *good*.'

'That's all?' Priyanka said. Her smile had left the building.

'I'm busy trying to get the system fixed.'

Everyone was staring at me.

'OK,' I said, 'OK, Priyanka. This is *great* news. I am *so* happy for you. *OK*?'

'You could have used a better tone,' Priyanka muttered, and walked away quickly towards the ladies room.

'What? Why is everyone staring at me?' I said as they all turned away.

The systems guy finally came out from under the table.

'Fixed?' I said.

'I need signal-testing equipment,' he said, wiping sweat

off his forehead. 'The problem could be external. Builders are digging all over this suburb right now, some contractor may have dug over our lines. Just take a break until I come back. Get your manager here as well,' he said and left.

I picked up the telephone to call Bakshi, but the line was busy so I left a voicemail.

Priyanka returned from the restroom and I noticed that she had washed her face. Her nose still had a drop of water on it.

'Sounds like an easy night. I hope it never gets fixed,' Radhika said, knitting ferociously.

'There's nothing better than a call-centre job when the phones aren't working,' Priyanka said and closed the box of sweets.

'So, tell us more. What's he like?' Esha said.

'Who? Ganesh?' Priyanka asked.

'His name is Ganesh? Nice,' Esha said and switched on her mobile phone. Everyone else followed suit and several opening tones filled the room. Normally agents couldn't use cellphones in the bay, but it was OK to do so when the system was down.

I had two text messages from Shefali: one wishing me goodnight, and another wishing me sweet dreams and a cuddly night. I cringed.

'Does Ganesh like to talk? Sometimes the software types are really quiet,' Radhika said.

'Oh yes, he talks a lot. In fact, I might get a call from him now because my phone is on,' Priyanka said and smiled. 'We're still getting to know each other, so any communication is good.'

'You sound *sooo* happy,' Esha said. Her 'so' lasted four seconds.

'I *am* happy. I can see what Radhika says now about getting a new family. Ganesh's mum came round today and gave me a big gold chain and hugged me and kissed me.'

'Sounds horrible,' Vroom said.

'Shut up, Vroom,' Esha said. 'Oh, Priyanka, you're so lucky.'

Vroom sensed that I wasn't exactly jumping with joy at the conversation.

'Cigarette?' he said.

I looked at my watch. It was 11:30, our usual time for taking a smoke. In any case, I preferred burning my lungs to sticking around to find out Ganesh's hobbies.

Chapter 8

11.31 p.m.

VROOM AND I WENT TO THE CALL-CENTRE parking lot. He leaned against his bike and lit two cigarettes with one match. I looked at his tall, thin frame. If he weren't so skinny you'd say he was a stud. Still, a cigarette looked out of place on his boyish face. Perhaps conscious of the people who had called him Baby Face before, he always wore one-day-old stubble. He passed a lit cigarette to me. I took a puff and let it out in the cold night air.

We stayed quiet for a moment and I was thankful to Vroom for that. One thing guys do know is when to shut up.

Vroom finally spoke, starting with a neutral topic. 'I need a break. Good thing I'm going to Manali next weekend.'

'Cool, Manali is really nice,' I said.

'I'm going with my school buddies. We might ride up there on bikes.'

'Bikes? Are you nuts? You'll freeze to death.'

'Two words: leather jackets. Anyway, when have you been there?'

'Last year. We went by bus, though,' I said.

'Who did you go with?' Vroom said as he looked for a place to flick ash. He found none. He stepped to a corner of the parking lot and plucked two large leaves from a tree. We tapped our cigarettes on the improvised ashtray.

'Priyanka,' I said and turned silent. Vroom didn't respond either for ten seconds.

'Was it good?' he finally said.

'Yeah, it was great. Apart from the aches from the bus ride,' I said.

'Why, what happened?'

'We took a bus at four in the morning. Priyanka was in her anti-snob phase, so she insisted we take the ordinary slow bus and not the deluxe fast one. She also wanted to enjoy the scenery slowly.'

'And then?'

'The moment the bus reached the highway, she leaned on my shoulder and fell asleep. My shoulder cramped and my body stiffened up, but apart from that it was great fun.'

'She's a silly girl,' Vroom said, letting out a big puff, his face smiling behind the smoke ring.

'She is. You should have seen her back then. She used to wear all these beads and earthy clothes she bought from Fab India all the time. And then she'd sit with the truck drivers and drink tea.'

'Wow. I can't imagine Priyanka like that now,' Vroom said.

'Trust me, the girl has a wild side,' I said, and paused as her face came to mind. 'Anyway, it's history now. Girls change.'

'You bet. She's all set now.'

I nodded. I didn't want to talk about Priyanka any more. At least one part of me didn't. The rest of me always wanted to talk about her.

'An expat Indian catch, Microsoft and all. Not bad,' Vroom continued as he lit another cigarette. I narrowed my eyes at him.

'What?' he said. 'It's in my daily quota. It is only my third of five.' He exhaled a giant cloud.

'It's a little too fast, isn't it?' I said.

'What? The cigarette? I need it today.'

'Not that. Priyanka's wedding. Don't you think she's moving too quickly?'

'C'mon, man, you don't get matches like that every day. He's in freakin' Microsoft. As good as they get. He is MS Groom 1.1 – deluxe edition.'

'What's the deal with Microsoft?'

'Dude, I'm sure he packs close to a hundred grand a year.'

'What is that? A hundred thousand US dollars a year?'

Vroom nodded. I tried to convert one hundred thousand US dollars to rupees and divide it by twelve to get the monthly salary, but there were too many zeros and it was a tough calculation to do in my head. I racked my brain for a few seconds.

'Stop calculating in rupees,' Vroom said and smiled. 'Priyanka's got a catch, I'm telling you.'

He paused and looked at me. His eyes were wet, brown and kind like a puppy's. I could see why girls flocked to him. It was the eyes.

'I'm going to ask you a question. Will you answer it honestly?' Vroom said.

'OK.'

'Are you upset she's getting married? I know you have feelings for her.'

'No,' I said and started laughing. 'I just find it a bit strange. But I wouldn't say I'm upset. That's too strong a word. It is not like we're together any more. No, I'm not *upset* upset.'

Vroom waited while I continued to laugh exaggeratedly. When I'd stopped he said, 'OK, don't bull-shit me. What happened to your re-proposal plans?'

I remained silent.

'It's OK, you can tell me.'

I sighed, 'Well, of course I feel for her, but they're just vestigial feelings.'

'Vesti what?'

'Like vestigial organs. They serve no purpose or value. But they can give you a pain in the appendix. It's the same with my feelings for Priyanka. I'm supposed to have moved on, but obviously I haven't. Meanwhile, Mr Indian in Seattle comes and gives me a kick in the rear end,' I said.

'Talk to her. Don't tell me you're not going to,' Vroom said and exhaled two smoke rings.

'I was planning to. I thought we'd submit the website user manual and hopefully that would have made it easier for Boston to approve my promotion. How did I know there would be milk cake distribution tonight? How was it by the way? I didn't touch it.'

'The milk cake was great. Never sulk when food is at stake, dude. Anyway, screw that. Listen, you still have some time. She's only just said yes.'

'I hope so. Though even as team leader it's hard to compete with Mr Microsoft,' I said.

We remained silent for a few more seconds. Vroom spoke again.

'Yeah, man. Girls are strategic. They talk about love and romance and all that crap, but when it comes to doing the deal, they'll choose the fattest chicken,' he said, and bunched up the leaf ashtray until it looked like a bowl.

'I guess I can only become fat, not a fat chicken,' I said.

'Yeah, you need to be fat, fresh and fluffy. Girls know their stuff. That's why you shouldn't feel so upset. We're not good husband material, just accept it.'

'Thanks, Vroom, that really makes my day,' I said. I did agree with him though. It was evolution. Maybe nature wanted dimple-cheeked, software-geek mini Ganesh babies. They were of far more value to society than depressed, good-for-nothing junior Shyams.

'And anyway, it's the girl who always gets to choose.

Men propose and women accept or, as in many cases, reject it.'

It's true. Girls go around rejecting men like it's their birthright. They have no idea how much it hurts us. I read once – or maybe saw it during one of my Discovery Channel phases – that the reason for this is that it takes a lot of effort for the female to bear their offspring. Hence they choose their mates carefully. Meanwhile, men dance around, spend cash, make them laugh, write stupid poems, anything to win them over. The only species where courting works in reverse is the sea horse. Instead of the female, the male sea horse bears the offspring: they carry baby sea horse eggs in their pockets. Guess what? The female sea horses are always hitting on the males, while the latter pucker their noses and get to pick the cutest female. I wish I were a sea horse. How hard can it be to carry a couple of eggs in a backpack?

Vroom interrupted my thoughts.

'But who knows? Priyanka isn't like other girls, or maybe she is after all. Either way, don't give up, man. Try to get her back,' Vroom patted my shoulder in encouragement.

'Speaking of getting her back, shouldn't we be heading back to the bay?' I said and looked at my watch. 'It's 11:45 p.m.'

As we returned from the parking lot, we passed the Western Computers main bay. The main bay sounded like a noisy school, except the kids weren't talking to one another, but to customers. Monitoring problems, viruses, strange error messages – there was nothing Connexions could not help you with.

'Still looks busy,' I said.

'Not at all. People have told me call traffic is down forty per cent. I think they'll cut a lot of staff or, worst-case scenario, cut everyone and shift the clients to the centre based in Bangalore.'

'Bangalore? What will happen here?' I said.

'They'll close this poorly managed madhouse down. What else? That's what happens when people like Bakshi spend half their time playing politics with other managers,' Vroom said. He spotted a good-looking girl in the Western Computers bay and pointed her out to me.

'Close down!' I echoed after studying the pretty girl for half a second. 'Are you serious, what will happen to the hundreds of jobs here?'

'Like they care. You think Bakshi cares?' he shrugged his lanky shoulders.

'Shit happens in life. It could happen tonight,' Vroom said as we reached the WASG.

Chapter 9

12. 15 a.m.

THE SYSTEMS GUY WAS UNDER THE TABLE AGAIN.

'No calls yet. They've asked for a senior engineer,' Priyanka said.

'It's an external fault. Some cables are damaged, I think. This area of Gurgaon is going nuts with all the building work,' the systems guy said as he emerged from under the table.

'Does Bakshi know?' I said.

'I don't know,' Priyanka said.

Vroom and I sat down at our desk.

'It's not too bad. Nice break,' Esha said as she filed her nails with a weirdly shaped nail cutter.

Priyanka's cell phone began to ring, startling everyone.

'Who's calling you so late?' Radhika said, still knitting her scarf.

'It's long distance, I think,' Priyanka said and smiled.

'Ooooh!' Esha squealed, like a two-year-old on a

86

bouncy castle. What's the big deal about a long-distance phone call? I thought.

'Hi, Ganesh. I've just switched my phone on,' Priyanka said. 'I can't believe you called so soon.'

I couldn't hear Ganesh's response, thank god.

'Fifteen times? I can't believe you tried my number fifteen times . . . so sorry,' Priyanka said, looking idiotic with happiness.

'Yes, I'm at work. But it's really chaotic today. The systems are down . . . Hello? . . . How come you're working on Thanksgiving? Oh, nice of the Indians to offer to work . . . hello?' Priyanka said.

'What happened?' Esha said.

'There's hardly any network,' Priyanka said, shaking her phone as if that would improve the reception.

'We're in the basement. Nothing comes into this black hole,' Vroom said. He was surfing the Internet, and was on the Formula I website.

'Use the landline,' Esha said, pointing to the spare phone on our desk. Every team in Connexions had a spare independent landline at their desk for emergency use. 'Tell him to call on the landline.'

'Here?' Priyanka asked, looking to me for permission.

Normally this would be unthinkable, but our systems were down so it didn't really matter. Also, I didn't want to look like a sore loser, preventing a new couple from starting their romance.

I nodded and pretended to be absorbed by my computer screen. As the ad-hoc team leader, I had some influence. I could approve personal calls and listen in on any line on the desk through my headset. However, I couldn't listen in on the independent emergency phone. Not unless I went under the table and tapped it.

Tap the landline, a faint voice echoed in my head.

'No, it's wrong,' I said.

But I could still hear one side of the conversation.

'Hello . . . Ganesh, call the landline . . . yes, 22463463 and 11 for Delhi . . . Call after ten minutes, our boss might be doing his rounds soon . . . I know ten minutes is six hundred seconds, I'm sure you'll survive.' She laughed uncontrollably and hung up. When women laugh non-stop, they're flirting.

'He sounds so *cuuute,*' Esha said, stretching the last word to five times its normal length.

'Enough is enough, I'm going to call Bakshi. We need to fix the systems,' I said and stood up. I couldn't bear the systems guy lurking under the table any more. More than that, I couldn't bear 600-seconds-without-you survival stories.

I was walking towards Bakshi's office when I noticed him coming towards me.

'Agent Sam, why aren't you at your desk?' Bakshi said.

'I was looking for you, sir,' I said.

'I'm all yours,' Bakshi said as his face broke into a smile. He came and placed his arm around my shoulder.

Bakshi and I returned to WASG. Bakshi's heavy steps were plainly heard by everyone. Radhika hid her knitting gear under the table. Esha put her nail file in her bag.

Vroom opened his screen to an empty MS Word document.

The systems guy came out from under the table and called his boss, the head of the IT department.

'Looks like we have technology issues here,' Bakshi said and the systems guy nodded his head.

The head of IT arrived soon after and he and the systems guy discussed geek stuff between themselves in so-called English. When the discussions were over, the IT head ranted out incomprehensible technical details to us. I understood that the system was under strain: 80 per cent of the WASG capacity was damaged, and the remaining 20 per cent could not handle the current load.

'Hmmm,' Bakshi said, his left hand rubbing his chin, 'hmmm . . . that's really bad, isn't it?'

'So, what do you want us to do?' the IT head asked.

All eyes turned to Bakshi. It was a situation Bakshi hated, where he was being asked to take a decision or recommend action.

'Hmmm,' Bakshi said and flexed his knees slowly to buy time. 'We really need a methodical game plan here.'

'We can shut down the WASG system tonight. Western Computers main bay is running fine anyway,' the junior IT guy suggested.

'But WASG has not lost all its capacity. Boston won't like it if we shut the bay,' the IT head said, referring to the Western Computers and Appliances headquarters in Boston.

'Hmmm,' Bakshi said again and pressed a sweaty palm

on my desk. 'Upsetting Boston isn't a good idea at this time. We're already on a slippery slope at Connexions. Let's try to be proactively oriented here.'

Vroom couldn't resist a snigger at Bakshi's jargon. He looked away and clenched his teeth.

'Sir, can I make a suggestion,' I said, even though I should have kept my trap shut.

'What?' Bakshi said.

'We could enlist Bangalore's help,' I said, referring to the location of the second Western Appliances and Computers call centre in India.

'Bangalore?' Bakshi and the IT head said in unison.

'Yes sir. It's Thanksgiving and the call volume is low, so Bangalore will be running light as well. If we pass most of our calls there, it will get busier for them, but it won't overload them. Meanwhile, we can handle a limited flow here,' I said.

'That makes sense. We can easily switch the flow for a few hours. We can fix the systems here in the morning,' the junior IT guy said.

'That's fine,' I said. 'And people will start their Thanksgiving dinner in the States soon, so call volumes will fall even more.'

Everyone at the desk looked at me and nodded. Secretly they were thrilled at the idea of an easy shift. Bakshi, however, had fallen into silent contemplation.

'Sir, you heard what Shyam said. Let's talk to Bangalore. That's our only option,' Priyanka said.

Bakshi remained silent and pondered for a few more

seconds. I would love to know what he's thinking about in these moments.

'See, the thing is,' Bakshi said and paused again, 'aren't we comparing apples to oranges here?'

'What?' Vroom looked at Bakshi with a disgusted expression.

I wondered what Bakshi was talking about. Was I the apple? Who was the orange? What fruit was Bangalore?

'I have an idea. Why don't we enlist Bangalore?' Bakshi said and snapped his fingers.

'But that's what Shyam—' the junior IT guy began, but Bakshi interrupted him. Poor junior IT guy, he isn't familiar with Bakshi's ways.

'See, it sounds unusual, but sometimes you have to think outside the box,' Bakshi said and tapped his head in self-admiration.

'Yes sir,' I said. 'That's a great idea. We have it all sorted now.'

'Good,' the IT guys said and began playing with the computer menus.

Before the IT guys left they told us that the WASG call volume would be super-light, maybe even less than twenty calls an hour. We were overjoyed, but kept a straight face before Bakshi.

'See, problem solved,' Bakshi said and spread his hands. 'That's what I'm here for.'

'Lucky us, sir,' Priyanka said.

We thought Bakshi would leave, but he had other plans.

'Shyam, as you are free tonight, can you help me with some strategic documents? It will give you some exposure.'

'What is it, sir?' I said, not happy about sacrificing my night.

'I've just printed out ten copies of monthly data sheets,' Bakshi said and held up some documents in his right hand. 'For some reason the sheets are no longer in order. There are ten page ones, then page twos and so on. Can you help fix this?'

'You haven't collated them. You can choose the option when you print,' Vroom said.

'You can choose to collate?' Bakshi asked, as if we'd told him about an option for brain transplants.

'Yes,' Vroom said and took some chewing gum from his drawer. He popped a piece into his mouth. 'Anyway, it is easier to take one printout and photocopy the rest. It comes out stapled too.'

'I need to upgrade my technical skills. Technology changes so fast,' Bakshi said. 'But Shyam, can you help re-order and staple them this time?'

'Sure,' I said.

Bakshi placed the sheets on my table and left the room. Priyanka looked at me with her mouth open.

'What?' I said.

'I can't believe it,' she shook her head. 'Why do you let him do that to you?'

'C'mon, Priyanka, leave Shyam alone. Bakshi runs his life,' Vroom said.

'Exactly. Because he lets him. Why can't people stand up for themselves?'

I don't know why I can't stand up for myself, but I definitely can't stand Priyanka's rhetorical questions. She doesn't understand the point, and then asks the world out loud.

I tried to ignore her. However, her words had affected me. It was difficult to focus on the sheets. I stacked the first set and was about to staple them when Vroom said, 'He can't take on Bakshi right now. Not at this time, Priyanka, while they're in the mood for firing people.'

'Yes, thanks, Vroom. Can someone explain the reality? I need to make a living. I don't have Mr Microsoft PowerPoint waiting for me in Seattle,' I said and pressed the stapler hard. I missed and the staple pin pierced my finger.

'Oww!' I screamed loud enough to uproot Military Uncle from his desk.

'What happened?' Priyanka said and stood up.

I lifted my finger to show the streaks of blood. A couple of drops spilt onto Bakshi's document.

The girls squealed 'eews' in rapid succession.

'Symbolism, man. Giving your lifeblood to this job,' Vroom said. 'Can someone give this guy a Band-Aid before he makes me throw up?'

'I have one,' Esha said as the girls came up and surrounded me. Women love to repair an injury, as long as it's not too gruesome.

'That looks bad,' Esha said, taking out a Band-Aid from her bag. She had fifty of them.

'It's nothing. Just a minor cut,' I said. I clenched my teeth hard.

Priyanka took out a few tissues from her bag. She held my finger and cleaned the blood around it.

'Ouch!' I screamed.

'Oh, the staple's still in there,' she said. 'We need tweezers. Tweezers, anyone?'

Esha had tweezers in her handbag, which I think she uses to rip her eyebrows out. Girls' handbags hold enough to make a survival kit for Antarctica.

Priyanka held the tweezers and went to work on my finger with a surgeon's concentration.

'Here's the culprit,' she said as she pulled out a staple pin drenched in blood. Priyanka wiped my finger and then stuck the Band-Aid on it. With no more bloodletting to see, everyone returned to their seats. I went back to collating sheets.

Esha and Radhika began talking about Bakshi.

'He had no idea what IT was saying,' Radhika said.

'Yeah, but did you see his face?' Esha said. 'He looked like he was doing a CBI investigation.'

I looked at Priyanka. The letters CBI brought back memories. Even as I collated Bakshi's sheets, my mind drifted to Pandara Road.

Chapter 10

My Past Dates with Priyanka – II

Havemore Restaurant, Pandara Road
Nine months earlier

'SHYAM,' PRIYANKA SAID as she tried to push me away.
'This is not the place to do these things. This is
Pandara Road.'

'Oh really,' I said, refusing to move away. We were
sitting at a corner table, partially hidden by a carved
wooden screen. 'What's wrong with Pandara Road?' I
said, continuing to kiss her.

'This is a family place,' she said, spreading a palm
on my face and pushing me back again, firmly this
time.

'So, families get made by doing these things.'

'Very funny. Anyway, you chose this place. I hope
the food is as good as you said it was.'

'It's the best in Delhi,' I said. We were in Havemore

95

Restaurant, one of the half-dozen overpriced but excellent restaurants on Pandara Road. We had done enough museums. After the Rail Museum, we had gone to the Planetarium – the dark empty theatre with its romantic possibilities was fun, I admit – the Natural History Museum, the Doll Museum and the Science Museum. According to Priyanka, museums offered good privacy, lovely gardens and cheap canteens.

'A hundred and thirty bucks for dhal!' Priyanka exclaimed as she opened the menu. Her kohl-lined eyes turned wide and her nostrils flared again: her face had the expression of a stunned cartoon character. It was embarrassing, especially as the waiter was already at our table to take the order.

'Just order, OK?' I said in a hushed voice.

Priyanka took five more minutes to place the order. Here is how she decides. Step one: sort all the dishes on the menu according to price. Step two: re-sort the cheaper ones based on calories.

'One naan, no butter. Yellow dhal,' she said as I glared at her.

'Okay, not yellow, black dhal,' she said. 'And . . .'

'And one shahi paneer,' I said.

'You always order the same thing, black dhal and shahi paneer,' she made a face.

'Yes, same girl, same food. Why bother experimenting when you already have the best?' I said.

'You are so cute,' she said. Her smile made her eyes

crinkle. She pinched my cheeks and fed me a little vinegar-onion from the table. Hardly romantic, but I liked it.

She moved her hand away quickly when she saw a family being led to the table adjacent to us. The family consisted of a young married couple, their two little daughters and an old lady. The daughters were twins, probably four years old.

The entire family had morose faces and no one said a word to each other. I wondered why they had bothered to go out when they could be grumpy for free at home.

'Anyway,' Priyanka said, 'what's the news?'

'Not much, Vroom and I are busy with the troubleshooting website.'

'Cool, how's it coming along?'

'Really well. Nothing fancy, though, the best websites are simple. Vroom even checked out sites meant for mentally handicapped people. He said if we can model it on them, Americans will surely be able to use it.'

'They're not *that* stupid.' Priyanka laughed. 'Americans invented computers, remember?'

The waiter arrived with our food.

'Yeah, there are ten smart guys in America. The rest call us at night,' I said as I tore off a piece of naan and dipped it in the daal.

'I agree the people who call us are pretty thick. I'm like, figure out where the power button is, hello?' she said.

She put micro-portions of food on her plate.

'Eat properly,' I said. 'Stop dieting all the time like Esha.'

'I'm not that hungry,' she said as I forcefully gave her human portions of food.

'Hey, did I tell you about Esha? Don't tell anyone,' she said, her voice dipping, eyebrows dancing.

I shook my head. 'You love to gossip. Don't you? Your name should be Miss Gossip FM 99.5,' I said.

'I *never* gossip,' she said, waving a fork at me solemnly. 'Oh my god, the food is so good here.'

My chest inflated with pride as if I had spent all night cooking the dishes myself.

'Of course you love to gossip. Whenever someone starts with "don't tell anyone", that to me shows a juicy titbit of gossip is coming,' I said.

Priyanka blushed and the tip of her nose turned tomato red. She looked cute as hell. I would have kissed her right then, but the grumpy family next to us was beginning to argue and I didn't want to spoil the sombre ambience for them.

'OK so maybe I gossip, but only a little bit,' Priyanka relented. 'But I read somewhere, gossip is good for you.'

'Oh really?' I teased.

'Yes, it's a sign you're interested in people and care for them.'

'That is so lame,' I burst out laughing, pointing my

spoon at her. 'Anyway, what about Esha. I know Vroom has the hots for her, but does she like him?'

'Shyam, that is old news. She's rejected Vroom's proposal before. The latest is that she had signed up for the Femina Miss India contest. Last week she got a rejection letter because she wasn't tall enough. She is five-five and the minimum is five-six. Radhika saw her crying in the toilet.'

'Oh wow! Miss India?'

'Come on, she's not that pretty. She should really stop this modelling thing. God, she is so thin, though. OK, I'm not eating any more.' She pushed her plate away.

'Eat, stupid. Do you want to be happy or thin?' I said, pushing her plate back towards her.

'Thin.'

'Shut up, eat properly. The name of the restaurant should tell you something. And as for Esha, well too bad Miss India didn't work out. However, trying doesn't hurt,' I said.

'Well, she was crying. So it hurt *her*. After all, she's come to Delhi against her parents' wishes. It's not easy struggling alone,' she said.

I nodded.

We finished our meal and the waiter reappeared like a genie to clear our plates.

'Dessert?' I said.

'No way. I'm too full,' Priyanka said, placing her hand on her neck to show just how full. She is way too

99

dramatic sometimes, just like her mum. Not that I dare tell her that.

'OK, one kulfi please,' I said to the waiter.

'No, order gulab jamun,' she said.

'Huh? I thought you didn't want . . . OK, one gulab jamun please.'

The waiter went back into his magic bottle.

'How's your mum?' I said.

'The same. We haven't had a cry fest since last week's showdown, so that alone is a reason to celebrate. Maybe I will have half a gulab jamun.'

'And what happened last week?'

'Last week? Oh yes, my uncles were over for dinner. So picture this, dinner ends and we are all having butterscotch ice cream at the dining table. One uncle mentioned that my cousin was getting married to a doctor, a cardiac surgeon or something,' Priyanka said.

The waiter came and gave us the gulab jamun. I took a bite.

'Ouch, careful, these are hot,' I said, blowing air out. 'Anyway, what happened then?'

'So I'm eating my ice cream and my mother screams "Priyanka, make sure you marry someone well settled".' The latter phrase was said in falsetto.

'I'm going to be a team leader soon,' I said and fed her a slice of gulab jamun.

'Relax, Shyam,' Priyanka said as she took a bite and patted my arm. 'It has nothing to do with you.

The point, is how could she spring it on me in front of everyone? Like, why can't I just have ice cream like the others? Why does my serving have to come with this hot guilt sauce? Take my younger brother, nobody says anything to him while he stuffs his face.'

I laughed and signalled for the bill.

'So what did you do then?' I said.

'Nothing. I slammed my spoon down on the plate and left the room.'

'You're a major drama queen,' I said.

'Guess what she says to everyone then? "This is what I get for bringing her up and loving her so much. She doesn't care. I nearly died in labour when she was born, but she doesn't care."'

I laughed uncontrollably as Priyanka imitated her mother. The bill arrived and my eyebrows shot up for a second as I paid the 463 rupees.

We stood up to leave and the grumpy family's voices reached us.

'What to do? Since the day this woman came to our house, our family's fortunes have been ruined,' the old woman was saying. 'The Agra girl's side were offering to set up a full clinic. I don't know where our brains were then.'

The daughter-in-law had tears in her eyes. She hadn't touched her food while the man was eating nonchalantly.

'Look at her now, sitting there with a stiff face. Go, go to hell now. Not only did you not bring anything, now you have dumped these two girls like two curses on me,' the mother-in-law said.

I looked at the little girls. They had identical plaits with cute pink ribbons in them. The girls were each holding one of their mother's hands and they looked really scared.

Priyanka was staring at them. I noticed they had ordered delicious, cold kulfi and wondered if I should have done the same and at least saved my scalded tongue.

'Say something now, you silent statue,' the mother-in-law said and shook the daughter-in-law's shoulders.

'Why doesn't she say anything?' Priyanka whispered to me.

'Because she can't,' I said. 'When you have a bad boss, you can't say anything.'

'Who will pay for these two curses? Say something now,' the mother-in-law said as the daughter-in-law's tears came down faster and faster.

'I'll say something,' Priyanka shouted, facing the mother-in-law.

The grumpy family turned to look at us in astonishment. I looked for a deep hole to hide myself from the embarrassment.

'Who are you?' the husband asked, probably his first words during the entire meal.

'We'll worry about that later,' Priyanka said, 'but who the hell are *you*? Her husband I presume?'

'Huh? Yes I am. Madam, this is a family matter,' he said.

'Oh really? You call this a family? Doesn't look like a family to me,' Priyanka said. 'I just see an old shrew and a loser wimp upsetting these girls. Don't you have any shame? Is this what you married her for?'

'See, she's another one,' the mother-in-law said. 'Look at the girls of today: they don't know how to talk. Look at her, eyes made up like a heroine's.'

'The young girls know how to talk and behave. It's you old people who need to be taught a lesson. These are your granddaughters and you are calling them a curse?' Priyanka said, her nose an even cuter red than before. I wanted to take a picture of that nose.

'Who are you, madam? What is your business here?' the husband said, this time in a firmer voice.

'I'll tell you who I am,' Priyanka said and fumbled in her handbag. She took out her call-centre ID card and flashed it for a nanosecond. 'Priyanka Sinha, CBI, Women's Cell.'

'What?' the husband said in half-disbelief.

'What is your number plate?' Priyanka said, talking in a flat voice.

'What? Why?' the bewildered husband asked.

'Or should I go outside to check,' she said and glanced at the keys on the table. 'It's a Santro, isn't it?'

'DGI 463. Why?' the husband said.

Priyanka took out her cell phone and pretended to

call a number. 'Hello? Sinha here. Please retrieve records on DGI 463 . . . yes . . . Santro . . . thanks.'

'Madam, what is going on?' the husband said, his voice quivering.

'Three years. Harassing women is punishable by three years. A quick trial, no appeal,' Priyanka said and stared at the mother-in-law.

The old woman pulled one of the twin granddaughters onto her lap.

'What? Madam this is just a f-f-f-family affair and—' the husband stammered.

'Don't say family!' Priyanka said, her voice loud.

'Madam,' the mother-in-law said, her tone now sweet, as if someone had soaked her vocal cords in gulab jamuns, 'we are just here to have a meal. I don't even let her cook see, we just had—'

'—Shut up! We have your records now. We will keep track. If you mess around, your son and you will have plenty of meals together – in jail.'

'Sorry, madam,' the husband said with folded arms. He asked for the bill and fumbled for cash. Within a minute they had paid and left.

I looked at Priyanka with my mouth open.

'Don't say anything,' she said, 'let's go.'

'CBI?' I said.

'Don't. Let's go.'

We sat in the Qualis I had borrowed from the call-centre driver.

'Stupid old witch,' Priyanka said. I started to

drive. Five minutes later, Priyanka turned to me. 'OK, you can say what you want now.'

'I love you,' I said.

'What? Why this now?'

'Because I love it when you stand up for something you feel strongly about. And that you do such a horrible job of acting like a CBI inspector. I love it when you want to order the cheapest dishes only because I'm paying for them. I love the kohl in your eyes. I love it when your eyes light up when you have gossip for me. I love it that you say you don't want dessert and then ask me to change mine so you can have half. I love your stories about your mother. I love it that you believe in me and are patient about my career. Actually, you know what, Priyanka?' I said.

'What?'

'I may not be a heart surgeon, but the one little heart I have, I have given it to you.'

Priyanka laughed aloud and put her hand on her face.

'Sorry,' she said and shook her head, still laughing. 'Sorry, you were doing so well, except for the heart surgeon line. Now, that is seriously cheesy.'

'You know what,' I said and removed one hand from the steering wheel to tweak her nose. 'They should put you in jail for killing romantic lines.'

Chapter 11

12.30 a.m.

'I CAN'T BELIEVE THIS,' Radhika said and threw her mobile phone on her desk, breaking up my Pandara Road dream.

Everyone turned to look at her. She covered her face with her hands and took a couple of deep breaths.

'What's up?' Priyanka said.

'Nothing,' Radhika said and heaved a sigh. She looked upset, but also younger at the same time. Five years ago, Radhika must have been pretty, I thought.

'Tell us,' Esha said.

'It's Anuj. Sometimes he can be so unreasonable,' she said and passed her phone to Esha. On the screen was a text message.

'What is it?' Priyanka said.

'Read it out,' Radhika said as she fumbled through her bag for her anti-migraine pills. 'Damn, I only have one pill left.'

'Really? OK,' Esha said and started reading the message:

'Show elders respect. Act like a daughter-in-law should. Goodnight.'

'What did I do wrong? I was in a hurry, that's all,' Radhika mumbled to herself as she took her pill with a sip of water.

Esha put a hand on her shoulder.

'What happened?' Esha asked softly. Women do this so well: a few seconds ago she was squealing in excitement over Ganesh, now she was whispering with concern over Anuj.

'Anuj is in Kolkata on tour. He called home and my mother-in-law told him, "Radhika made a face when I told her to crush the almonds more finely." Can you believe it? I was running to catch the Qualis and still made time to prepare her milk,' Radhika said and started to press her forehead.

'Is this what mother and son talk about?' Priyanka said.

Radhika continued, 'And then she told him, "I am old, if the pieces are too big they will choke my food pipe. Maybe Radhika is trying to kill me." Why would she say something so horrible?'

'And you're still knitting a scarf for her?' Vroom said, pointing at the knitting needles.

'Trust me, being a daughter-in-law is harder than being a model,' Radhika said. The pill was starting to have an effect and her face looked calm again. 'Anyway, enough of my boring life. What's up? Is Ganesh calling soon or what?'

'Are you OK?' Esha said, still holding Radhika's arm.

'Yes, I'm fine. Sorry guys, I overreacted. It's just a little miscommunication between Anuj and me.'

'Looks like your mother-in-law likes melodrama. She should meet my mother,' Priyanka said.

'Really?' Radhika said.

'Oh yes. She is the Miss Universe of melodrama. We cry together at least once a week. Though today she's on cloud nine,' Priyanka said, pulling the landline closer to her.

My attention was diverted by a call flashing on my screen.

'I'll take it,' I said, raising my hand. 'Western Appliances, Sam speaking, how may I help you?'

It was one of my weird calls of the night. The caller was from Virginia and was having trouble defrosting his fridge. It took me four long minutes to figure out the reason. It turned out the caller was a 'big person', which is what Americans call fat people, and his fingers were too thick to turn the tiny knob in the fridge's compartment which activates the defrosting mechanism. I suggested that he use a screwdriver or a knife and fortunately that solution worked after seven attempts.

'Thank you for calling Western Appliances, sir,' I said and ended the call.

'More politeness, agent Sam. Be more courteous,' I heard Bakshi's voice and felt his heavy breath on my neck.

'Sir, you again?' I said and turned around. Bakshi's face was as shiny as ever. It was so oily, he probably slipped off his pillow every night.

'Sorry, I forgot something important,' he said. 'Have you guys done the Western Computers website manual? I am finally sending the project report to Boston.'

'Yes sir. Vroom and I finished it yesterday,' I said and took out a copy from my drawer.

'Hmm,' Bakshi said as he scanned the cover sheet.

Western Computers Troubleshooting Website
User Manual and Project Details

Developed by Connexions, Delhi

Shyam Mehra and Varun Malhotra
(Sam Marcy and Victor Mell)

'Do you have a soft copy that you can email me?' Bakshi said. 'Boston wants it urgently.'

'Yes, sir,' Vroom said, pointing to his computer, 'I have it stored here. I'll send it to you.'

'Also, did you do the collation, Sam?'

'Yes, sir,' I said and passed him the ten sets.

'Excellent. I empowered you, and you delivered the output. Actually, I have another document, the board meeting invite. Can you help?'

'What do I have to do?' I said.

'Here's a copy,' Bakshi said and gave me a five-page document. 'Can you photocopy ten copies for me please? My secretary is off today.'

'Er. Sure, sir, just photocopying, right?'

Bakshi nodded.

'Sir,' Vroom said, 'what's the board meeting for?'

'Nothing, just routine management issues,' Bakshi said.

'Are people going to get fired?' Vroom asked, his direct question making everyone spring to attention.

'Er . . .' Bakshi said, as usual, lost for words when asked something meaningful.

'There are rumours in the Western Computers main bay. We just want to know if we will be fine,' Vroom said.

'Western Appliances won't be affected, right?' Esha said.

Bakshi took a deep breath and said, 'I can't say much. All I can say is we are under pressure to rightsize ourselves.'

'Rightsize?' Radhika asked in genuine confusion.

'That means people are getting fired, doesn't it?' Vroom said. Right size never meant otherwise.

Bakshi did not respond.

'Sir, we need to increase our sales force to get new clients. Firing people is not the answer,' Vroom said with a boldness that was high even by his standards.

Bakshi had a smirk on his face as he turned to Vroom. He put his hand on Vroom's shoulder. 'I like your excitement, Mr Victor,' he said, 'but a seasoned management has to study all underlying variables and come up with an optimal solution. It's not so simple.'

'But sir, we can get more . . .' Vroom was saying as Bakshi patted his shoulder twice and left.

Vroom waited to ensure that Bakshi was out of the room before he spoke again.

'This is insanity. Bakshi's fucked up, so they're firing innocent agents!' he shouted.

'Stay calm,' I said, and started assembling the sheets.

'Yes, stay calm. Like Mr photocopy Boy here, who finds acceptance in everything,' Priyanka said.

'Excuse me,' I said looking up. 'Are you talking about me?'

Priyanka kept quiet.

'What is your problem? I come here, make fifteen grand a month and go home. It sucks that people are being fired and I'm trying my best to save my job. Overall, yes, I accept my situation. And Vroom, before I forget, can you email Bakshi the user manual please?'

'I'm doing it,' Vroom said as he clicked his mouse, 'though what's going on here is still wrong.'

'Don't worry. We've finished the website. We should be safe,' I said.

'I hope so. Damn, it will suck if I lose my fifteen grand a month. If I don't get my pizza three times a week I'll die,' Vroom said.

'You have pizza that often?' Esha said.

'Isn't it unhealthy?' Radhika asked. Despite her recent text, she was back to knitting her scarf. Knitting habits die hard, I guess.

'No way. Pizzas are the ultimate balanced diet. Look at the contents: grain in the crust, milk protein in the cheese, vegetables and meat as toppings. It has all the food

111

groups. I read it on the Internet: pizza is good for you.'

'You and your Net,' Esha said. It was true. Vroom got all his information off the Internet – bikes, jobs, politics, dating tips and, as I had just learned, pizza nutrition as well.

'Pizzas are not healthy. I gain weight really fast if I eat a lot of it,' Priyanka said, 'especially with my lifestyle. I hardly get time to exercise and on top of that I work in a confined space.'

Priyanka's last two words made my heart skip a beat. 'Confined space' means only one thing to me: that night at the 32nd Milestone disco.

Chapter 12

My Past Dates with Priyanka – III

32nd Milestone, Gurgaon Highway
Seven months earlier

I SHOULDN'T REALLY CALL THIS ONE a date, since this time it was a group thing with Vroom and Esha joining us. I argued earlier with Priyanka about going out with work people, but she told me I should be less antisocial. Vroom picked 32nd Milestone and the girls agreed because the disco doesn't have a 'door-bitch'. According to Priyanka, a door-bitch is a hostess who stands outside the disco, screening every girl who goes in, and if your waist is more than twenty-four inches, or if you aren't wearing something cool, the door-bitch will raise an eyebrow at you like you're a fifty-year-old auntie.

'Really? I've never noticed those door girls before,' I said as we sat on stools at the bar.

'It's a girl thing. They size you up, and unless you're drop dead gorgeous, you get that mental smirk,' Priyanka said.

'So why should you care? You *are* gorgeous,' I said. She smiled and pinched my cheek.

'Mental smirk? Girls and their coded communication. Anyway, drink anyone?' Vroom said.

'Long Island Iced Tea please,' Esha said and I noticed how stunning she looked in her make-up. She wore a black fitted top and black pants that were so tight she'd probably have to roll them down to take them off.

'Long Island? Want to get drunk quick or what?' I said.

'Come on. I need to de-stress. I ran around like mad last month chasing modelling agencies. Besides, I have to wash down last week's one thousand calls,' Esha said.

'That's right. Twelve hundred calls for me,' Vroom said. 'Let's all have Long Islands.'

'Vodka cranberry for me please,' Priyanka said. She wore camel-coloured pants and a pistachio-green sequinned kurti. I'd given her the kurti as a gift on her last birthday. She had just a hint of eyeliner and a light gloss of lipstick, which I preferred to Esha's Asian Paints job.

'Any luck with the modelling assignments?' I asked Esha idly.

'Not much. I did meet a talent agent, though, and

he said he would refer me to some designers and fashion show producers. I need to be seen in those circles,' Esha said as she pulled her top down to cover her navel.

Vroom went to the bartender to collect our drinks while I scanned the disco. The place had two levels: a dance floor on the mezzanine and a lounge bar on the first floor. A remixed version of 'Dil Chahta Hai' played in the background. As it was Saturday night, the disco had more than 300 customers. They were all rich, or at least had rich friends who could afford drinks priced at over Rs 300 a cocktail. Our budget was a lavish thousand bucks each: a treat for making it through the extremely busy summer period at the call centre.

I noticed some stick-thin models on the dance floor. Their stomachs were so flat, if they swallowed a pill you'd probably see an outline of it when it landed inside. Esha's looks are similar, except she's a bit short.

'Check it out. She is totally anorexic. I can bet on it,' Priyanka said, pointing to a pale-complexioned model on the dance floor. She wore a top without any sleeves or neck or collar – I think the girls call it 'off-the-shoulder'. Defying physics, it didn't slip off, though most men were waiting patiently.

The model turned, displaying a completely bare back.

'Wow, I wish I were that thin. But oh my god, look at what she's wearing,' Esha said.

'I can't believe she's not wearing a bra. She must be totally flat,' Priyanka said.

'Girls!' I said.

'Yes?' Esha and Priyanka turned to me.

'I'm bored. Can you choose more inclusive conversation topics,' I pleaded. I looked for Vroom who had collected the drinks and was waving maniacally at us for help.

'I'll go,' Esha said and went over to Vroom.

Finally, to my relief, it was only Priyanka and me.

'So,' she said as she leaned forward to peck at my lips. 'You're feeling left out with our girlie talk?'

'Well, this was supposed to be a date. I forced myself to come with them. I haven't caught up with you in ages.'

'I told you, Vroom asked me and I didn't want to be anti-social,' Priyanka said as she ruffled my hair. 'But we'll go out for a walk in a bit. I want to be alone with you too, you know?'

'Please, let's go soon.'

'Sure, but they're back now,' Priyanka said as Vroom and Esha arrived. Vroom passed us our drinks and we said 'cheers', trying to sound lively and happy, as people at a disco should.

'Congrats on the website, guys. I heard it's good,' Esha said as she took a sip.

'The website is cool,' Vroom said. 'The test customers love it. No more dialling. And it's so simple, just right for those spoon-feed-me Americans.'

'So, a promotion finally for Mr Shyam here,' Priyanka said. I noticed she had finished a third of her drink in just two sips.

'Now Mr Shyam's promotion is another story,' Vroom said. 'Maybe Mr Shyam would like to tell it himself.'

'Please, man. Some other time,' I said as Priyanka looked at me expectantly.

'OK, well Bakshi said he is talking to Boston to release a headcount. But it will take a while.'

'Why can't you just be firm with him?' Priyanka said.

'Like how? How can you be firm with your own boss?' I said, my voice loud with irritation.

'Cool it, guys,' Vroom said. 'It's a party night and—'

A big noise interrupted our conversation. We noticed a commotion on the dance floor as the DJ turned off the music.

'What's up?' Vroom said and we all went towards the dance floor where a fight had broken out. A gang of drunken friends accused someone of pawing one of the girls with them and grabbed his collar. Soon, Mr Accused's friends came to his defence and, as the dance floor was too noisy for vocal arguments, people expressed themselves with fists and kicks instead. The music stopped when someone knocked one guy flat on the floor. Several others were on top of each other and bouncers finally disentangled everyone and restored peace while a stretcher emerged to carry away the knocked-out guy.

'Man, I wish it had gone on a bit longer,' Vroom said.

It's true. The only thing better than watching beautiful people in a disco is watching a fight, because a fight means the party is totally rocking.

Five minutes later the music resumed and the anorexic girls' brigade were back on the floor.

'That's what happens to kids with rich dads and too much money,' Vroom said.

'Come on, Vroom. I thought you said money's a good thing. That's how we'll beat the Americans, right?' Priyanka said with the confidence that comes from drinking a Long Island Iced Tea in seven minutes.

'Yes, doesn't money pay for your mobile phones, pizzas and discos?' I asked.

'Yes, but the difference is that I've earned it. These rich kids, they don't have a clue how hard it is to make cash,' Vroom said and held up his glass. 'This drink is three hundred bucks – it takes me almost a full night of two hundred irritating Americans screaming in my ear to earn it. Then I get this drink. Which is full of ice-cubes anyway. These kids can't make that comparison.'

'Oh, I feel so guilty drinking this now,' Priyanka said.

'C'mon, you get good money. Significantly more

than the eight grand you made as a journalist trainee,' I said.

'Yes,' Vroom said as he took a big hundred-and-twenty-rupee sip. 'We get paid well, fifteen thousand a month. Fuck, that's almost twelve dollars a day. Wow, I make as much a day as a US burger boy makes in two hours. Not bad for my college degree. Not bad at all. Fucking nearly double what I made as a journalist anyway.' He pushed his empty glass and it slid to the other end of the table.

Everyone was silent for a minute. Vroom on a temper trip is unbearable.

'Stop being so depressed. Let's dance,' Esha said and tugged at Vroom's hand.

'No,' Vroom said.

'Come for one song,' Esha said and stood up from her stool.

'OK, but if anyone teases you, I'm not getting into a fight,' Vroom said.

'Don't worry, no one will. There are prettier girls here,' Esha said.

'I don't think so. Anyway, let's go,' Vroom said as they went to the dance floor. The song playing was 'Sharara Sharara', one of Esha's favourites.

Priyanka and I watched them dance from our seats.

'Want to go for a walk now?' Priyanka said after a few minutes.

'Sure,' I said. We held hands and walked out of 32nd Milestone. The bouncer at the door stamped our palms so that we could re-enter the disco and we headed to the parking lot, where the music was softer. My ears had never felt so good.

'It's so calm here,' Priyanka said. 'I don't like it when Vroom gets all worked up. The boy needs to control his temper. Too much unchecked aggression going on there.'

'He's young and confused. Don't worry, life will slap him into shape. I think he regrets moving to Connexions sometimes. Besides, he hasn't taken his dad and mum's separation so well. It shows now and then.'

'Still, he should get a grip on himself. Get a steady girlfriend maybe, that will help him relax.'

'I think he likes Esha,' I said.

'I don't know if Esha is interested. She's really focused on her modelling.'

We reached our Qualis and I opened the door to take out a pack of cigarettes.

'No smoking near me,' she said and grabbed the pack from me.

'See, maybe it is not such a good idea to have a steady girlfriend,' I said.

'Really? So Mr Shyam is having second thoughts?' she said, tilting her head.

'No,' I said and opened the Qualis again. I took out a bottle.

'What's that?' she asked.

'Some Bacardi we keep handy. It's three hundred

bucks for a drink inside, the cost of this whole bottle.'

'Cool. You guys are smart,' Priyanka said and pulled at my cheek, then she took a sip from the bottle.

'Careful. There's no need to get drunk just because it's free.'

'Trust me. There is a need when you have a psycho parent.'

'What's going on now?'

'Nothing. I don't want to talk about her today. Let's do a shot.' The bottle's lid acted as one cup, and I broke the top of a cigarette packet for another. We poured Bacardi into both and warmth travelled down from my lips to my insides.

'I'm sorry about the Bakshi comment I made inside,' she said.

'It's all right. Doesn't matter,' I said, and wondered if we should do shot number two now or later.

'I can be a bitch sometimes, but I do make it up to you. I'm a loving person, no?' she said, high from mixing her drinks.

'You're just fine,' I said and looked at her moist eyes. Her nose puckered up a bit and I could have looked at it for ever.

'So,' she said.

'So what?' I said, still hypnotized by her nose.

'Why are you looking at me like that?' she said and smiled.

'Like what?'

'The come-hither look. I see mischief in your eyes,

mister,' she said playfully, grabbing both my hands.

'There's no mischief, that's just your imagination,' I said.

'We'll see,' she said and came up close. We hugged as she kissed me on my neck.

'Listen,' she said.

'What?' I mumbled.

'When was the last time we made love?'

'Oh, don't even ask. It's really pathetic – over a month ago.'

It was true. The only place we made love was in my house when it was empty. However, recently my mum had started staying at home more because of the cold. She'd even given up her favourite pastime of meeting relatives.

'Have you ever made love in a confined space?'

'*What*?' I said loudly, right into her ear.

'Ouch!' she said, rubbing her ear. 'Hello? You heard me right?'

'What are you talking about?'

'Well, we have the time, soft music and a desolate spot.'

'So?'

'So, step into the Qualis, my friend,' she said and opened the door. I climbed into the backseat and she followed me.

Our Qualis was parked right behind the disco, and we could hear the music if we were quiet. The song changed to 'Mahi Ve' from the movie *Kaante*.

'I love this song,' she said and sat astride my lap, facing me.

'It's a pole dancer's song. You know that?' I said.

'Yes. But I like the lyrics. Their love is true, but fate has something else in store.'

'I never focus on the lyrics.'

'You just notice the scantily clad girls in the video,' she said and ran her fingers through my hair.

I stayed silent.

'So, you didn't answer my question – have you made love in a confined space?' she said.

'Priyanka, are you crazy or are you drunk?'

She unbuttoned the top few buttons of my shirt. 'Both. OK, mister, the thing about being in a confined space is that you have to cooperate. Now move your hands out of the way,' she said.

We were quiet, apart from our breathing.

She confirmed that the windows were shut and ordered me to remove my shirt. She took off her kurti first, and then slowly unhooked her bra.

'Be careful with your clothes. We'll need to find them quickly afterwards,' she said.

'Are you mad?' I gasped as I raised my arms so she could pull my shirt over my head. She moved to kick my shirt aside and her foot landed on my left baby toe.

'Ouch!' I screamed.

'Oops, sorry,' she said in a naughty-apologetic

tone. As she moved her foot away, her head hit the roof.

'Ouch,' she said. 'Sorry, this isn't as elegant as in the *Titanic* movie.'

'It's all right. Clumsy sex is better than choreographed sex, and it's certainly better than no sex at all,' I said as I pulled her close.

'By the way, do you have a condom?' she said.

'Yes, sir. We live in constant hope,' I said as I pulled out my wallet.

We laughed as she embraced me. She started kissing me on my face, I kissed her shoulders and in a few moments, I forgot I was in the company Qualis.

Twenty minutes later we collapsed in each other's arms on the backseat.

'Amazing. That was simply amazing, Ms Priyanka.'

'My pleasure, sir,' she said and winked at me. 'Can we lie here and talk for a while?'

'Sure,' I said, reaching for my clothes.

She cuddled me again after we had dressed.

'Do you love me?' she asked. Her voice was serious.

'More than anybody else on this planet, and that includes me,' I said, caressing her hair.

'You think I'm a caring person?' she said. Her voice told me she was close to tears.

'Why do you keep asking me that?' I said.

'My mother was looking at our family album today. She stopped at a picture of me when I was three years old: I'm sitting on a tricycle and my mother is pushing me. She saw that picture, and d'you know what she said?'

'What?'

'She said I was so cute when I was three.'

'You're cute now,' I said and pressed her nose like a button.

'And she said I was so loving and caring then and that I wasn't so loving any more. She said she always wondered what had made me so heartless,' Priyanka said and burst into tears.

I held her tight and felt her body shake. I thought hard about what I could say. Guys can never figure out what to say in such emotional moments and always end up saying something stupid.

'Your mother is crazy . . .'

'Don't say anything about my mother. I love her. Can you just listen to me for five minutes?' Priyanka said.

'Of course. Sorry . . .' I said as her sobs grew louder. I swore to myself to stay quiet for the next five minutes. I started counting my breath to pass time. Sixteen a minute is my average; eighty breaths would mean I had listened to her for five minutes.

'We weren't always like this. My mum and I were best friends once – until class eight I think. Then as I became older, she became crazier,' she said.

I wondered if I should point out that she had just told me not to call her mum crazy. However, I had promised myself I would keep quiet.

'She had different rules for me and my brother, and that began to bother me. She would comment on everything I wore, everywhere I went, whereas my brother . . . she would never say anything to him. I tried to explain it to her, but she just became more irritating, and by the time I reached college I couldn't wait to get away from her.'

'Uh-uh,' I said, calculating that almost half my time must have passed. My leg was cramping. When sex is over, being in a confined space is a pain.

'All through college I ignored her and did what I wanted. In fact, this whole don't-care phase was born out of that. But at one level I felt so guilty. I tried again to connect with her after college, but she had a problem with everything: my thinking, my friends, my boyfriend.'

The last word caught my attention. I had to speak, even though only fifty-seven breaths had passed.

'Sorry, but did you say boyfriend?'

'Well, yeah. She knows I'm with you. And she has this thing about me finding someone settled.'

Settled? The word rewound and repeated itself in my head several times. *What does that mean anyway?* Just someone rich, or someone who gets predictable cash flows at the end of every month. Except parents do not say it that way because it sounds like they're trading their daughter to the highest bidder, which in some ways they are. They don't give a damn about love or feelings or crap like that. 'Show me the money

and keep our daughter for the rest of your life.'
That's the deal in an arranged marriage.

'What are you thinking about?' she said.

'I'm a loser according to your mum, aren't I?' I
said.

'That's not what I said.'

'Don't you bring up Bakshi and my promotion
every time we have a conversation?' I said, moving
away.

'Why do you get so defensive? Anyway, if Bakshi
doesn't promote you, you can look for another job.'

'I'm tired of job hunting. There's nothing good out
there. And I'm tired of rejections. Moreover, what is
the point of joining another call centre? I'd just have
to start as a junior agent all over again – without you,
without my friends. And let me tell you this, I may not
be team leader, but I am happy. I'm content. Do you
realize that? And tell your drama-queen mum to come
and tell me to my face that I'm a loser. And she can
send you off with whichever fucking settled-annuity-
income earner she likes. I am what I am,' I said, my
face beetroot-red.

'Shyam, please can you try and understand?'

'Understand what? Your mother? No, I can't. And
you can't either, but I suspect deep down you might
agree with her. Like, what am I doing with this loser?'
I said.

'Stop talking nonsense,' Priyanka shouted. 'I just
made love to you, for God's sake. And stop using that

loser word,' she said and burst into tears again.

Two brief knocks on the window disturbed our conversation. It was Vroom and Esha was standing next to him.

'Hello? I thought we came together. You love birds are inseparable, eh?' he said.

Chapter 13

12.45 a.m.

THE LOUD RING OF THE LANDLINE telephone brought me back from 32nd Milestone. Priyanka grabbed the phone. 'Hiiiii, Ganesh,' she said, her stretched tone too flirty, if you ask me. But then who the hell cares for my opinion anyway?

I wondered what *his* tone was like. *Get under the table. Tap the phone, Shyam,* a voice told me. I immediately scolded myself for such a horrible thought.

'Of course I knew it was you. No one else calls on this emergency line,' Priyanka said and ran her fingers through her hair. Women playing with their hair while talking to a guy is an automatic female preening gesture; I saw it once on the Discovery Channel.

'Yeah,' Priyanka said after a few seconds, 'I like cars. Which one are you planning to buy? ... A Lexus?'

'A Lexus! The dude is buying a Lexus!' Vroom

screamed, loud enough for me to understand that this was an expensive car.

'Ask him which model, ask him, please,' Vroom said, and Priyanka looked at him, startled. She shook her head at Vroom.

'Let them talk, Vroom. They've got better things to discuss than car models,' Esha said.

'What colour? C'mon, it's your car. How can I decide for you?' Priyanka said as her fingers started playing with the curled telephone wire. Over the next five minutes Ganesh did most of the talking, while Priyanka kept saying monosyllabic yeses or the equivalent.

Tap the phone, the voice kept banging in my head. I hated myself for it, but I wanted to do it. I wondered when Priyanka would step away from the desk.

'No, no, Ganesh, it's fine, go for your meeting. I'll be here, call me later,' Priyanka said as she ended her call. I guess Mr Microsoft did have some work to do after all.

'Vroom, is the Lexus a nice car?' Priyanka said.

Vroom was already on the Net, surfing Lexus pictures. He turned his monitor to Priyanka. 'Check this out. The Lexus is one of the coolest cars. The guy must be loaded.'

Priyanka looked at Vroom's screen for a few seconds and then turned to the girls. 'He wants me to choose the colour. Can you believe that? I don't think I should, though,' she said.

Vroom pushed himself back in his swivel chair. 'Go for black or silver. Nothing is as cool as the classic colours.

But I'll check out some more for you,' he said. 'And tell him the interiors have to be dark leather.'

Meanwhile, my interiors were on fire. I felt like throwing up.

I wondered when I could tap the phone. It was totally wrong, and Priyanka and the rest of the girls would probably kill me if they found out, but I had to do it. It was masochistic, but I just had to hear that ass woo my ex-girlfriend with the promise of expensive cars.

I tried to set the stage so I had an excuse to get under the table.

'Why have there been no calls in the last ten minutes?' I said. 'I should check if the connections are fine.'

'Leave it alone,' Esha said. 'I'm enjoying the break.'

'Yes, me too,' Radhika said. 'And the connection is fine. Bangalore is just over-eager and picking up all the calls.'

'Bio?' Priyanka said to Esha. It was their code word for a visit to the toilet together for a private conversation.

'Sure.' Esha sensed the need for gossip and got up from her chair.

'I'll come too,' Radhika said and stood up. She turned to me: 'The girls want a bio break, team leader.'

'You're *all* going?' I said, pretending to be reluctant, but secretly thrilled. This was my chance. 'Well, OK, since nothing much is happening right now.'

As soon as the girls were out of sight I dived under the table.

'What are you doing?' Vroom said.

'Nothing. I don't think the connections are firm,' I said.

131

'And what the hell do you know about the connections?' Vroom said. He bent down to look under the table. 'Tell me honestly what you're doing.'

I told him about my uncontrollable urge to tap the phone. Vroom scolded me for five seconds, but then got excited by the challenge and joined me under the table.

'I can't believe I'm helping you with this. The girls will kill us if they find out,' Vroom said.

'They won't have a clue,' I said, and connected the wires. 'Look, it's almost done.'

Vroom picked up the landline and we tested the arrangement. I could select an option on my computer and listen in on the landline via my headset. Mr Microsoft was in the bag.

'Why are you doing this?' Vroom said.

'I don't know. Don't ask me.'

'And why are the girls taking so long?'

'You know them, they have their girl talk in the toilet.'

'And you don't want to hear what they're saying? I'm sure they're discussing Mr Microsoft there.'

'Oh no,' I said, worried about what I could be missing. 'Although how would we be able to eavesdrop?'

'From the corner stall of the men's toilet,' Vroom said. 'It shares a wall with the girls' toilet. If you press your ear hard against the wall, you can hear them.'

'Really?' I said, my eyes lighting up.

Vroom nodded.

'It'll be wrong, though, eavesdropping through a stall,' I said.

'Yes, it will.'

'But who cares? Let's go,' I said and Vroom and I jumped off our chairs.

Vroom and I squeezed in and bolted the door in the corner stall of the WASG men's toilet. We pressed our ears against the wall until I could hear Radhika's voice.

'Yes, he sounds like a really nice guy,' she was saying.

'But I shouldn't tell him what colour to get, no? It's his car and it's so expensive. But do you know what he said?' Priyanka said.

'What?' Radhika said.

'He said, "No, it is *our* car," and then he said, "You have brought colour to my life, so you get to choose the colour."'

'Oh, he sounds so romantic,' Esha said.

'That is such a lame loser line. Colour to my life, my ass,' I said to Vroom.

'Shh. They'll hear us, stupid. Keep quiet,' Vroom said and put his hand on my mouth.

'Anyway, how's Anuj?' Priyanka said. I could hear the jingle of her bangles. She was probably brushing her hair.

'Anuj is fine,' Radhika said. 'He's at a dealer conference in Kolkata. I think he has to be up late as some dealers can't seem to have enough to drink.'

'Sales jobs are tough,' Esha said. 'OK, excuse me, but I have to change this . . . ouch!'

'What's going on?' I said.

Vroom shrugged his shoulders.

'Esha, your wound hasn't healed for days. Just a

133

Band-Aid isn't enough,' Priyanka said. I guessed Esha was changing the Band-Aid on her shin.

'No, I'm fine. As long as it heals before the Lakme fashion week,' Esha said.

'Let's go back, girls, it is almost 1:00 a.m.,' Radhika said. 'Otherwise the boys will grumble.'

'The boys always grumble. Like they never have a cigarette break,' Esha said.

'But today they are extra grumbly. At least *someone* is,' Radhika said.

Vroom pointed a finger at me. Yes, the girls were talking about me.

I grumbled in lip-sync.

'You think Shyam is not taking the news well?' Priyanka said, her voice becoming fainter as they walked towards the toilet's exit.

'You tell us. You know him better than we do,' Esha said.

'I wish I knew him now. I don't know why he sulks and acts so childishly sometimes,' Priyanka said as they left the toilet.

'Childish? Me? I am childish?' I said to Vroom, jumping up and down in the stall. 'What the hell. Mr Microsoft says his cheesy lines and he's cute and romantic. I say nothing and I'm childish,' I banged a fist on the stall door.

'Shyam, don't behave like a kid,' Vroom said.

We came out of the stall and I jumped back a step as I saw Bakshi by the sink.

Through the mirror, Bakshi saw both of us. His jaw dropped as he turned towards us.

'Hello, sir,' Vroom said and went up to the sink next to him.

'Sir, it's not what you think,' I said, pointing back at the stall.

'I'm not thinking anything. What you do in your personal lives is up to you. But why aren't you at the desk?' Bakshi said.

'Sir, we just took a short break. The call traffic is very low today,' I said.

'Did you log your break? The girls are missing from the bay as well,' Bakshi said. His face was turning from shiny pink to shiny red.

'Really? Where did the girls go?' Vroom said.

Bakshi turned away from us and walked to the urinal stalls. I went to the stall adjacent to him.

'Didn't you just use the toilet?' Bakshi said.

'Sir,' I said and hesitated. 'Sir, that was different, with Vroom.'

'Please. I don't want to know,' Bakshi said.

'Sir, no,' I said.

Now this is something women never have to deal with: standing next to your boss in the toilet as he pees is one of the world's most awkward situations. What are you supposed to do? Leave him alone or give him company and entertain him? Is it OK to talk to him while he is doing his business or not?

'Sir, how come you're using this restroom?' I said,

135

as I hadn't seen him there before.

'I didn't mean to. I always use the executive toilet,' Bakshi said.

'Yes, sir,' I said and nodded my head. I had acknowledged his magnanimous gesture of peeing in the same bay as us. But why was he here?

'Anyway, I came to your desk to drop off a courier delivery for Esha.'

'Courier?' Vroom said from his position at the sink. 'At this time?'

'I've left the parcel on her desk. Just let her know,' Bakshi said as he zipped up.

'And, Shyam, can you tell the voice agents to come to my office for a team meeting later, say 2:30 a.m., OK?' Bakshi said.

'What's up, sir?' Vroom said.

'Nothing. I want to share some pertinent insights with the resources. Anyway, can I ask you a couple of questions on the website? You know it well, don't you?'

'Yes, sir. And most questions will be answered in the FAQ section of the user manual we sent you,' Vroom said.

'FAQ?'

'Frequently asked questions.'

'Good. Boston may have some queries. I will rely on you smart people to answer them. For instance, how do you update the site for new computer models?'

'It's easy, sir. Any systems person can modify the website backend and change the queries to suit the model,' Vroom said.

Bakshi asked us a few more questions. They were simple enough for Vroom or me to answer, especially as we had built the website from scratch.

'Good, good. I'm impressed by your knowledge. Anyway, thanks for the user manual, I've already sent it to Boston,' Bakshi said and shook his hands dry. I moved away to avoid any droplets falling on me.

'You did?' both of us said in unison.

'Sir, if you could have copied us in on the email . . . we'd like to be kept in the loop,' Vroom said. Good one.

'Oh, didn't I? I'm so sorry. I'm not good with emails. I'll just forward it to you. But you guys man the bay now, OK?'

'Of course, sir,' I said.

'And have you finished the ad-hoc task I gave you?' Bakshi said.

'What, sir?' I said, and then realized he meant the photocopying of the board meeting invite. 'Almost done, sir.'

Bakshi nodded and left us behind in the restroom. I thought it was weird that Bakshi hadn't copied us in on the email with the attached website proposal, but it didn't surprise me.

'Is he a total moron or what? Can't cc people on an email?' Vroom said.

'Easy, man. Let's get back to the bay,' I said.

Chapter 14

1.00 a.m.

WE RETURNED FROM THE MEN'S ROOM to find the call flow had resumed at the WASG. Radhika explained to a caller how to open his vacuum cleaner. Priyanka advised a lady not to put hot pans in the dishwasher. Esha taught an old man to pre-heat an oven and simultaneously dodged his telephonic your-voice-is-so-sexy pass.

Another call flashed on my screen.

'I know this guy. Can I take this call?' Vroom said.

'Who is it?' I raised my eyebrows.

'A prick called William Fox. Listen in if you want,' Vroom said.

I selected the option on my computer.

'Good afternoon, Western Appliances, Victor speaking. How may I help you today, Mr Fox?' Vroom said.

'You'd better darn well help me, smart ass,' the man on the phone said. He had a rough voice with a heavy southern American accent; he sounded like he was in his mid-thirties and I would guess he was drunk.

'Who is he?' I whispered, but Vroom shushed me.

'Sir, if I may confirm, I am speaking to Mr William Fox?'

'You bet you are. You think just 'cos you know my name it's OK to sell me crap hoovers?'

'What is the problem with your vacuum cleaner, sir? It's a VX100?'

'It doesn't suck dust any more. It just doesn't.'

'Sir, do you remember when you last changed the dust bags?' Vroom said.

'Like fuck I remember when I changed the bags. It's just a crap machine, you dumbass.'

Vroom took three deep breaths and remembered the suggested line to use in such situations. 'Sir, I request you not to use that language.'

'Oh really? Then make your fucking hoover work.'

Vroom pressed a button on his phone before he spoke again. 'Fuck you first, you sonofabitch prickhead,' he said.

'What are you doing?' I said, panicking.

'Just venting, don't worry it's on mute,' Vroom smirked. 'Back to normal now.' He pressed the button again and said, 'Sir, you need to change the dust bags when they are full.'

'Who am I speaking to?' the voice on the phone became agitated.

'Victor, sir.'

'Tell me your fucking name. You're some kid in India, ain't ya?'

'Sir, I'm afraid I can't disclose my location.'

'You're from India. Tell me, boy.'

'Yes sir. I am in India.'

'So what did you have to do to get this job? Fucking degree in nuclear physics?'

'Sir, do you need help with your cleaner or not?'

'C'mon son, answer me. I don't need your help. Yeah, I'll change the dust bag. What about you guys? When will you change your dusty country?'

'Excuse me, sir, but I want you to stop talking like that,' Vroom said.

'Oh really, now some brown kid's telling me what to do—' William Fox's voice stopped abruptly as I cut off the call.

Vroom didn't move for a few seconds. His whole body trembled and he was breathing heavily, then he placed his elbows on the table and covered his face with his hands.

'You don't have to talk to those people. You know that,' I said to Vroom.

The girls glanced at us while they were still on their calls.

'Vroom, I'm talking to you,' I said.

He raised his face and slowly turned to look at me. Then he banged his fist on the table. 'Damn!' he screamed and kicked hard under the table.

'What the . . .' Priyanka said. 'My call just got cut off.'

Vroom's kick had dislodged the power wires, disconnecting all our calls. I wanted to check the wires, but had to check on Vroom first. Vroom stood up and his six-foot-plus frame towered above us.

'Guys, there are two things I cannot stand,' he said and showed us two fingers. 'Racists. And Americans.'

Priyanka started laughing.

'What is there to laugh at?' I said.

'Because there is a contradiction. He doesn't like racists, but can't stand Americans,' Priyanka said.

'Why?' Vroom said, ignoring Priyanka. 'Why do some fat-ass, dim-witted Americans get to act superior to us? Do you know why?'

Nobody answered.

Vroom continued, 'I'll tell you why. Not because they are smarter. Not because they are better people. But because their country is rich and ours is poor. That is the only damn reason. Because the losers who have run our country for the last fifty years couldn't do better than make India one of the poorest countries on earth.'

'Stop overreacting, Vroom. Some stupid guy calls and—' Radhika said.

'Screw Americans,' I said and gave him a bottle of water. 'Look, you've broken down the entire system.' I pointed to the blank call screens.

'Someone kicked the Americans a bit too hard. No more calls for now,' Priyanka said, rolling her eyes.

'Let me take a look,' I said and went under the table. I was more worried about the wires tapping the emergency phone. However, they were intact.

'Shyam, wait,' Esha said, 'we have a great excuse for not taking calls. Leave it like it is for a while.'

Everyone agreed with her. We decided to call systems after twenty minutes.

'Why was Bakshi here? I saw him come out of the men's toilet,' Priyanka said.

'To drop off a courier delivery for Esha,' I said. 'And he said there's a team meeting at 2:30 a.m. Oh man, I still have to photocopy the board meeting invite.'

I assembled Bakshi's sheets again.

'What delivery,' Esha said. 'This?'

She lifted a brown packet that was lying near her computer.

'Must be,' Vroom said, 'though what courier firm delivers stuff at this time of night?'

Esha opened the packet and took out two bundles of hundred-rupee notes. One bundle had a small yellow Post-it note on it. She read the Post-it and her face went pale.

'Wow, someone's rich,' Vroom said.

'Not bad. What's the money for?' Radhika said.

'It's nothing. Just a friend returning money she borrowed from me,' Esha said.

She dumped the packet in her drawer and took out her mobile phone. Her face was pensive, as if she was debating whether or not to make a call. I collected my sheets to go to the photocopying room.

'Want to help me?' I called out to Vroom.

'No thanks. People I used to work with are becoming national TV reporters, but look at me. I'm taking calls from losers and being asked to help with loser jobs,' Vroom said and looked away.

Chapter 15

1.30 a.m.

I SWITCHED ON THE PHOTOCOPIER in the supplies room and put Bakshi's stack in the document feeder. I'd just pressed the 'start' button on the agenda document when the copier creaked and groaned to a halt. 'Paper Jam: Tray 2' appeared in big, bold letters on the screen.

The copier in our supplies room is not a machine, it's a person. A person with a psychotic soul and a grumpy attitude. Whenever you copy more than two sheets, there's a paper jam. After that, the machine teases you: it gives you systematic instructions on how to unjam it – open cover, remove tray, pull lever – but if it knows so much, why doesn't it fix itself?

'Damn,' I mumbled to myself as I bent down to open the paper trays. I turned a few levers and pulled out whatever paper was in sight.

I stood up, rearranged the documents on the feeder tray and pressed 'start' again, not realizing that my ID was resting on Bakshi's original document. As the machine re-started it sucked in my ID along with the paper. The ID pulled at the strap, which tightened around my neck.

'Aargh,' I said as I choked. The ID went inside the machine's guts, and the strap curled tighter around my neck. I screamed loudly and pulled at my ID, but the machine was stronger. I was sure it wanted to kill me and was probably making a copy of my ID for my obituary while it was at it. I started kicking the machine hard.

Vroom came running into the room. 'What the . . .' he appeared nonplussed. He saw A4 sheets spread all over the room, a groaning photocopier and me lying down on top of it, desperately tugging at my ID strap.

'Do something,' I said in a muffled voice.

'Like what?' he said and bent over to look at the machine. The screen was flashing the poetic words 'Paper Jam' while my ID strap ran right into the machine.

Vroom looked around the supplies room and found a pair of scissors.

'Should I?' he said and smiled at me. 'I really want the others to see this.'

'Shut . . . up . . . and . . . cut,' I said.

Snap! In one snap my breath came back.

'OK now?' Vroom asked as he threw the scissors back in the supplies tray.

I nodded as I rubbed my neck and took wheezing breaths. I rested my head on the warm, soothing glass of the photocopier, but I must have rested it too hard, or maybe my head is too heavy, because I heard a crack.

'Fuck,' Vroom said, 'you broke the glass.'

'What?' I said as I lifted my head.

'Get off,' Vroom said and pulled me off the machine. 'What is it with you, man? Having a bad office supplies day?'

'Who knows?' I said, collecting Bakshi's document. 'I really am good for nothing. I can't even do these loser jobs. I almost died. Can you imagine the headline: COPIER DECAPITATES MAN, AND DUPLICATES DOCUMENT.'

Vroom laughed and put his arm around my shoulder.

'Chill out, man. I apologize.'

'For what?' I said. Nobody has ever apologized to me in the past twenty-six years of my life.

'I'm sorry I was rude and didn't come and help you. First there are these rumours about the call centre closing down, then my old workmate Boontoo makes it to NDTV and Bakshi sends the document without copying us in. Meanwhile, some psycho caller screams curses at me. It just gets to you sometimes.'

'What gets to you?' I asked. I was trying to copy Bakshi's document again, but the photocopier was hurling abusive messages at the screen every time I pressed a button. Soon it self-detected a crack in the glass and switched itself off altogether. I think it had committed suicide.

'Life,' Vroom said, sitting down on one of the stools in the supplies room, 'life gets to you. You think you're perfectly happy – you know, good salary, nice friends, life's a party – but all of a sudden, in one tiny snap, everything can crack, like the stupid glass pane of this photocopier.'

I didn't fully understand Vroom's glass-pane theory of

life, but his face told me he was upset. I decided to soothe the man who had just saved my life.

'Vroom, you know what your problem is?'

'What?'

'You don't have real love in your life. You need to fall in love, be in love and stay in love. That's the void in your life,' I said firmly, as if I knew what I was talking about.

'You think so?' Vroom said. 'I've had girlfriends. I'll find another one soon – you know that.'

'Not those kind of girls. Someone you really care about. And I think we all know who that is.'

'Esha?' he said.

I kept quiet.

'Esha isn't interested. I've asked her. She has her modelling and says she has no time for a relationship. Besides, she has other issues with me,' Vroom said.

'What issues?' I said.

'She says I don't know what love is. I care for cars and bikes more than girls.'

I laughed. 'You do.'

'That's such an unfair comparison. It's like asking women what they prefer, nice shoes or men. There's no easy answer.'

'Really? So we are benchmarked to footwear?'

'Trust me, women can ignore men for sexy shoes. But come to the point – Esha.'

'Do you think you love her?' I said.

'Can't say. But I've felt something for her for over a year now.'

'But you dated other girls last year.'

'Those girls weren't important. They were like TV channels you surf while looking for the programme you really want to see. You're with that Curly Wurly chick, even though you still have feelings for Priyanka,' Vroom said.

The statement startled me.

'Shefali is there to help me move on,' I said.

'Screw moving on. That girl is enough to put you off women for ever. Maybe that will help you get over Priyanka,' Vroom said.

'Don't change the subject. We're talking about you. I think you should ask Esha again for a real relationship. Do it, man.'

Vroom looked at me for a few seconds. 'Will you help me?' he said.

'Me? You're the expert with girls,' I said.

'This one is different. The stakes are higher. Can you be around when I talk to her? Just listen to our conversation, then maybe we can analyse it later.'

'OK, sure. So, let's do it now.'

'Now?'

'Why not? We have free time. Afterwards the calls will begin and we'll be busy again. Worst case, the management may fire us. So we'd better act fast, right?' I said.

'OK. Where do we do it?' Vroom said as he put his hand on his forehead to think. 'The dining room?'

The dining room made sense. I could be nearby, but inconspicuous.

Chapter 16

1.45 a.m.

'Is everything ok? I heard a noise,' Esha said, as we returned from the supplies room. She stretched back on her chair, so her top slid up, revealing her twinkling navel ring.

'The photocopier died. Anyone for a snack?' I said.

'Yes, let's go. I need a walk. Come on, Priyanka,' Esha said and tried to pull Priyanka up by her upper arm.

'No, I'll stay here,' Priyanka said and smiled. 'Ganesh might call.'

A scoop of hot molten lead entered through my head and left from my toes. *Try to move on*, I reminded myself. At the same time, I had the urge to pick up the landline and smash it into fifty pieces.

Radhika was about to get up when I stopped her.

'Actually, Radhika, can you stay here? If Bakshi walks by, at least he'll see some people at the desk,' I said.

Radhika sat down puzzled as we left the room.

* * *

The dining area at Connexions is a cross between a restaurant and a college hostel mess. There are three rows of long granite-covered tables, with seating on both sides. The chairs are plush, upholstered in black leather in an attempt to give them a hip designer look. The tables have a small vase every three feet. Management recently renovated the place when some overpriced consulting firm (full of MBAs) recommended that a bright dining room would be good for employee motivation. A much cheaper option would have been to just fire Bakshi, if you ask me.

Vroom took a cheese sandwich and chips – they don't serve Indian food, again for motivational reasons – on his tray and sat at one of the tables. Esha just took soda water and sat opposite Vroom. I think she eats once every three days. I took an unhealthy-sized slice of chocolate cake. I shouldn't have, but justified it as a well-deserved reward for helping a friend.

I sat at the adjacent table, took out my phone and started typing fake text messages.

'Why isn't Shyam sitting with us?' Esha said to Vroom, twisting on her seat to look at me.

'Private texting,' Vroom said. Esha rolled her eyes and nodded.

'Actually, Esha, I wanted to tell you something,' Vroom said, fingering the chips on his plate. I'd already finished half my cake – I was probably a pig with a reverse eating disorder in my previous life.

'Yeah?' Esha said to Vroom, dragging the word as an eyebrow rose in suspicion. The invisible female antennae were out and suggesting caution. 'Talk about what?'

'Esha,' Vroom said, clearing his throat. 'I've been thinking about you a lot lately.'

'Really?' she said and looked sideways to see if I was eavesdropping. Of course I was, but I made an extra effort to display a facial expression that showed I was focusing on my cake. She watched as I joyfully downed what was probably her entire weekly calorific consumption in just a few seconds.

'Yes really, Esha. I may have met a lot of girls, but no one is like you.'

She giggled and, taking a flower out from the vase, began plucking out its petals.

'Yes,' Vroom continued, 'and I think rather than fool around I could do with a real relationship. So I'm asking you again, will you go out with me?'

Esha was quiet for a few minutes. 'What do you expect me to say?'

'I don't know. How about a yes?'

'Really? Well, unfortunately that word didn't occur to me,' Esha said, her expression serious.

'Why?' Vroom said. I could tell he thought it was over already. He had told me once, if a girl hints she's not interested, it's time to cut your losses and leave. Never try the persuasion game.

'I've told you before. I have to focus on my modelling

career. I can't afford the luxury of having a boyfriend,' she said, her voice unusually cold.

'What is with you, Esha? Don't you want someone to support you . . .' Vroom said.

'That's right, with three different girlfriends last year I'm sure you will always be there for me,' Esha said.

'The other girls were just for fun. They meant nothing, they're like pizza or movies or something. They're channel surfing, you're more serious,' Vroom said.

'So what serious channel am I? The BBC?' Esha said.

'I've known you for more than a year. We've spent hundreds of nights together . . .'

I thought Vroom's last phrase came out odd, but Esha was too preoccupied to notice.

'Just drop it, Vroom,' Esha said and put the flower back in the vase. Her voice was breaking, though she wasn't crying yet.

'Are you OK?' Vroom said and extended his hand to hold hers. She sensed the move and pulled her hand away nanoseconds before he reached it.

'Not really,' Esha said.

'I thought we were friends. I just wanted to take it to the next level . . .' Vroom said.

'Please stop it,' Esha said, and covered her eyes with her hands. 'You chose the worst time to talk about this.'

'What's wrong, Esha? Can I help?' Vroom said, his voice now full of concern rather than the nervousness of romance.

She shook her head frantically.

I knew Vroom had failed miserably. Esha wasn't interested and was in a really strange mood. I finished my thousand-calorie chocolate cake and went to the counter to get water. By the time I returned, they had left the dining room.

Chapter 17

2.00 a.m.

I RETURNED TO THE WASG BAY with the taste of chocolate cake lingering in my mouth. I sat down at my desk and began surfing irrelevant websites. Radhika was giving Priyanka recommendations on the best shops in Delhi for bridal dresses, while Esha and Vroom were silent. My guilt over the chocolate cake combined with my guilt for not reporting the systems failure, and when guilt combines, it multiplies manifold. I finally called IT to fix our desk. They were busy, but promised to come in ten minutes.

The spare landline's ring startled us all.

'Ganesh,' Priyanka said as she scrambled to pick up the phone. I kept a calm face while I selected the option to listen in on the call.

'Mum,' Priyanka said, 'why aren't you sleeping? Who gave you this number?'

'Sleeping? No one has slept a wink today,' her mother said in an excited voice.

The tapped line was exceptionally clear. Her mother sounded elated, which was unusual for a woman who, according to Priyanka, had spent most of her life in self-imposed, obsessive-compulsive depression.

Priyanka's mother explained how Ganesh had just called her and given her the emergency line number. Ganesh's family in India had also not slept; they'd been calling Priyanka's parents at least once an hour. Ganesh had told Priyanka's family that he was 'on top of the world'. I guess the sad dude really had no other life.

'I'm so happy today. Look how God sent such a perfect match right to our door. And I used to worry about you so much,' Priyanka's mother said.

'That's great, Mum, but what's up?' Priyanka said. 'I'll be home in a few hours. How come you called here?'

'Can't a mother call her daughter?' Priyanka's mum said. 'Can't a mother' is one of her classic lines.

'No Mum, I just wondered. Anyway, Ganesh and I have spoken a couple of times today.'

'And?'

'And what?'

'Did he tell you his plans?'

'What plans?'

'He is coming to India next month. Originally he'd planned the trip so he could see girls, but now that he has made his choice, he wants to get married instead on the same trip,' Priyanka's mum announced, her voice turning breathless.

'What?' Priyanka said, 'next month?' and looked

around at all of us with a shocked expression. Everyone returned puzzled looks, as if they didn't know what was going on. I also pretended to look confused.

'Mum, no!' Priyanka wailed. 'How can I get married next month? That's less than five weeks away.'

'Oh you don't have to worry about that. I am there to organize everything. You wait and see, I'll work day and night to make it a grand event.'

'Mum, I'm not worried about organizing a party. I have to be *ready* to get married. I hardly know Ganesh,' Priyanka said, entwining her fingers nervously in the telephone wire.

'Huh? Of course you're ready for it. When the families have fixed the match and bride and groom are happy, why delay? And the boy can't keep visiting again and again. He's in an important position after all.'

Yeah right, I thought. He was probably one of the thousands of Indian geeks coding away at Microsoft. But to his in-laws, he was Bill Gates himself.

'Mum, please. I can't go ahead with it next month. Sorry, but no,' Priyanka said, 'and I have to put the phone down now.'

'What do you mean no? This is too much. Do you have to disagree with me always or what?'

'Mum, how does this have anything to do with disagreeing with you? In fact, how does it have anything to do with you? It's my life, and sorry, I can't marry anyone I have only known for five weeks.'

Priyanka's mother stayed silent for a while. I thought

she would retaliate, but then I figured out that the silence was working more effectively than words. She knows how to put an emotional slasher knife right at Priyanka's neck.

'Mum, are you there?' Priyanka asked after ten seconds.

'Yes, I'm still here. I'll be dead soon, but unfortunately I'm still here.'

'Mum, c'mon now . . .'

'Don't even make me happy just by chance,' Priyanka's mother said. What a killer line, I thought. I almost applauded.

Priyanka threw a hand up in the air in exasperation, then grabbed a stress ball lying near Vroom's computer across the table and squeezed it hard. I tugged the headset closer to my ear as Priyanka's voice turned softer.

'Mum, please. Don't do this.'

'You know I prayed for one hour today . . . praying you stay happy . . . for ever,' Priyanka's mother said as she broke into tears. Whoever starts crying first always has an advantage in an argument. This works for Priyanka's mother, who at least has obedient tear glands, if not an obedient daughter.

'Mum, don't create a scene. I'm at work. What do you want from me? I have agreed to the boy. Now why is everyone pushing me?'

'Isn't Ganesh nice? What's the problem?' her mother said in a tragic tone that could put any Bollywood hero's mother to shame.

'Mum, I didn't say he isn't nice, I just need time.'

'You aren't distracted, are you? Are you still talking to

that useless call-centre chap, what's his name? Shyam?'

I jumped.

'No, Mum. That's over. I've told you so many times. I've agreed to Ganesh, right?'

'So, why can't you agree to next month – for everyone's happiness? Can't a mother beg her daughter for this?'

There you go: can't-a-mother No. 2 for the night.

Priyanka closed her eyes to compose herself and spoke slowly, 'Can I think about it?'

'Of course. Think about it. But think for all of us, not just yourself.'

'OK. I will. Just . . . just give me some time.'

Priyanka hung up the phone and kept still while the girls asked her for details.

She looked around and threw the stress ball at her monitor.

'Can you believe it? She wants me to get married next month. Next month!' Priyanka said and stood up. 'They brought me up for twenty-five years, and now they can't wait more than twenty-five days to get rid of me. What is it with these people? Am I such a burden?' Priyanka repeated her conversation to Esha and Radhika. Vroom checked his computer to see if Bakshi had sent us any emails.

'It doesn't matter, right? You have to marry him any-way. Why drag it out?' Radhika said to Priyanka.

'Yes, you get to drive the Lexus sooner, too,' Vroom said, without looking up from his screen. Screw Vroom. I gave him a firm glare out of the corner of my eye.

'What will I wear?' Esha said. Her sombre mood had lightened with the new announcement. Give her a chance to dress up and she'll ignore people dying all around her. 'This is too short notice,' she continued. 'I need a new dress for every ceremony.'

'Get your *designer friends* to lend you a few dresses,' Vroom said to Esha with a hint of sarcasm in his voice.

Esha's face dropped again. Only I saw it, but her eyes became wet. She took a tissue from her purse, pretended to fix her lipstick and casually wiped away her tears.

'I'm so not ready for this. In one month I'll be someone's wife. Gosh, little kids will call me auntie,' Priyanka said.

Everyone discussed the pros and cons of Priyanka getting married in four weeks' time. Most of them felt getting married so quickly wasn't such a big deal once she had chosen the guy. Of course, most people didn't give a damn about me.

In the midst of the discussions the systems guy returned to our desk.

'What happened here?' he said from under the table. 'Looks like someone ripped these wires apart.'

'I don't know,' I said. 'See if we can get some traffic again.'

Priyanka's mother and her words – 'the useless call-centre boy' – resounded in my head. I remembered the time when Priyanka told me her mother's views about me. It wasn't long ago: it was one of our last dates at Mocha Café.

Chapter 18

My Past Dates with Priyanka – IV

Mocha Café, Greater Kailash I
Five months earlier

WE PROMISED TO MEET ON ONE CONDITION: we wouldn't fight. No blame games, no sarcastic comments and no judgemental remarks. She was late again. I fiddled with the menu and looked around. Mocha's décor had a Middle Eastern twist, with hookahs, velvet cushions and coloured glass lamps everywhere. Many of the tables were occupied by couples, sitting with intertwined fingers, obviously deeply in love. The girls laughed at whatever the guys said. The guys ordered the most expensive items on the menu. Every now and then their eyes met and giggles broke out. It was perfect, like all they needed to be happy was each other. Aren't the silly delusions in the initial stage of a relationship amazing?

My life was nowhere near perfect, of course. For

starters, my girlfriend, if I could still call her that, was late. Plus I could sense she was itching to dump me. Priyanka and I had ended eight of our last ten phone calls with one of us hanging up on the other.

I hadn't slept the entire day, which isn't a big deal for most people, but considering I work all night, it hadn't left me feeling too good. My job was going nowhere, with Bakshi bent on sucking every last drop of my blood. Maybe he was right – I just didn't have the strategic vision or managerial leadership or what-ever crap things you are supposed to have to do well in life. Maybe Priyanka's mum was right too, and her daughter was stuck with a loser.

These thoughts enveloped me as she came in. She had just had a haircut and her waist-length hair was now just a few inches below her shoulders. I liked her with long hair, but she never listened to me. I told you, I didn't have the leadership skills to influence *anyone*. Anyway, her hair still looked nice. She wore a white linen top and a flowing lavender skirt with lots of crinkly edges. She wore a thin silver necklace, with the world's tiniest diamond pendant hanging from it. I stared at my watch as a sign of protest.

'Sorry, Shyam,' she said as she put a giant brown bag on the table, 'that ass hairdresser took so long. I told him I had to leave early.'

'No big deal. A haircut has to be more important than me,' I said without any emotion in my voice.

'I thought we said no sarcasm,' she said, 'and I did say sorry.'

'That's right. One sorry every half an hour seems fair. In fact, go and get a two-hour facial done while you're at it, then you can come back and say sorry four times.'

'Shyam, please. I know I'm late. We promised not to fight. Saturday is the only day I get time for a haircut.'

'I told you to keep your hair long,' I said.

'I did for a long time, but it's so hard to maintain, Shyam. I'm sorry, but you have to understand, I had the most boring hair and I couldn't do anything with it. It took a whole hour to oil the damn thing, and it's so hot in the Delhi heat.'

'Whatever,' I said in a dismissive voice, looking at the menu. 'What do you want?'

'I want my Shyam to be in a good mood,' she said and held my hand. We didn't intertwine fingers, though.

'My' Shyam. I guess I still count, I thought. Girls sure know how to sweet-talk.

'Hmm,' I said and let out a big sigh. If she was trying to make peace, I guess I had to do my bit. 'We can have their special freeze-dried Maggi noodles.'

'Maggi? You've come all this way to eat Maggi?' she said, and took the menu from me. 'And check this out: ninety bucks for Maggi?' She said the last phrase so loudly that the tables and a few waiters next to us heard.

'Priyanka, we earn now. We can afford it,' I said.

'Order chocolate brownies and ice cream,' she said. 'Or at least something you don't get at home.'

'I thought you said you'll have whatever I want,' I said.

'Yes, but Maggi?' she said and made a quirky face. Her nostrils contracted for a second. I had seen that face before, and I couldn't help but smile. I saved myself time by ordering the brownie.

The waiter brought the chocolate brownie and placed it in front of Priyanka – half a litre of chocolate sauce dripping over a blob of vanilla ice cream placed precariously on top of a huge slice of rich chocolate cake. It was a heart attack served on a plate. Priyanka had two spoons and slid the dish towards me.

'Look at me, eating away like a cow,' she said.

'Did you have a heart to heart with your mum?' I said.

Priyanka wiped her chocolate-lined lips with tissue. I felt like kissing her right then. However, I hesitated. When you hesitate in love, you know something is wrong.

'Me and my mum,' she said, 'are incapable of having a rational, sane conversation. I tried to talk to her about you and my plans to study further. It sounds like a simple conversation, right?'

'What happened?'

'In seven minutes we were crying. Can you believe it?'

'With your mother, I can. What exactly did she say?'

'You don't want to know.'

'But I have to know,' I insisted.

'She said she has never liked you because you aren't settled, and because since the day I started dating you I have changed and become an unaffectionate, cold person.'

'Unaffectionate? What the . . . ?' I shouted, my face turning red. 'How the hell have I changed you?'

The second comment cut me into slices. Sure, I hated the 'not settled' tag, but there was some truth to that.

But how could she accuse me of turning Priyanka into a cold person?

She didn't say anything, but her face softened and I heard tiny sobs. It was so unfair, I was the one being insulted: I should be the one getting to cry. However, I guess only girls look nice crying on dates.

'Listen, Priyanka, your mum is a psycho,' I said.

'No she's not. It's not *because* of you, but I *have* changed. Maybe it is because I'm older, and she confuses it with my being with you. We used to be so close, and now she doesn't like anything I do,' she said and broke down into full-on crying. Everyone in the café must have thought I had cheated on my girlfriend and was dumping her or something. I got some you-horrible-men looks from girls at other tables.

'Calm down, Priyanka. What does she want?

And tell me honestly, what do you want?' I said.

Priyanka shook her head and remained silent.

The effort it sometimes takes to make women speak up is harder than interrogating terrorists.

'Please, talk to me,' I said, looking at the brownie. The ice cream had melted into a gooey mess.

She finally spoke. 'She wants me to show that I love her. She wants me to make her happy and marry someone she chooses for me.'

'And what do you want?' I said.

'I don't know,' she told the tablecloth.

What the hell? I thought. All I get for four years of togetherness is an 'I don't know'?

'You want to dump me, don't you? I'm just not good enough for your family.'

'It isn't like that, Shyam. She married my dad, who was just a government employee, because he seemed like a decent human being. But her sisters waited and married better-qualified boys, and they are richer today. Her concern for me comes from that. She is my mother. It's not as if she doesn't know what's good for me. I want someone doing well in his career too.'

'So your mother is not the only cause for the strain in our relationship. It's you as well.'

'A relationship never flounders for one reason alone, there are many issues. You don't take feedback. You're sarcastic. You don't understand my ambitions. Don't I always tell you to focus on your career?'

'Just get lost, OK,' I said.

My loud voice attracted the attention of the neighbouring tables. All the girls at Mocha were probably convinced I was the worst possible male chauvinist pig.

Her tears came back until she noticed people watching us and composed herself. A few wipes with a tissue and she was normal again.

'Shyam, it's this attitude of yours. At home, my mother doesn't understand, and now it's you who doesn't. Why have you become like this? You've changed, Shyam, you are not the same happy person I first met,' she said, her voice restrained but calm.

'Nothing has happened to *me*. It's you who finds new faults in me every day. I have a bad boss and I'm trying to manage as happily as possible. What has happened to you? You used to eat at truck drivers' dhabas, now all of a sudden you need to marry an expat cardiac surgeon to make ends meet?'

We stared at each other for two seconds.

'OK, it's my fault. That's what you want to prove, isn't it? I'm a confused, selfish, mean person, right?' she said.

I couldn't believe I had loved her and those flared nostrils for four years, and now it was difficult to say four sentences without disagreeing.

I sighed. 'I thought there was to be no arguing, blaming or sarcasm, but that's all we've done.'

'I care for you a lot,' she said and held my hand.

'Me, too,' I said, 'but I think we need to take care of other things in our life as well.'

We asked for the bill and made cursory conversation about the weather, traffic and the café decor. We talked a lot, but we weren't communicating at all.

'Call me in the evening if you're free,' I said as I paid the bill and got up to leave.

It had come to this: now we had to tell each other to call. Previously, not a waking hour had passed without one of us texting or calling the other.

'OK, or I'll text you,' she said.

We had a basic hug without really touching. A kiss was out of the question.

'Sure,' I said, 'it's always nice to get your messages.'

Sarcasm. Man, will I never learn?

Chapter 19

1.59 a.m.

MOCHA CAFÉ AND ITS COLOURED ARABIAN LIGHTS faded away from my mind as I returned to WASG's tube-lit interiors. I checked the time: it was close to 2 a.m. I got up to take a short walk. I didn't know what was more disgusting: thinking about Priyanka's mother or hearing the girls obsess about Priyanka's marriage. I went to the corner of the room where Military Uncle sat and we nodded to each other. I looked at his screen and saw pictures of animals – chimps, rhinos, lions and deer.

'Are those your customers?' I said and laughed at my own unfunny joke.

Military Uncle smiled back. He was in one of his rare good moods.

'These are pictures I took at the zoo. I scanned them to send to my grandson.'

'Cool. He likes animals?' I said and bent over to take a

closer look at the chimp. It bore an uncanny resemblance to Bakshi.

'Yes, I'm sending it by email to my son. But I'm having trouble as our emails don't allow more than four-megabyte attachments.'

I decided to help Uncle, if only to avoid going back to my seat until the systems guy had fixed the phones.

'Hmm, these are large files,' I said, as I took over his mouse. 'I could try to zip them, though that won't compress images much. The other way is to make the pictures low resolution. Otherwise, you could leave a few animals out.'

Military Uncle wanted to keep them high resolution, so we agreed to leave out the deer and the hippos as those weren't his grandson's favourite animals.

'Thanks so much, Shyam,' Military Uncle said, as I successfully pressed 'send' on his email. I looked at his face and there was genuine gratitude. It was hard to believe he had been booted out because he was too bossy with his daughter-in-law – a piece of gossip Radhika had once passed on to me.

'You're welcome,' I said. I noticed Vroom signal to me to come back. Hoping that the topic of Priyanka's wedding was over, I returned to the desk.

'Bakshi has sent us a copy of the proposal,' Vroom said.

I sat at my desk and opened my inbox. There was a message from Bakshi.

The calls had not resumed, so the systems guy had gone back to his department to get new wires.

'Let's see which white bozos he sucked up to. Who has he sent it to?' Vroom's voice was excited.

I opened the mail to see who had been the original recipients. It was like a *Who's Who* of Western Computers and Appliances in Boston: the sales manager, the IT manager, the operations head and several others. Bakshi had sent it to the entire directory of people in our client base. I have to say, he makes a better mass sucker-upper than he would a gangbang porn star.

'He's copied in everyone. Senior management in Boston in the "To" field, and India senior management in the "Cc" field,' I said.

'And yet somehow he forgot to copy us in,' Vroom said.

I read out the contents of his short mail:

```
Dear All,
Attached please find the much-awaited user
manual of the customer service website
that has altered the parameters of customer
service at Western Appliances. I have only
just completed this and would love to
discuss it further on my imminent trip
to . . .
```

I let out a silent whistle.

'Boston? Why is that ass going to Boston?' Vroom said.

The girls heard us.

'What are you talking about?' Priyanka said.

'Bakshi's going to Boston,' Vroom said. 'Any of you ladies want to tag along?'

'What?' Esha said. 'What's he going to Boston for?'

'To talk about our website. Must have swung a trip for himself,' I said.

'What the hell is going on here anyway? On the one hand we're downsizing to save costs, on the other hand there's cash to send idiots like Bakshi on trips to the US?' Vroom said and threw his stress ball on the table. It hit the pen stand, spilling the contents.

'Careful,' Esha said, sounding irritated as a few pens rolled towards her. She had her mobile phone in her hand; she was probably still trying to call someone.

'Madness, that is what this place is. Boston!' Priyanka said and shook her head. She was surfing the Internet. I wondered which sites she was looking at: wedding dresses, lifestyle in the US, or the official Lexus website?

I was about to close Bakshi's message when Vroom stopped me.

'Open the document,' Vroom said, 'just open the file he sent.'

'It's the same file we sent him. The user manual,' I said.

'Have you opened it?'

'No, what's the point?'

'Just open it,' he roared so loudly that Esha looked at us. I wondered who she was calling this late.

I opened the file containing our user manual.

'Here, it's exactly the same,' I said and scrolled down. As

170

I reached the bottom of the first page, my jaw dropped, partly in horror and partly in preparation for some major cursing.

Western Computers Troubleshooting Website
Project Details and User Manual

Developed by Connexions, Delhi

Subhash Bakshi
Manager, Connexions

'Like fuck it's the same,' Vroom said and threw the pens he'd picked up back on the table. One landed on Esha's lap, who by this time had tried to connect to a number at least twenty times. She threw an angry look at Vroom and hurled the pen back at him. He ignored her, his eyes fixed on my screen.

'It says it's by fucking Subhash Bakshi,' Vroom said, tapping his finger hard on my monitor. 'Check this out. Mr Moron, who can't tell a computer from a piano, has created this website and this manual. Like crap he has.'

Vroom banged his fists on the table. In a mini-fit, he violently swept the table with his hands. Now the pens were on the floor.

'What is wrong with you?' Esha said and pulled her chair away. She got up and went to the conference room, desperately shaking the phone to get a connection.

'He passed off our work as his, Shyam. Do you realize that?' he said and shook my shoulder hard.

I stared numbly at the first page of our, or rather Bakshi's, manual. This time Bakshi had surpassed himself. My head felt dizzy and I fought to breathe.

'Six months of work on this manual alone,' I said and closed the file. 'I never thought he'd stoop this low.'

'And?' Vroom said.

'And what? I don't really know what to do. I'm in shock. And on top of all this, there's the fear he may downsize us,' I said.

'Downsize us?' Vroom said and stood up. 'We've worked on it for six months, man. And all you can say is we can't do anything "as he may downsize us"? That fucking loser Baskhi is turning *you* into a loser. Mr Shyam, you are turning into a mousepad, people are rolling over you every day. Priyanka, tell him to say something. Go to Bakshi's office and have it out with him.'

Priyanka looked up at us, and for the second time that night our eyes met. She had that look; that same gaze that used to make me feel so small. Like what was the point of even shouting at me.

She shook her head and gave a wry smile. I knew that wry smile, too, like she'd known this was coming all along. I had the urge to shake her. It's frigging easy to give those looks when you have a Lexus waiting for you, I wanted to say. But I didn't say anything. Bakshi's move had hurt me – it wasn't just the six months of toil, but that the prospects for my promotion were gone. And that meant – poof! – Priyanka was gone, too. But right now the people around me just wanted to see me get angry. People see you as weak if you express hurt. They always want to see you strong, as in a raging temper. Maybe I don't have it in me? That's why I'm not a team leader, that's why no girls distribute sweets in the office for me.

'Are you there, Mr Shyam?' Vroom said. 'Let's email all the recipients of this message and tell them what's going on.'

'Just cool down, Vroom. There's no need to act like a hero,' I snapped.

'Oh really? So, who should we act like? Losers? Tell us, Shyam, you should be the expert on that,' Vroom said.

A surge of anger choked me. 'Just shut up and sit down,' I said. 'What do you want to do? Send another email to the whites and tell them about the infighting going on here? Who are they going to believe? Someone who's on his way to Boston for a meeting or some frustrated agent who claims he did all the work? Get real, Mr Varun. You'll get fired and that's it. Bakshi is management, but all he manages is only his own career, not us.' I was so caught up in the argument I didn't even notice Radhika, who was standing next to me with a bottle of water in her hand.

'Thanks,' I said and took a few noisy sips.

'Feeling better?' Radhika said.

I raised my hand to stop her from saying more. 'I don't want to talk about this any more. This is between Bakshi and us. And I don't need the opinions of random people

173

whose life is just one big party.' I sat down and glared at Vroom.

He opened a notepad and drew a 2x2 matrix.

'What the fuck is that?' I said.

'I think I've finally figured Bakshi out. Let me explain with the help of a diagram,' Vroom said.

'I'm not in the mood for diagrams,' I said.

'Just listen,' Vroom said as he labelled the matrix.

On the horizontal axis he wrote 'good' and 'evil' next to each box. On the vertical axis, he wrote 'smart' and 'stupid'.

'OK, here is my theory about people like Bakshi,' Vroom said and pointed at the matrix with his pen. 'There are four kinds of bosses in this world, based on two dimensions: a) how smart or stupid they are, and b) whether they are good or evil. Only with extreme good luck do you get a boss who is smart *and* a good human being. However, Bakshi falls into the most dangerous and common category. He is stupid, as we all know, but he is evil, too,' Vroom said, tapping his pen in the relevant quadrant of the matrix.

'Stupid and evil,' I echoed.

'Yes, we've underestimated him. He is frightening. He's like a blind snake: you feel sorry for it, but it still has a poisonous bite. You can see it – he is stupid, hence the call centre is so mismanaged, but he is also evil, so he'll make sure all of us go down instead of him.'

I shook my head.

'Forget it. Destiny has put an asshole in my path. What can I say?'

Radhika took the bottle from my desk. 'Sorry to interrupt your discussion, guys, but I hope you weren't talking about me when you mentioned people whose lives are one big party. My life is not a party, my friend. It really isn't—'

'It wasn't you, Radhika. Shyam most clearly meant me,' Priyanka interrupted.

'Oh forget it,' I said and stood up. I moved from the desk, just to get away from everyone. As I left, I could hear Vroom's words, 'If I could just once have the opportunity to fuck with Bakshi's happiness, I'd consider myself the luckiest person on earth.'

Chapter 20

2.10 a.m.

As I walked away from the WASG desk, my mind was still in turmoil. I felt like chopping Bakshi up into little bits and feeding them to every street dog in Delhi. I approached the conference room to find the door was shut. I knocked and waited for a few seconds.

'Esha?' I said and turned the knob to open the door.

Esha was sitting on one of the conference-room chairs. Her right leg was bent and resting on another chair as she examined the wound on her shin. She held a blood-tipped Stanley knife in her hand and I noticed a used Band-Aid on the table. There was fresh blood coming out of the wound on her shin.

'Are you OK?' I said, moving closer.

Esha turned to look at me with a blank expression.

'Oh hi, Shyam,' she said in a calm tone.

'What are you doing here? Everyone's looking for you.'

'Why? Why would anyone be looking for me?'

'No particular reason. What are you doing here anyway? And your wound is bleeding, do you want some lotion or a bandage?' I said and looked away. The sight of blood nauseates me. I don't know how doctors show up to work every day.

'No, Shyam, I like it like this. With lotion it may stop hurting,' Esha said.

'What?' I said. 'But you want to stop the pain, don't you?'

'No,' Esha smiled sadly. She pointed to the wound with the knife. 'This pain takes my mind away from the real pain. Do you know what real pain is, Shyam?'

I really had no idea what she was on about, but I knew that if she didn't cover the wound up soon, I'd throw up my recently consumed chocolate cake.

'Listen, I'll get the first-aid kit from the supplies room.'

'You haven't answered my question. What is real pain, Shyam?'

'I don't know, what is it?' I said, shifting anxiously as I saw fresh drops of blood trickle down her smooth leg.

'Real pain is mental pain,' Esha said.

'Right,' I said, trying to sound intelligent. I sat down on a chair next to her.

'Ever felt mental pain, Shyam?'

'I don't know if I have. I'm a shallow guy, you see. There are lots of things I don't feel,' I said.

'Everyone feels pain, because everyone has a dark side to their life.'

'Dark side?'

'Yes, dark side – something you don't like about yourself, something that makes you angry or that you fear. Do you have a dark side, Shyam?'

'Oh, let's not go there. I have so many, like half a dozen dark sides. I am a dark-sided hexagon,' I said.

'Ever felt guilt, Shyam? Real, hard, painful guilt?' she said as her voice became weak.

'What's happened, Esha?' I said, as I finally found a position that allowed me to look at her face but avoid a view of her wound.

'Do you promise not to judge me if I tell you something?'

'Of course,' I said. 'I'm a terrible judge of people anyway.'

'I slept with someone,' she said and let out a sigh, 'to win a modelling contract.'

'What?' I said, as it took me a second to figure out what she meant.

'Yes, my agent said this man was connected and I just had to sleep with him once to get a break in a major fashion show. Nobody forced me, I chose to do it. But ever since, I've felt this awful guilt. Every single moment. I thought it would pass, but it hasn't. And the pain is so bad that this wound in my leg feels like a tickle,' she said and took the knife to her shin where she started scraping the skin around her wound.

'Stop it, Esha, what are you doing?' I said and snatched the knife from her. 'Are you insane? You'll get tetanus or gangrene or whatever other horrible things they show on TV in those vaccination ads.'

'This is tame. I'll tell you what's dangerous. My own fucked-up brain, the delusional voice that says I have it in me to become a model. You know what the man said afterwards?'

'Which man?' I said as I shoved the knife to the other side of the table.

'The guy I slept with – a forty-year-old designer. He told my agent I was too short to be a catwalk model,' Esha said, her voice rising as anger mingled with sadness. 'Like the bastard didn't know that before he slept with me.' She began crying. I don't know what's worse, a shouting girl or a crying one. I'm awful at handling either. I placed my hands on Esha's shoulders, ready for a hug in case she needed it.

'And that son of a bitch sends some cash as compensation afterwards,' she said, sobbing. 'And my agent tells me, "This is part of life." Sure it's part of life – part of Esha the failed model's fucked-up life. Give me the knife back, Shyam,' she said, holding out her palm.

'No, I won't. Listen, now I'm not really sure what to do in this situation, but just take it easy,' I said. It was true; nobody would ever demand to have sex with me. Therefore, feeling-guilty-after-demanded-sex was completely unfamiliar territory.

'I hate myself, Shyam. I just hate myself. And I hate my face, and the stupid mirror that shows me my face. I hate myself for believing people who told me I could be a model. Can I get my face altered?'

I don't know of any plastic surgeons who specialize in

making pretty girls ugly, so I kept quiet. After ninety seconds she stopped crying, around about the same time any girl would stop crying if you ignored her. She took a tissue from her bag and wiped her eyes.

'Shall we go? They must be waiting,' I said. She reached for my hand to stand up.

'Thanks for listening to me,' Esha said. Only women think there is a reason to thank people when someone listens to them.

Chapter 21

2.20 a.m.

TO MY DISGUST, Priyanka's wedding was still the topic of discussion when Esha and I returned to the bay.

Esha sat down quietly.

'Now where were you?' Priyanka asked Esha.

'Still here. I wanted to make a private call,' Esha said.

'I'm taking mother-in-law tips from Radhika,' Priyanka said. 'I'm so not looking forward to that part. She seems nice now, but who knows how she'll turn out.'

'C'mon, you're getting so much more in return. Ganesh is such a nice guy,' Radhika said.

'Anyway I'd take three mothers-in-law for a Lexus. Bring it on, man,' Vroom said.

Radhika and Priyanka started laughing.

'I'll miss you, Vroom,' Priyanka said, still laughing, 'I really will.'

'Who else will you miss?' Vroom said and all of us fell silent.

Priyanka shifted on her seat: Vroom had put her on the spot. 'Oh I'll miss all of you,' she said, diplomacy queen that she is when she wants to be.

'Whatever,' Vroom said.

'Anyway, don't wish for three mothers-in-law, Vroom. It would be like asking for three Bakshis,' said Radhika. 'Or at least it can be for some women.'

'So your mother-in-law is evil?' Vroom said.

'I never said she's bad. But she did say those things to Anuj. What will he think?'

'Nothing. He won't think anything. He knows how lucky he is to have you,' Priyanka said firmly.

'It's hard sometimes. She isn't my mum, after all.'

'Oh, don't go there. I can get along with anyone else's mum better than my own. My mum's neurosis has made me mother-in-law proof,' Priyanka said, and everyone on the desk laughed. I didn't, though, as there's nothing funny about Priyanka's mum to me. Emotional manipulators like her should be put in jail and made to watch daytime TV all day.

'Anuj will be OK now, right? Tell me, guys: he won't hate me?' Radhika said.

'No,' Priyanka got up and went to Radhika. 'He loves you and he will be fine.'

'D'you want to check if he's okay?' Vroom said. 'I have an idea.'

'What?' Radhika said.

I looked at Vroom. What the hell did he have to say about Anuj and Radhika?

'Let's play radio jockey,' Vroom said. Radhika was baffled.

'I'll call Anuj and pretend I'm calling from a radio show. Then I'll tell him he's won a prize, a large bouquet of roses and a box of Swiss chocolates which he can send to anyone he loves, anywhere in India, with a loving message. So then, we'll all get to hear the romantic lines he has for you.'

'C'mon, it will never work,' Priyanka said. 'You can't sound like a DJ.'

'Trust me, I'm a call-centre agent. I can be a convincing DJ,' Vroom said.

I was curious to see how Vroom would do.

'OK,' Vroom said as he got ready, 'It's show time, folks. Take line five everyone, and no noise. Breathe away from the mouthpiece, OK?'

Radhika gave him the number as we listened in and Vroom dialled Anuj's mobile.

We glued the earpiece to our ears. The telephone rang five times.

'He's sleeping,' Priyanka whispered.

'Shhh,' Vroom went as we heard someone pick up.

'Hello?' Anuj said in a sleepy voice.

'Hello there, my friend, is this 98101 46301?' Vroom said in an insanely cheerful, DJ's voice.

'Yes, who is it?' Anuj said.

'It's your lucky call for tonight. This is DJ Max calling from Radio City 98.5 FM, and you, my friend, have just won a prize.'

'Radio City? Are you trying to sell me something?' Anuj said. I guess, being a salesperson himself, he was sceptical.

'No, my friend, I'm not selling anything – no credit cards, no insurance policies and no phone plans – I'm just offering you a small prize from our sponsor Interflora and you can request a song, too, if you want to. Man, people doubt me so much these days,' Vroom said.

'Sorry, I just wasn't sure,' Anuj said.

'Max is the name. What's yours?' Vroom said.

'Anuj.'

'Nice talking to you, Anuj. Where are you right now?'

'Kolkata.'

'Oh, the land of sweets, excellent. Anyway, Anuj, you get to send a dozen red roses, with your message, to anyone in India. This service is brought to you by Interflora, one of the world's largest flower delivery companies.'

Vroom was like a pro, I must admit.

'And I don't pay anything? Thanks, Interflora,' Anuj said with suitable gratitude.

All of us had our mouths shut tight and the headset mouthpiece covered with our hands.

'No, my friend, no payment at all. So do you have the name and address of your special person?'

'Yes, sure. I'd like to send it to my girlfriend, Payal.'

I think the earth shook beneath us. I looked at Vroom's face: his mouth was wide open and he was waving a hand in confusion.

'Payal?' Vroom said, his speech slowing to a more

normal pace as he dropped the exuberant hyperactive DJ act.

'Yes, she's my girlfriend. She lives in Delhi. She's a modern type of girl, so please make the bouquet fashionable.'

Radhika couldn't stay silent any longer.

'Payal? What did you just say, Anuj? Your girlfriend, Payal?' Radhika said.

'Who's that . . . ? Radhika . . . ?'

'Yes, Radhika. Your fucking wife, Radhika.'

'What's going on here? Who is this Max guy, hey, Max?' Anuj said.

I think the Max guy just died. Vroom put his hand on his head, wondering what to say next.

'You talk to me, you asshole,' Radhika said, probably cursing for the first time since she'd got married. 'What message were you going to send this Payal?'

'Radhika, honey, listen, this is a prank. Max? Max?'

'There is no Max. It's Vroom here,' Vroom said in a blank voice.

'You bastar—' Anuj began before Radhika stood up and cut the line. She sat back down on her chair, stunned. A few seconds later she broke down in tears.

Vroom looked at Radhika. 'Damn, Radhika, I am so sorry,' he said.

Radhika didn't answer, she just cried and cried. In between, she lifted the half-knitted scarf to wipe away her tears. Something told me Radhika would never finish the scarf.

Esha held Radhika's hand tightly. Maybe the tear bug passed through their hands because soon Esha started crying as well. Priyanka went to fetch some water, then Radhika cried a glassful of tears, and drank the glass of water.

'Take it easy. It's probably a misunderstanding,' Priyanka said. She looked at Esha, puzzled as to why she was so upset about Payal. I guess Esha's 'real pain' was back.

Radhika rifled through her bag looking for her headache pills. She could only find an empty blister pack, cursed silently and threw it aside.

'Radhika?' Priyanka said.

'Just leave me alone for a few minutes,' Radhika said.

'Girls, I really need to talk,' Esha said as she wiped her tears away.

'What's up?' Priyanka said as she looked at Esha. They exchanged glances: Esha used the female telepathic network to ask Priyanka to come to the toilet. Priyanka tapped Radhika's shoulder and the girls stood up.

'Now where are you girls going?' Vroom said. 'I created this situation. Can't you talk here?'

'We have our private stuff to discuss,' Priyanka said firmly to Vroom and left the desk.

'What's up? What's the deal with Esha?' Vroom said to me after the girls were out of sight.

'Nothing,' I said.

'Come on, tell me, she must have told you in the conference room.'

'I can't tell you,' I said and looked at my screen. I tried to change the topic. 'Do you think Bakshi expects us to prepare for his team meeting?'

'I think Esha is feeling sorry for having said no to me,' Vroom said.

I smirked.

'Then what is it?' Vroom said. I shrugged my shoulders.

'Fine. I'll use our earlier technique. I'm going to the toilet to find out,' Vroom said.

'No, Vroom, no,' I said, trying to grab his shirt, but he pulled away and went to the men's room.

I didn't chase after him. I didn't care if he found out. I figured he ought to know what his love interest was up to anyway. I called systems and told them the calls had still not resumed. They promised to come to my desk with the new cable in 'five minutes maximum'. They must be busy. Computers are supposed to help men, but computers need help from men, too.

With no one at the desk and the systems down, I decided to take a walk around the room. I passed by Military Uncle's station and noticed him slouched at his desk. This was typical of him. I went closer. His head was resting on the desk.

'Everything OK?' I said. There were already enough problems tonight. Military Uncle raised his head. I looked at his face: his wrinkles seemed more pronounced, making him look older.

'My son replied to the email I sent,' he said. 'I think the file was too big.'

'Really? What did he say?' I said.

Military Uncle shook his head and put it back on the desk. The message on his screen caught my eye.

```
Dad, You have cluttered my life enough,
now stop cluttering my mailbox. I do not
know what came over me that I allowed
communication between you and my son. I
don't want your shadow on him. Please stay
away and do not send him any more emails.
```

'It's nothing,' Uncle said, as he closed all the windows on his screen. 'I should get back to work. What's happened? Your systems are down again?'

'A lot is down tonight, not just the systems,' I said and returned to my seat.

Chapter 22

2.25 a.m.

'DID YOU KNOW?' Vroom whispered to me as he returned from the men's toilet.

'What?' I said.

'Esha's big bad story.'

'I'd rather not discuss it. It's her private matter.'

'No wonder she won't go out with me. She needs to romp her way to the ramp, doesn't she? Bitch.'

'Mind your language,' I said, 'and where are the girls?'

'Coming back soon. Your chick was consoling Radhika when I left.'

'Priyanka is not my chick, Vroom. Will you just shut up?' I said.

'OK, I'll shut up. That is what a good call-centre agent does, right? Crap happens around him and he just smiles and says, "How can I help you?" Like someone's just slept with the one girl I care for, but it's OK, right? Pass me the next dumb customer.'

I saw the girls on their way back to the desk. 'The girls are coming. Pretend you know nothing about Esha.'

The desk was silent as the girls took their seats. Vroom was about to say something, but I signalled for him to be quiet. The systems guy finally showed up with new kick-proof wires and reinstalled our systems. I was relieved as calls began to trickle in. Sorting Americans' oven and fridge problems was easier than solving our life problems.

I looked over at Priyanka once; she was busy with a caller. 'My chick.' I smirked to myself at Vroom's comment. She was no longer my chick. She was going to marry a rich, successful guy – someone who was no competition for a loser like me. Certainly not after Bakshi backstabbed me with his website, I thought. But had I given up? Did I still feel for her? I shook my head at the irrelevant questions. What did it matter if I still felt something for her? I didn't deserve her and I wasn't going to have her. That was reality and, as is often the case with me, reality sucks.

Esha was still subdued after returning from the toilet. Priyanka was trying to cheer her up.

'Get a flowing lehnga for the engagement. But what will you wear for the wedding? A sari?' Priyanka asked Esha between calls.

'My navel ring will show,' Esha said.

I'm constantly amazed at the ability of women to calm down. All they need to do is talk, hug and cry it out for ten minutes, and then they can face any of life's crap. Esha's 'real pain' was obviously much better, or she was at least distracted from it, given that she could discuss her dress plans for Priyanka's big day.

'Don't do anything elaborate,' Priyanka said, 'I'm going to tell my mother I want a simple sari. Of course, she will freak out. Hey, Radhika, are you OK?' Priyanka said as she noticed Radhika massaging her forehead.

'I'll be fine. I'm just out of migraine pills,' Radhika said as she picked up a call. 'Western Appliances, Regina speaking. How may I help you?'

The landline telephone's ring caught everyone's attention.

'This is my call. Guys, I know the system is live, but can I take this call?' Priyanka said.

'Sure. The call flow is so light anyway,' Vroom said as the landline continued to ring.

Priyanka's hand reached for the telephone. I casually switched the option on my screen to listen in to the conversation.

'By the way, dark blue mica is also a good colour,' Vroom said as Priyanka lifted the receiver.

'What?' Priyanka said.

'I saw the Lexus website, dark blue mica is their best colour,' Vroom said.

I threw Vroom a disgusted glance.

'At least that's what I think,' Vroom's voice dropped as he intercepted my look.

'Hello, my centre of attention,' Ganesh's beaming voice came over Priyanka's and my phones.

'Hi, Ganesh,' Priyanka said sedately.

'What's up, Priya? You sound serious,' Ganesh said.

Priyanka hates it when people shorten her name to Priya. This moron had yet to learn that.

'Nothing. Just having a rough day . . . sorry, night. And please call me Priyanka,' she said.

'Well, I'm having a rocking day here. Everyone in the office is so excited for me. They keep asking me, "So when is the date?" and "Where is the honeymoon?"'

'Yeah, Ganesh, about the date,' Priyanka said, 'my mum's just called.'

'She did. Oh no. I thought I'd give you the good news myself.'

'What good news?'

'That I'm coming to India next month. We should get married then. How about having our honeymoon straight from there? People say the Bahamas is amazing, but I've always wanted to go to Paris, because what could be more romantic than Paris?'

'Ganesh,' Priyanka said, her voice frantic.

'What?'

'Can I say something?'

'Sure. But first tell me, Paris or the Bahamas?'

'Ganesh.'

'Please tell me where you'd rather go.'

'Paris. Now can I say something?' Priyanka said.

Esha and Radhika raised their eyebrows when they heard the word Paris. It wasn't difficult to guess that honeymoon planning was in progress.

'Sure. What do you want to say?' Ganesh said.

'Don't you think it's a little rushed?'

'What?'

'Our marriage. We've only talked to each other for a week. I know we've spoken quite a bit, but still.'

'You've said yes to me, right?' Ganesh said.

'Yes, but . . .'

'Then why wait? I don't get much leave here, and considering I now spend my every living moment thinking about you, I'd rather bring you over at the earliest opportunity.'

'But this is marriage, Ganesh, not just a vacation. We have to give each other time to prepare,' Priyanka said and twirled a strand of hair with her finger. I used to love playing with her hair when we were together.

'But', Ganesh said, 'you've spoken to your mother, right? You heard how happy she is about us getting married next month. My family is excited as well. Marriage is a family occasion, too, isn't it?'

'I know. Listen, maybe I'm just having a rough night. Let me sleep on it.'

'Sure. Take your time. But have you thought of a colour?'

'For what? The car?'

'Yeah, I'm going to pay the deposit tomorrow so it's here when you arrive, assuming you agree to next month, of course.'

'I can't say. Wait, I heard dark blue mica is nice.'

'Really? I kind of like black,' Ganesh said.

'Well then, take black. Don't let me—' Priyanka said.

'No, dark blue mica it is. I like that colour. I'll tell the dealer it's my wife's choice.'

The words 'my wife' sizzled my insides the way they fry French fries at McDonald's. I closed my eyes for a few seconds. I couldn't bear to hear another man talk like this to Priyanka.

'Hey, Ganesh, it's 2:25 a.m. here. I have to get ready for a 2:30 meeting with the boss. Can we talk later?' Priyanka said.

'Sure. I might leave work early today. Maybe look at some tiles for the pool. But I'll call you when I get home, OK?'

'Pool?' Priyanka said as she took the bait.

'Yes, we have a small swimming pool in our house.'

'Our house? You mean you have a private pool?'

'Of course. Can you swim?'

'I have never been in a pool in my life,' Priyanka said.

'Well I can teach you. I'm sure there are many interesting possibilities in the pool.'

The French fries were burned charcoal black from being over-fried.

'Bye, Ganesh.' Priyanka smiled and shook her head. 'You guys are all the same.'

She hung up.

'What's the matter?' Esha said as she filed her nails.

'Nothing, same stuff. First tell me, are you OK?' Priyanka said.

'I'm fine. Please keep me distracted. I heard Paris.'

'Yes, as a honeymoon destination. And, of course, more

194

pressure to get married next month. I don't want to, but I just might have to give in.'

'Well, if it means seeing Paris sooner rather than later . . .' Esha said and looked over at us. 'Right, guys?'

'Sure,' Vroom said. 'What do you think, Shyam?'

Stupid ass, I hate Vroom.

'Me?' I said as everyone looked round. Esha stared at me for five seconds non-stop. I didn't want to come across as a sulker – or childish, my new tag for the night – so I responded.

'Sure, might as well get it done. Then go to Paris or the Bahamas or whatever.'

Damn. I kicked myself as the words left my mouth. Priyanka looked at me and her nose twitched as she thought hard.

'What did you just say, Shyam?' Priyanka said slowly, looking straight at me, her nostrils flaring big-time.

'Nothing,' I said, avoiding eye contact. 'I just said get married and go to Paris sooner.'

'No, you also said the Bahamas. How did you know Ganesh mentioned the Bahamas?' she asked.

I kept quiet.

'Answer me, Shyam. Ganesh also suggested the Bahamas, but I didn't tell that to you guys. How did you know what he said?'

'I don't know anything. I just randomly said it,' I replied, my shaking voice giving me away.

'Were you . . . listening to my conversation? Shyam, have you played around with the phone?' Priyanka said and got up. She lifted the landline phone and pulled it away from the table. The wire followed her. She looked down under the table and tugged at the wires again. A little wire tensed up all the way back to my seat. Damn, busted, I thought.

'Shyam!' Priyanka screamed at the top of her voice and banged the landline instrument on the table.

'Yes,' I said as calmly as possible.

'What is going on here? I cannot believe you could sink so low. This is the height of indecency,' she said.

At least I'd achieved the heights in something, I thought.

Radhika and Esha looked at me. I threw up my hands, pretending to be ignorant of the situation.

Vroom stood and went up to Priyanka. He put his arm around her shoulder, 'C'mon, Priyanka, take it easy. We're all having a rough night.'

'Shut up. This is insane,' she said and turned to me. 'How could you tap into my personal calls? I could report this and get you fired.'

'Then do it,' I said, 'what are you waiting for? Get me fired. Do whatever.'

Vroom looked at Priyanka and then at me. Realizing there wasn't much he could do to help, he returned to his seat.

Esha pulled Priyanka's hand, making her sit down again.

'What the . . . he . . .' Priyanka said, anger and impending tears showing in her voice. 'Can't one expect just a little decency from our colleagues?'

I guess I was just a colleague now. An indecent colleague at that.

'Say something,' Priyanka said to me.

I stayed silent and disconnected the tapped wire. I showed her the unhooked cable and threw it on the table.

Our eyes met. Even though we were silent, our eyes communicated.

My eyes asked, Why are you humiliating me?

Her eyes said, Why are you doing this, Shyam?

I think eye-talk is more effective than word-talk. But Priyanka was in no mood to be silent.

'Why, Shyam, why? Why do you do such childish, immature things? I thought we were going to make this amicable. We agreed to some terms and conditions, didn't we?'

I didn't want to discuss our terms and conditions in public. I wanted her to shut up, so I could scream. 'We said we would continue to work together, and that just because we'd ended our relationship, it didn't mean we had to end our friendship. But this . . . ?' she said and lifted the wire on the table, then threw it down again.

'Sorry,' I said, or rather whispered.

'What?' she said.

'Sorry,' I said, this time loud and clear. I hate it when she does this to humiliate me. Fuck it, if you've heard an apology, just accept it.

'Do me a huge favour. Stay out of my life, please. Will you?' Priyanka said, her voice heavy with the sarcasm she had picked up from me.

I looked up at her and nodded. I felt like putting her and Ganesh in their dark blue mica Lexus, wrapping it with the landline and drowning it in Ganesh's new pool.

Vroom sniggered, even as he continued clicking his mouse. A smile rippled over Esha and Radhika as well.

'What's so funny?' Priyanka said, her face still red.

'It's OK, Priyanka. C'mon, can't you take it in a bit of good humour?' Vroom said.

'Your humour', Priyanka said and paused, 'has a tumour. It isn't funny to me at all.'

'It's 2:30, guys,' Esha said and clapped her hands, 'time to go to Bakshi's office.'

Priyanka and I gave each other one final glare before we got up to leave.

'Is Military Uncle needed?' Esha said.

'No. Just the voice agents,' I said. I looked at Military Uncle at the end of the room. I could see he was busy at the chat helpline.

'Let's go, Radhika,' Vroom said.

'Do you think he loves her? Or is it just sex? Some good, wild sex that they share?' Radhika said.

'You OK, Radhika?' I said.

'Yes, I'm fine. I'm surprised that I am, actually. I think I must be in shock. Or maybe nobody has taught me an appropriate reaction for this situation. My husband is cheating on me. What am I supposed to do? Scream? Cry? What?'

'Do nothing for now. Let's just go to the meeting,' Vroom said as we turned to go to Bakshi's room.

198

My brain was still fumbling with Priyanka's words – 'we had terms and conditions' – as if our break-up was a business contract. Every moment of our last date was replaying itself in my mind as I walked to Bakshi's office. We had gone to a Pizza Hut, and pizzas have never tasted the same since.

Chapter 23

My Past Dates with Priyanka – V

Pizza Hut, Sahara Mall, Gurgaon
Four months earlier

SHE ARRIVED ON TIME THAT DAY. After all, she had a purpose. This wasn't a date: we were meeting to formally break up. Actually, there was nothing left in our relationship to break any more. Still, I had agreed, if only to see her face as she told me. She also wanted to discuss how we were to interact with each other and move forward. Discuss, interact, move forward – when you start using words like that, you know the relationship is dead.

We chose Pizza Hut because it was, well, convenient. For break-ups, location takes priority over ambience. She had come to shop in Sahara Mall, where half of Delhi descends whenever there's a public holiday.

'Hi,' she said and looked at her watch. 'Wow! Look, I'm actually on time today. How are you?' She held her shirt collar and shook it for ventilation. 'I can't believe it's so hot in July.'

Priyanka cannot tolerate awkward silences; she'll say anything to fill in the gaps. *Cut the bullshit*, I wanted to say but didn't.

'It's Delhi. What else do you expect?' I said.

'I think most people who come to malls just come for the air-conditioning—'

'Can we do this quickly?' I said, interrupting her. Consumer motives of mall visitors did not interest me.

'Huh?' she said, startled by my tone.

The waiter came and took our order. I ordered two separate small cheese and mushroom pizzas. I did not want to share a large pizza with her, even though, per square inch, it works out cheaper.

'I'm not good at this break-up stuff, so let's not drag this out,' I said. 'We've met for a purpose. So now what? Is there a break-up line I'm supposed to say?'

She stared at me for two seconds. I avoided looking at her nose. Her nose, I had always felt, belonged to me.

'Well, I just thought we could do it in a pleasant manner. We can still be friends, right?' she said.

What is it with women wanting to be friends for ever? Why can't they make a clear decision between a boyfriend and no-friend?

'I don't think so. Both of us have enough friends.'

'See, this is what I don't like about you. That tone of voice,' she said.

'I thought we decided not to discuss each other's flaws today. I have come here to break up, not to make a friend or get an in-depth analysis of my behaviour.'

She kept silent until the pizzas arrived on our table. I bit into a slice.

'Perhaps you forget that we work together. That makes it a little more complicated,' Priyanka said.

'Like how?'

'Like if there's tension between us it will make it difficult to focus on work – for us and for the others,' she said.

'So what do you suggest? Should I resign?' I said.

'I didn't say that. Anyway, I'm only going to be at Connexions for another nine months. By next year I will have saved enough to fund my B.Ed, so the situation will automatically correct itself. But if we can agree to certain terms and conditions, like if we can remain friendly in the interim . . .'

'I can't force myself to be friendly,' I interrupted her. 'My approach to relationships is different. Sorry if it's not practical enough for you, but I can't fake it.'

'I'm not telling you to fake it,' she said.

'Good. Because you are past the stage of telling me what to do. Now, let's just get this over with. What are we supposed to say? I now pronounce us broken up?'

I pushed my plate away. I'd completely lost my appetite and felt like tossing the pizza to the end of the room like a frisbee.

'What? Say something,' I said. She had gone silent for ten seconds.

'I don't know what to say,' she said, her voice cracking.

'Really? No words of advice, no last-minute preaching, no moral high ground in these final moments for your good-for-nothing unsettled boyfriend? Come on, Priyanka, don't lose your chance to slam the loser.'

She collected her bag and stood up. She took out a hundred-rupee note and put it on the table – her contribution for the pizza.

'OK, she leaves in silence again. Once again I get to be the prick,' I mumbled, loud enough for her to hear.

'Shyam,' she said, slinging her bag onto her shoulder.

'Yes?' I said.

'You know how you always say you're not good at anything? I don't think that's true, because there is something you are very good at,' she said.

'What?' I said. Perhaps she wanted to give me some last-minute praise to make me feel better, I thought.

'You are damn good at hurting people. Keep it up.'

With that, my ex-girlfriend turned around and left.

Chapter 24

2.30 a.m.

WE REACHED BAKSHI'S OFFICE AT 2:30 A.M. The size of a one-bedroom flat, it's probably the largest unproductive office in the world. His desk, on which he has a swanky flat-screen PC, is in one corner, and behind the desk is a bookshelf full of scarily thick management books. Some of them are so heavy you could use them as assault weapons. The thought of slamming one hard on Bakshi's head had often crossed my mind during previous team meetings. Apart from blonde threesomes, I think beating up your boss is the ultimate Indian male fantasy.

At another corner of the room is a conference table and six chairs, and in the centre of the table is a speakerphone for multi-party calls with other offices.

Bakshi was not in his office when we got there.

'Where the hell is he?' Vroom said.

'Maybe he's in the toilet?' I said.

'Executive toilet, it's a different feeling,' Vroom said as I nodded in agreement.

We sat around Bakshi's conference table. All of us had brought notebooks to the meeting. We never used them, but it always seems necessary to sit in meetings with an open notebook.

'Where is he?' Priyanka asked.

'I don't know. Who cares,' Vroom said and stood up. 'Hey, Shyam, want to check out Bakshi's computer?' he said as he walked over to Bakshi's desk.

'What?' I said. 'Are you crazy? He'll be here any minute. What can you see so quickly anyway?'

'Do you want to know what websites Bakshi visits?' Vroom said and leaned over so he could reach the keyboard. He opened up Internet Explorer and pressed Ctrl+H to pull out the history of visited websites.

'Have you gone nuts? You'll get into trouble,' I said.

'Come back Vroom,' Esha said.

'OK, I've just fired a printout,' Vroom said and sprinted across the room to Bakshi's printer. He fetched the print-out and leaped back to the conference table.

'Are you stupid?' I said.

'OK, guys, check this out,' Vroom said as he held the A4 sheet in front of him. 'Timesofindia.com, rediff.com, and then we have Harvard business review website, Boston weather website, Boston places to see, Boston real estate—'

'What's with him and Boston?' Esha said.

'He's going there on a business trip soon,' Radhika reminded her.

'And what other websites?' I said.

'There are more. Aha, here's what I was looking for: awesomeindia.com – the best porn site for Indian girls – adultfriendfinder.com – a sex personals site – cabaret-lounge.com – a strip club in Boston – porn-inspector.com – hello, the list goes on in this department.'

'What's with him and Boston?' I repeated Esha's words.

'Who knows?' Vroom said and laughed. 'Hey, check this out: he visited the official website for Viagra six hours ago.'

'I'll try and ask him about Boston,' Priyanka said.

We heard Bakshi's footsteps and Vroom quickly folded up the sheet of paper. We turned quiet and opened our notebooks to fresh blank pages.

Bakshi took quick steps as he entered his office.

'Sorry, team. I had to visit the computers bay team leaders for some pertinent managerial affairs. So, how is everyone doing tonight?' Bakshi said as he took the last empty seat at his conference table.

No one responded. I nodded my head to show I was doing fine, but Bakshi wasn't looking at me.

'Team, I've called you today to tell you about a few changes that are about to take place at Connexions. We need to rightsize people.'

'So, people are getting fired; it wasn't a rumour,' Vroom said.

Radhika's face turned white. Priyanka and Esha looked shocked.

'We never want to fire people, Mr Victor. But we have to right size sometimes.'

'Why? Why are we firing people when clearly there are other things we can do?' Vroom said.

'We have carefully evaluated all the plausible and feasible alternatives, I'm afraid,' Bakshi said and took out a pen. We retreated nervously. The last thing we needed was another Bakshi diagram.

'Cost-cutting is the only alternative,' Bakshi said and began to draw something. However, his pen wasn't working. He tried to shake it into action, a pointless thing to do with a ball pen. The pen refused to cooperate, perhaps it, too, was sick of Bakshi's abuse.

I was going to offer my own pen but Esha, who was sitting at my side, sensed the movement and quickly pulled at my elbow to stop me. Bakshi continued to lecture us. He spoke non-stop for six minutes (or ninety-six breaths), going into various management philosophies, schools of thought, corporate governance methods and other deeply complicated stuff that I know nothing about. His point was that we should make the company more efficient. He just didn't have an efficient way to say it.

Vroom had promised me he wouldn't mention the website to Bakshi that night, at least until the lay-offs were over. However, this didn't stop him from taking him on.

'Sir, but cost-cutting is useless if we have no sales growth. We need more clients, not non-stop cuts until there's no company left,' Vroom said after Bakshi had finished his lecture. I guess somewhere within him was a diehard optimist who really thought Bakshi would listen to him.

'We've thought of every alternative,' Bakshi said. 'A sales force is too expensive.'

'Sir, we can create a sales force. We have thousands of agents. I'm sure some of them are good at selling. We talk to customers every day, so we know what they want . . .'

'But our clients are in the US, we have to sell there.'

'So what? Why don't we send some agents to the US to try and increase our client base. Why not, guys?' Vroom said and looked at us, as if we would furiously nod our heads in approval. I was the only one listening, but I remained quiet.

Radhika was doodling on her pad, drawing a pattern that looked like this:

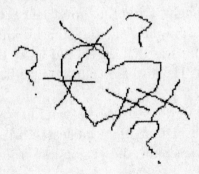

Priyanka was making a table of numbers on her notepad. I think she was making a calendar to figure out the day she was getting married. I felt like ripping her notebook to shreds. Esha was digging the nib of her pen deep into her notepad, so that it came out the other end.

'Send agents to the US? Move them to Boston?' Bakshi said and laughed.

'Well a few of them, at least on a trial basis. Some of them are really smart. Who knows, they may get that one client that could save a hundred jobs. Right, Shyam?' Vroom said.

'Huh?' I said, startled to hear my name.

'Mr Victor, as a feedback-oriented manager I appreciate your input, however, I don't think it's such a good idea,' Bakshi said.

'Why not?' Vroom demanded with the innocence of a primary school kid.

'Because if it was such a good idea, someone would have thought of it before. Why didn't it strike me, for instance?' Bakshi said.

'Huh?' Vroom said, completely flabbergasted. I'd heard it all before so it didn't move me. I was aware of every red, white, and black blood cell in Bakshi's body.

'What's the plan, sir, when do we find out who gets fir— I mean right-sized?' I said.

'Soon. We're finalizing the list, but we'll let you know by this morning or early tomorrow night,' Bakshi said, his forehead showing relief that I hadn't challenged him.

'How many people will lose their job, sir? What percentage?' Radhika said, her first words in the meeting.

'Thirty to forty is the plan, as of now,' Bakshi said in a

practised, calm voice as if he was announcing the temperature outside.

'That's hundreds of people,' Vroom said. As if it was a difficult calculation.

'Such is corporate life, my friend,' Bakshi said and got up, indicating that the meeting was over. 'You know what they say: it's a jungle out there.' I don't know who said that, but when I looked at Bakshi, I realized there are buffoons in that jungle as well.

The girls collected their notebooks primly and stood up. Vroom sat there for a few more seconds, then crushed the printout of websites visited by Bakshi in his hand and stuffed it in his pocket.

'Thank you, sir,' Esha said.

'You're welcome. As you know, I am an ever-approachable manager. Here or in Boston, you can contact me any time.'

We were at the door when Priyanka asked a question.

'Sir, are you going to Boston soon?'

Bakshi was back at his desk and had picked up the telephone, but paused when he heard Priyanka's question. 'Oh yes, I need to tell you, I'm transferring to Boston soon. Maybe in a month or so.'

'Transferring to Boston?' Vroom, Radhika, Esha, Priyanka and I all spoke together.

'Yes. You see, I don't like to blow my own trumpet, but it seems they have recognized my contribution to the value-addition cycle of the company,' Bakshi said, a smug smile sliding across his shiny face. I thought of toppling the entire bookshelf onto his head.

'But details will come later. Anyway, if you don't mind, I need to make a call. I'll keep you posted.'

Bakshi signalled us to shut the door as we left. As I closed it, I felt like someone had slapped my face. We walked away from his office in slow motion.

Chapter 25

2.45 a.m.

WHEN WE RETURNED TO WASG AFTER OUR MEETING with Bakshi, calls were flashing on the screen, but no one attended to them. I sat at my seat and opened my email. I couldn't read anything – my mind was having a systems overload.

I looked at the time, it was 2.45 a.m.

Vroom sat at his desk and mumbled inaudible curses. He opened the internal web page of Connexions on his computer. It had the map of the US on it. He held up a pen and tapped at a point on the US east coast.

'This is Boston,' he said and clenched his fist tight around the pen. 'This is where our boss will be while we are on the road looking for jobs.'

Everyone stayed quiet.

'Can I ask why everyone is so bloody quiet?' Vroom said.

'I think we should start picking up a few calls,' I

said and started fumbling with the controls on the telephone.

'Like fuck we should,' Vroom said and jabbed his pen hard at the monitor. A loud ping startled everyone on the desk. Shattered glass made a nine-inch wide spider's web pattern on Vroom's monitor, while the rest of his screen worked as if nothing had happened.

'What happened?' the girls said and came around to Vroom's computer.

'Damn it,' Vroom said and threw his pen hard on the ground so it broke into two pieces.

'Oh no. The monitor is totally gone,' Esha said. She put her hand on Vroom's shoulder, 'Are you OK?'

'Don't you dare touch me, you slut,' Vroom said and pushed her hand away.

'What?' Esha said. 'What did you just say?'

'Nothing. Just leave me alone, all right? Go and pray for your jobs or whatever. Bloody bitch will be a hooker soon.' He moved his chair away from Esha.

For a few seconds the girls stood there, stunned. Then, slowly, they walked back to their seats.

'What's wrong with him?' Priyanka asked Esha in a whisper audible to us.

'I told you he proposed to me again. Maybe he's not taking my rejection so well,' Esha said to Priyanka.

'Oh really?' Vroom shouted and stood up. 'You think this is about the proposal? Like I don't know about your escapades. Everyone here knows about it – Shyam, Radhika and Priyanka. You thought I wouldn't find out? I wish I'd known before I proposed to a certified slut who'll bang for bucks. I feel sick.'

Esha looked at all of us, shocked, and tears appeared in her eyes. She started shaking and Radhika helped her sit down. It's way more elegant to cry sitting down than standing up.

Priyanka went up to Vroom's seat and stared at him, her face red. Slap! She deposited a hand across Vroom's face.

'Learn how to talk to women. You say one more nasty thing and I'll screw your happiness, understand?' Priyanka said.

Vroom stared at Priyanka, his hand covering his cheek. He was too shocked to retaliate. I inserted myself between the two of them. 'Guys, can we have some peace here?' I said. 'Things are already messy. Please let's sit down and get some work done.'

'I can't work. I don't know if I'll still have a job in a few hours,' Priyanka said and moved back to her seat.

'At least sit down,' I said.

'I want him to apologize to Esha. The idiot has to watch what he says.'

Esha continued to cry as Radhika tried to console her.

'What do you care about a job? You're getting married. Women have it easy,' Vroom said.

'Don't you start that with me now,' Priyanka said. She had reached her seat but refused to sit down. 'You think this is easy?' She pointed a finger at Esha and Radhika.

Vroom kept quiet and looked down.

'Radhika has found out her husband is cheating on her when she works for him and his family day and night, and Esha can't get a fair break unless she sleeps with creepy men. But they aren't breaking monitors and yelling curses, Vroom. Just because we don't make a noise doesn't mean it's easy,' she said at the top of her voice.

'Can we not talk for two minutes. Don't take calls, but at least keep quiet,' I pleaded.

Radhika gave Esha a glass of water and she stopped crying. Priyanka sat down and opened her hand-made calendar. When he saw the shattered pieces of glass on his desk, Vroom went silent.

The silence gave me a chance to reflect on Bakshi's meeting. If I lost my job, what would I do? Become an agent again? I could probably forget about being a team leader.

'I'm sorry,' Vroom mumbled.

'What?' Esha said.

'I'm sorry, Esha,' Vroom said, clearing his throat. 'I said horrible and hurtful things. I was upset about something. Please forgive me.'

'It's OK, Vroom. It only hurts because there's some truth in it,' Esha said with a wry smile.

'I meant to say those horrible things to myself. Because,' Vroom said and banged two fists simultaneously on the table, 'because the real hooker is me, not you.'

'What?' I said.

'Yes, this salary has hooked me. Every night I come here and let people fuck me,' Vroom said and picked up the telephone headset. 'The Americans fuck me with this, in my ears hundreds of times a night. Bakshi fucks me with his management theories, backstabbing and threats to fire us. And the funny thing is, I let them do it. For money, for security, I let it happen. Come fuck me some more,' Vroom said and threw the headset on the table.

'Do you want some water?' Radhika said and handed him a glass.

Vroom took it and drank the contents in one gulp. I wondered if he would throw the empty glass on the floor and shatter it to pieces too. Luckily he just banged it on the table.

'Thanks,' Vroom said. 'I needed that. I need a break, otherwise I'll go mad. I can't take this right now.'

'I need a break, too,' Priyanka said. 'It's all right, Vroom. Only a few more hours left and the shift will be over.'

'No. I want a break now. I want to go for a drive. C'mon people, let's all go for a drive. I'll get the Qualis,' Vroom said and stood up.

'Now? It's close to 3 a.m.,' I said.

'Yes, now. Who gives a damn about the calls? You may not even have a job soon. Let's go.'

'Actually, if someone is going, can you please get some pills for me from the 24-hour chemist?' Radhika said.

'No, all of us are going,' Vroom said. 'Get out of your chair, Shyam. If you come, everyone will come.'

'I'm game,' Esha said.

'OK, I'll come, too. Just for a bit of fresh air,' Priyanka said.

I paused for a second. 'OK, let's go. But we have to be back soon,' I said.

'Where are we going?' Esha said, 'I heard the new lounge bar Bed is close by.'

'No way, we're just going for a drive,' I said, but Vroom interrupted me.

'Great idea. Let's go to bed; it's a damn cool place.'

'But I need a real bed,' Radhika said and stretched her arms.

We all got up from our chairs, deciding to leave individually to prevent suspicion.

'Come on, Military Uncle,' Vroom said as he went to his desk.

'Huh?' Uncle said, getting up. Normally he would have scoffed at Vroom, but I guess he was in too much pain over his son's email to give a conscious reaction.

'We're all going for a drive. The others will tell you everything. I'll get the Qualis,' Vroom said and switched off Uncle's monitor.

Chapter 26

3.00 a.m.

At 3:00 A.M. SHARP, we were outside the main entrance of Connexions when a white Qualis drove up and stopped beside us.

'Get in,' Vroom said, reaching over to open the doors.

'It's so cold. What took you so long?' Esha said, getting in the front.

'You try shifting a sound-asleep driver to another Qualis,' Vroom said.

Radhika, Priyanka and I took the middle row, while Military Uncle preferred to sit by himself at the back. He looked slightly dazed. Maybe we all did.

Vroom drove past the executive parking area and we saw Bakshi's white Mitsubishi Lancer.

'Bakshi's got a flash car,' Esha said.

Vroom inched the Qualis forward and stopped close to the Lancer. He switched on the Qualis headlights. Bakshi's car shone bright.

'Can I ask a question? What's the penalty for running someone over?' Vroom said.

'Excuse me?' I said.

'What if we ran this Qualis over Bakshi? We could do it when he comes to pick up his car in the morning. How many years in jail are we talking?' Vroom said.

It was a silly conversation, but Priyanka led him on anyway.

'It depends on how the court sees it. If they see it as an accident and not as homicide or murder, about two years,' she said.

Vroom restarted the engine and turned towards the exit gate.

'Two years is not a lot. Can we divide it among the six of us? Four months each?' Vroom said.

'I don't know. Ask a lawyer,' Priyanka shrugged.

'Four months is nothing if it means getting rid of Bakshi.' Esha blew away a strand of hair that had fallen against her lips.

'Just sixteen weekends of sacrifice. Weekdays are like jail anyway,' Vroom said. 'How about it, guys?'

By now we were on the highway, which was empty apart from a few trucks. India has a billion people, but at night, 99 per cent of them are fast asleep. Then this land belongs to a chosen few: truck drivers, late shift workers, doctors, hotel staff and call-centre agents. We, the nocturnal, temporarily rule the roads and the country. Vroom accelerated the Qualis to eighty kilometres an hour.

'I doubt you can split the sentence. The driver gets all of it,' Priyanka said, still on the stupid Bakshi-homicide topic. 'And if they know it's premeditated, you're talking ten years plus.'

'Hmmm. Now ten years is a totally different equation. How about it, Shyam, still not too bad to eliminate Bakshi?'

'OK, enough of this stupidity,' I said. 'I thought you were taking us out for a drink.'

'I'm just . . .' Vroom said, raising one hand from the steering wheel.

'Shut up and drive. I need a drink,' I said.

'Chemist first, please,' Radhika requested, giving herself a head massage.

We dropped the topic of taking out Bakshi, though if the law allowed me one free murder in my life, I am clear he would have been top of the list. No wait, I'm forgetting my ex-girlfriend's mum. I really wouldn't know who to kill first, that's the truth. Vroom took a sharp right turn onto a road that led to a 24-hour chemist.

Radhika was quiet as she waited. I guess Payal occupied half her mind, while the other half had a migraine.

'There it is,' Esha said as we sighted a neon red cross.

'Trust me. I know this area,' Vroom said and accelerated the Qualis to a hundred kph. 'Roads and girls are so much more fun at night.'

'That's sick,' Priyanka said.

'Sorry, couldn't help it,' Vroom said and grinned.

He parked the Qualis near the chemist, where a

sleep-deprived boy, no more than seventeen, manned the shop. A few medical entrance exam guides lay on the counter in front of him and a fly swatter served as a bookmark. He looked bored and grateful to see us.

Vroom and Radhika got out of the Qualis. I stepped out to stretch my legs as well.

Radhika walked up to the boy quickly.

'What do you need, Radhika? Saridon?' Vroom said as we reached the counter.

'No,' she shook her head. Turning to the boy, she said, 'Three strips of Fluoxetine, and five strips each of Sertraline and Paroxetine. Urgently, please.' She began to tap on the counter anxiously, her red bangles jingling.

The boy looked inquisitively at Radhika, then he turned around and started rifling through the shelves.

Vroom and I moved a few steps away to escape the smell of medicine. Vroom lit a cigarette and we shared a few puffs.

The boy returned with a stack of tablets and placed them on the counter. Radhika reached out to grab them, but he put his right hand on top of the pile of medicines and slid them away from her. 'This is pretty strong stuff, madam. Do you have a prescription?' he asked.

'It's three in the morning,' Radhika said in an irritated voice. 'I ran out of pills at work. Where the hell do you expect me to find a prescription?'

'Sorry, madam. It's just that sometimes young kids come here to pick up strange medicines before going to discos . . .'

'Look at me,' Radhika said, pointing to her face, 'do I look like a teenager in the mood to party?'

Radhika did not look like a party-hard teenager to me – she looked ill, with dark circles under her eyes. I wished the boy would just give her the medicines.

'But these are still very strong drugs, madam. What do you need them for? I mean, what's wrong with you?' the boy said.

'Fuck you,' Radhika said and banged her fist hard on the glass counter. The glass shook but survived the impact. However two of Radhika's red bangles shattered into a million pieces, scattering bits of bright glass along the counter.

The noise scared the boy, who jumped back two steps. Vroom crushed his cigarette and we joined them at the counter.

'Excuse me, madam,' the boy said.

'Fuck you. You want to know what's wrong with me, you little punk? You want to know what's wrong with *me*?'

'What's up, Radhika, everything OK?' Vroom said.

'This dumbass wants to know what's wrong with me,' Radhika said, pointing her finger at the boy. 'Who the hell is he? What does he know about me?'

'Calm down, Radhika,' I said, but she didn't hear me. That's the story of my life: half the things I say go unnoticed.

'What does he know about right and wrong? Everything is wrong with me, you moron. My husband is shagging some bitch while I slog my guts out. Happy now?' Radhika said, her face more red than her broken bangles. She held her head for a few seconds, then removed her hands from her head and grabbed the medicines. The boy at the counter didn't protest this time.

'Water. Can I have some water?' Radhika said.

The boy ran inside his shop and returned with a glass of water.

Radhika tore a few pills out of her new stack. One, two, three – I think she popped in three of them. Some migraine cure this was, I thought.

'Four hundred and sixty-three rupees, madam,' the boy said, his voice sounding a little fearful.

'I am alive because of this stuff. I need it to survive, not to party,' Radhika said.

She paid for the medicines and walked back to the Qualis. Vroom and I followed a few steps behind her.

'What sort of medicine is it?' I said.

'What the hell do I know? I'm not a doctor,' Vroom said.

'You sure she has a prescription for those?' I said.

'Ask her, if you have the guts,' Vroom said.

'No way. Let's get to the lounge bar right now.'

'Everything OK?' Esha said as we got into the Qualis. 'We heard an argument.'

'Nothing. As Bakshi would say, only a few communication issues. But now, let's get to Bed,' Vroom said as he turned the Qualis around.

Radhika put the medicines in her bag, her face calming as the pills started to kick in.

Vroom pushed the Qualis to one hundred and ten, the

maximum it would do without the engine crying for mercy.

'Slow down, Vroom,' Esha said.

'Don't use the words slow and Vroom in one sentence,' Vroom said.

'Dialogue,' I said, 'should we clap?'

A truck stuffed with bags of hay rumbled past us like an inelegant elephant. Our headlights made the huge bags glow in the dark.

'See, even that truck is driving faster than us. I am a safe driver,' Vroom said.

'Sorry, guys,' Radhika said, her voice becoming more normal as the drugs took effect. 'I apologize for creating a scene back there.'

'What did you buy, Radhika? Why did the chemist make such a fuss?' I said, unable to control my curiosity.

'Antidepressants. Chemists ask questions because they're prescription drugs, but most of the time they don't care.'

'Wow!' Vroom said. 'You mean happy drugs like Prozac and stuff.'

'Yes, Fluoxetine is Prozac. Except it's the Indian version, so it's a lot cheaper.'

'Like all of us,' Vroom said and laughed at his own joke.

'But it's dangerous to take it without medical supervision,' Priyanka said. 'Isn't it addictive?'

'It's legal addiction. I can't live without it and, yes, it's really bad for you. But it's still better than having to deal with my life,' Radhika said.

'Leave them, Radhika, they'll harm you,' Military Uncle spoke for the first time on our drive.

'I have cut down, Uncle. But sometimes you need a bigger dose. Can we just talk about something else? How far is this Bed place?'

'Just two kilometres from here. Ninety seconds if I'm driving, a lot more if Shyam is,' Vroom said. I ignored his comment, as I preferred him to keep his eyes on the road. Some inebriated truckies drove past, and Vroom dodged them.

'I heard the Bed is really snooty,' Priyanka said. 'I'm not dressed up at all.' She adjusted her salwar kameez. I noticed the border of glittering stone-work on her dark green chiffon dupatta.

'You look fine,' Esha reassured her, 'the chiffon look is really in. I should be worried. I look so grungy.'

'Don't worry, Esha. No one with a navel ring is ever denied entry to a disco,' Vroom said.

'Well, if you girls are in doubt, they definitely won't allow in a boring housewife like me,' Radhika said.

'Don't worry. As long as we've got cash to spend, we'll all be welcome. Plus, the DJ at Bed is my classmate from school,' Vroom said.

'All your school classmates have such funky jobs,' I said.

'Well, that's the problem: they all have rich dads. I have to work hard to match their lifestyle. If only my dad hadn't walked out on us,' Vroom said. 'Anyway, guys, welcome to Bed. And courtesy of your humble driver, it's just 3:23 a.m.' He flashed the headlights at a sign. It said 'Bed Lounge and Bar: Your Personal Space'.

'Oh no, I didn't realize we were here already,' Esha said. She fished out a mirror from her purse and examined her lips. How did women manage before mirrors were invented?

'How is my hair? Is it as horrible as usual?' Priyanka said to Radhika.

I looked at her long curly hair. Priyanka always said how she had the 'most boring hair in the world', and how she could 'do nothing with it'. I never understood it as I liked her hair, loved it actually. I felt the urge to run my fingers through it just as I had done a hundred times before. But I couldn't, as someone called Ganesh would be doing it for me in a few weeks' time. The oil for the McDonald's French fries started simmering again in my gut.

'Your hair is beautiful. Anyway, it'll be dark inside. Let's go,' Radhika said. 'C'mon, Military Uncle, we're going inside.'

Chapter 27

3.30 a.m.

WE FOLLOWED VROOM TOWARDS the huge black door that was the entrance to Bed. It was painted black so that it blended with the wall, and an ultra-beefy bouncer and a skinny woman stood beside it.

'Are you a member, sir?' the underfed woman addressed Vroom. She was the hostess – or door-bitch, as Priyanka called them – and she wore a black dress. She was about 5' 4", but looked way taller because of her thin frame and heels the size of Coke bottles.

'No, we've just come for a quick drink,' Vroom said and took out his credit card. 'Here, you can open the tab on this.'

'I'm sorry, sir, tonight is for members only,' she replied. The bouncer looked at us with a blank, daft glare.

'How do you become a member?' I said.

'You have to fill in a form and pay the annual

membership fee of fifty thousand,' the hostess said, as calmly as if she'd asked us for small change.

'What? Fifty grand for this place in the middle of nowhere?' Priyanka said and pointed her finger to the door. She had draped her dupatta in reverse, in an attempt to look hip.

'I suggest you go somewhere else then,' the hostess said. She looked at Priyanka scornfully. A fully clad female is a no-no at discos.

'Don't you look at me like that,' Priyanka said.

'Hey cool it, Priyanka,' Vroom said and turned to the bouncer. 'What's the deal? Is DJ Jas inside? I know him.' The bouncer looked at us anxiously. It was obviously the most challenging question anyone had asked him in months.

'You know Jas?' the hostess said, her voice warmer now.

'School buddy of seven years. Tell him Vroom is here,' Vroom said.

'Cool. Why didn't you tell me that before, Vroom?' the hostess said and flashed him a flirtatious smile. She leaned over to release the velvet ropes, revealing the skeletal structure of her upper torso. There would be no need of an X-ray, if she broke a bone.

'Can we go in now?' Esha asked the hostess in a monotone.

'Yes. Though, Vroom, next time, please tell your friends to dress up for Bed,' the hostess said and glanced meaningfully at Priyanka and Radhika.

'I could wring her tiny neck. One twist and it would snap like a chicken bone,' Priyanka said.

As we were walking in, the bouncer frisked us. I finally understood his function. When he'd done us, he approached Priyanka.

'What?' I said to the bouncer.

'I need to check this lady,' he said. 'She looks like a troublemaker.' He towered over Priyanka.

And then, I'm not sure how it happened but the following words came out of my mouth.

'You're not touching her, you understand,' I said.

The bouncer was startled and he turned to me. He had biceps the size of my thighs and I shuddered to think how much it would hurt if he delivered a punch.

'What's up now?' the hostess came towards us.

'Nothing, just teach your Mr Tarzan out here how to behave in female company,' I said and pulled at Priyanka's hand. In a second we were inside.

The interior design of Bed was a cross between *Star Trek* and a debauched king's harem, illuminated by ultra-violet bulbs and candles. As my eyes adjusted to the semi-darkness I noticed two rows of six beds. Only five were occupied, so I couldn't understand the big fuss at the entrance. I guess it's never easy to get people into bed.

We chose a corner bed, which had two hookahs next to it.

'Why is the hostess so nasty?' Esha said as she hoisted herself onto the bed. She took two cushions to rest her elbows on. 'Did you hear her? "Go somewhere else". Is that how you treat customers?'

'It's their job. They're paid to be nasty. It gives the place attitude,' Vroom said carelessly as he lit up a hookah. I looked at the hot, smouldering coals and thought of Ganesh. I don't know why, but I thought it would be fun to drop some down his trousers.

'I want a job that pays me to be nasty. All they tell us in the call centre is, "Be nice, be polite, be helpful," but being mean is so much more fun,' Radhika said and reclined along one of the cushions. For someone who had just had a really tough night she looked good, although I'm not sure it's possible to look ugly in ultraviolet candlelight. I wondered how a moron called Anuj could cheat on her.

Only Esha and Radhika got to lie down. The rest of us sat cross-legged on the bed.

Vroom went to say hi to DJ Jas, who was playing some incomprehensible French-African-Indian fusion music, and returned with twelve kamikaze shots. Military Uncle declined, and we didn't protest as it meant more alcohol for us. Vroom took Uncle's extra shots and drank them in quick succession.

We had barely finished our kamikazes when another thin woman – a Bed speciality – came up to us with another six drinks.

'Long Island Iced Teas,' she said, 'courtesy of DJ Jas.'

'Nice. You have friends in the right places,' Radhika said as she started gulping her Long Island like it was a glass of water. When you don't get to drink on a regular basis, you go crazy at the chance.

'These Long Islands are very strong,' I said after a few sips. I could feel my head spin. 'Easy, guys,' I said, 'our shift isn't over. We said one quick drink, so let's make our way back soon.'

'Cool it, man. Just one last drink,' Vroom said as he ordered another set of cocktails.

'I'm feeling high,' Priyanka said. 'I'm going to miss this. I'm going to miss you guys.'

'Yeah, right. We'll see when you move to Seattle. Here, guys, try this, it's apple flavoured,' Vroom said as he took a big drag from the hookah. He passed it around, and everyone, except Military Uncle, whose expression was growing more resigned by the minute, took turns smoking it. DJ Jas's music was mellow, which went well with the long drags from the hookah.

There were two flat LCD screens in front of our bed, one tuned to MTV and the other to CNN. A Bollywood number was being played on MTV, as part of its 'Youth Special' programme and a girl was gradually stripping off her clothing as the song progressed. The news breaking on CNN was about the US invasion of Iraq. I noticed Vroom staring at the news.

'Americans are sick,' Vroom said, as he pointed to a US politician who had spoken out in support of the war. 'Look at him. He'd nuke the whole world if he could have his way.'

'No, not the whole world. I don't think they'd blow up

China,' Priyanka said, sounding high. 'They need the cheap labour.'

'Then I guess they won't blow up Gurgaon either: they need the call centres,' Radhika said.

'So we're safe,' Esha said, 'that's good. Welcome to Gurgaon, the safest city on earth.'

The girls started laughing and even Military Uncle smiled.

'It's not funny, girls. Our government doesn't realize this, but Americans are using us. We're sacrificing an entire generation to service their call centres,' Vroom said, convincing me that one day he could be a politician.

Nobody responded.

'Don't you agree?' Vroom said.

'Can you please stop this trip . . .' I began. As usual, I was put on mute.

'C'mon, Vroom. Call centres are useful to us, too,' Esha said. 'You know how hard it is to make fifteen grand a month outside. And here we are, sitting in an air-conditioned office, talking on the phone, collecting our pay and going home. And it's the same for hundreds and thousands of us. What's wrong with that?'

'An air-conditioned sweatshop is still a sweatshop. In fact, it's worse, because nobody sees the sweat. Nobody sees your brain getting rammed,' Vroom said.

'Then why don't you leave? Why are you still here?' I said.

'Because I need the money. Money is what gets me into places like this,' Vroom said.

'It's just Bakshi. You're worked up about him and now you're blaming it on the call centre,' I said.

'Screw Bakshi, he is not the only bad boss around. Come on, the whole world is being run by a bad, stupid-evil boss,' he said, pointing to CNN. 'Look at them, scared out of their guts, ready to bomb everyone. Meanwhile, all we do is talk on the phone all night while the world snores,' Vroom said.

'Stop complaining about night work. Doctors do it, hotel people do it, airplane pilots do it, factory workers . . . hell, even that door bitch works at night,' Priyanka said.

'There's nothing wrong with working at night. And I agree the money is good. But the difference is, we don't have jobs that allow us to show our potential. Look at our country, we're still so behind the Americans. Even when we know we are no less than them,' Vroom said, gesturing wildly at the TV screen.

'So? What other kinds of jobs are there?' Esha said with a hairclip in her mouth. She had begun the ritual of untying and retying her hair.

'Well, we should be building roads for a start. Power plants, airports, phone networks, metro trains. And if the government moves its rear end in the right direction young people in this country will find jobs. Hell, I would work day and night for that, as long as I know that what I'm doing is helping build something for my country, for its future. But the government doesn't believe in doing any real work, so they allow these Business Process

233

Outsourcing places to be opened and think they have taken care of the youth. Just like stupid MTV thinks showing a demented chick do a dance in her underwear will turn the programme into a youth special. Do you think they really care?'

'Who?' I said. 'The government or MTV?' I got up and signalled for the check – in bars you always ask for the 'check', never the 'bill'. It was 3:50 a.m. and I had had enough of Vroom's lecture. I wanted to get back to the call centre soon.

Vroom paid the bill with his credit card and we promised to split it later.

'Neither of them give a fuck,' Vroom said as we left.

The door bitch and the bouncer gave us a puzzled look as we walked out.

Chapter 28

4.00 a.m.

Vroom drove us away from bed and we were soon back on the highway. Every now and then the Qualis would sway to the left or right of the road.

'Careful,' Esha said. 'You OK, Vroom?'

'I'm fine. Man, I love driving,' Vroom said dreamily.

'I can drive if you . . .' I said.

'I said I'm fine,' Vroom said in a firm voice. A few minutes later we passed by Sahara Mall, the biggest shopping mall in Gurgaon. Vroom brought the Qualis abruptly to a halt.

'I feel nauseous,' Vroom said. I think we were all feeling a little nauseous after Vroom's erratic driving.

'Whatever you do, don't throw up in the Qualis. The driver will kill you,' Esha said.

Vroom rested his head on the steering wheel and the horn blew loud enough to wake up the street dogs.

'Let's go for a walk, Vroom,' I said and tapped his shoulder. We got out of the Qualis.

I made Vroom walk around the perimeter of the Sahara Mall. We passed by several advertising hoardings: a smiling couple who had just bought a toothbrush; a group of friends giggling over their mobile phones; a family happily feeding their kid junk food; a young graduate jumping with joy, clutching a credit card; a girl holding seven shopping bags and beaming. All the ads had one thing in common: everyone looked incredibly happy.

'What the hell are they so happy about?' Vroom said. 'Look at that toothbrush couple. My mum and dad were never that happy.'

'Just take deep breaths and walk in a straight line, Vroom. You're drunk,' I said.

'I'm fine,' he said, 'but Mum and Dad . . . Shyam, why do they hate each other so much?'

'Grown-ups, man, they are way more complicated than we are. Don't even try figuring them out,' I said.

Vroom stopped walking and straightened up. He told me to pause as well, and continued, 'Think about this: The people who gave birth to me can't stop hating each other. What does that tell you about me? Half my genes must be fighting with the other half. No wonder I'm so fucking messed up.'

'We're all messed up, man, let's go,' I said and prodded his shoulders.

He walked faster to be a few steps ahead of me.

At the corner of Sahara Mall we passed by a Pizza Hut. It was closed. Vroom stood in front of it. I wondered if he'd really gone crazy; was he expecting pizza at this time?

We loitered near the entrance. To our right was a thirty-foot-wide metal hoarding of a cola company. A top Bollywood actress held a drink bottle and looked at us with inviting eyes, as if a fizzy drink was all it took to get her into bed.

Vroom walked up to the actress's face.

'What's up, dude?' I said.

'You see her?' Vroom said, pointing to the actress.

I nodded.

'There she is, looking at us like she's our best friend. Do you think she cares about us?'

'I don't know. She's a youth icon, man,' I shrugged my shoulders.

'Yes, youth icon. This airhead chick is supposed to be our role model. Like she knows a fuck about life and gives a fuck about us. All she cares about is cash. She just wants you to buy this black piss,' Vroom said, pointing to the cola bottle.

'Black piss?' I said and smiled. I sat down on some steps nearby.

'Do you know how much sugar there is in one of those drinks?' Vroom said.

I shook my head.

'Eight spoons of sugar in every bottle – and nothing else. And yet they convince us it's important. It isn't.'

Vroom looked around and noticed a pile of bricks. He

lifted one and threw it hard at the cola hoarding. Bang! It hit the actress's cheek, creating a dimple you would almost think was natural. She was still smiling.

'Careful, for fuck's sake. Let's go back. Someone will see us and get us arrested.'

'Like I care. Nobody cares,' Vroom said and staggered towards me. I looked at his lanky outline in the street-lights. 'The government doesn't care for anybody,' he continued. 'Even that "youth special" channel doesn't care. They say "youth" because they want the Pizza Huts, Cokes and Pepsis of the world to advertise on their channel. Ads that tell us if we spend our salary on pizza and coke we'll be happy. Like young people don't have a fucking brain. Tell us what crap to have and we'll have it.'

Vroom sat down in front of the Pizza Hut steps. 'Shyam,' he said, 'I'm going to throw up.'

'Oh no,' I said and moved three feet away from him.

'Unnh . . .' Vroom said as he threw up. Puke spread out-side the entrance like a 12″ thin-crust pizza with special toppings.

'Feeling better?' I said as I carefully helped him up. Vroom nodded.

He stood up, jerked his shoulders free from me and lifted another brick. He hurled it high, and with one wide swing smashed it into the Pizza Hut restaurant. Crash! A window shattered and bits of glass fell down like a beautiful ice fountain. An alarm began to ring.

'Damn! Vroom, have you gone mad? Let's get the hell out of here,' I said.

Vroom was startled by the alarm as well, and his body sprang to attention.

'Fuck, let's run,' Vroom said and we sprinted towards the Qualis.

'I thought you liked pizza,' I said when we reached the Qualis.

'I like pizza. I love it. I like jeans, mobiles and pizzas. I earn, I eat, I buy shit and I die. That's all the fuck there is to Vroom. It's all bullshit, man,' Vroom said, panting and holding his stomach. He didn't look too good, but at least the run seemed to have sobered him up.

'Seriously, dude, can I drive now?' I said, as Vroom opened the front door of the Qualis. He was taking noisy, heavy breaths.

'No way, man,' Vroom said and pushed me away.

The car jerked ahead as Vroom turned on the ignition while it was in gear.

'Are you OK?' Esha said.

Vroom nodded and raised his hand in apology. He waited for a few seconds, and then started the engine carefully. He promised to drive slowly and soon we were on the road again.

'Did you like Bed?' Vroom said, more to change the topic from his inebriated state.

'Great place,' Esha said, 'just the kind of high I needed. Hey, Vroom, have you got any music in the Qualis?'

'Of course. Let me see,' Vroom said and shuffled through the glove box. He took out a tape and held it up. 'Musafir lounge?' he said.

'Cool,' Esha and Radhika said.

'No,' Priyanka and I said at the same time.

'Come on, guys. You two not only hate each other, you hate the same things, too?' Vroom said and smiled. He put the tape in and turned on the music. A song called 'Rabba' started playing.

We sat in the same order as before, except this time I sat next to Priyanka. With every beat of the song, I could feel her body along my entire right side, like soft electric sparks. I had the urge to grab her hand again, but restrained myself. I opened the window for some fresh air.

'Don't open the window,' Esha said, 'it's cold.'

'Just for a minute,' I said and let the breeze in.

I focused on the lyrics of the song. The singer spoke of why no beloved should ever enter his life. That if one did, she should damn well stay and never leave. Somehow the lyrics were too close to my heart. But I was more worried about the next song. It was 'Mahi Ve', which would bring back memories of the 32nd Milestone parking lot.

I saw Priyanka's face change from the corner of my eye. She looked nervous. Yes, this was going to be hard.

'I love this song,' Vroom declared as it filled the Qualis.

I pressed the rewind-and-play button in the privacy of my head. Every moment of that night at 32nd Milestone replayed itself. I remembered how Priyanka had sat on my lap, stubbed my toe and hit her head on the roof. I recalled every little second of her careful, slow and yet amazing lovemaking. I missed her breath on my stubble, her eyes when they looked into mine, the pleasurable pain when she bit my ears. What is it about music that makes you remember things you'd prefer to forget? I wished I'd been promoted. I wished Priyanka had never left me. I wished my world were a happier place.

I turned my face to look outside. The breeze felt cold, particularly along two lines on my cheeks. I touched my face. Damn, I couldn't believe I was crying.

'Can we please close the window now? It's ruining my hair,' Esha said.

I slid the window shut and I tried to keep my eyes shut as well, but I couldn't hold back the tears. I never realized I was such a wuss.

I looked at Priyanka. Maybe it was my imagination, but her eyes seemed wet too. She turned towards me and then quickly looked away. I couldn't bear to meet her eyes right now, and I certainly couldn't look at that nose.

Vroom pulled out two tissues from the tissue box in front and swung his arm back to hand them over to us.

'What?' I said.

'I have a rear-view mirror. I can see everything,' he said.

'We can all see,' Radhika and Esha said together and burst out laughing.

'You keep driving, OK?' I said. I took the tissue on the pretext of wiping my nose, and then wiped my eyes. Priyanka took one and swabbed her eyes, too.

Esha reached behind her seat and rubbed Priyanka's arm.

'You guys are funny. Remind me again how you met in college?' Vroom said.

'Forget it,' I said.

'C'mon, Shyam, just tell. You guys never told me,' Radhika said.

'At the campus fair,' Priyanka and I spoke at the same time.

I looked at her. We gave each other a formal smile.

'You tell them,' Priyanka said.

'No, you. You tell it better,' I said.

Priyanka sat up straight to tell a story we had told a hundred times but never tired of repeating.

'We met at the campus fair in the second year. Both of us had stalls. Mine was on female empowerment and showed slides of problems faced by rural women in India. Shyam had a video games counter. However, nobody was coming to visit either of us – people just headed for the food stalls.'

'Then?' Esha said, her eyes focused on Priyanka.

'Then Shyam and I made a deal that we would visit each other's stalls six times a day. Shyam would come and see slides on hardworking farm women and female education programmes, and I would go and play Doom II on the PlayStation at his stall. By the end of the fair I was so good I could beat him,' Priyanka said.

'No way,' I said. 'I can take you on at Doom II any day.'

'Well, anyway, so over three days we visited each other's stalls three dozen times, and by the end of it we felt . . .' Priyanka said and paused.

'What?' Radhika said.

'We felt that both the stalls belonged to us, and that as

242

long as we were together we didn't need anyone else to visit,' Priyanka said and her voice choked up.

My throat already had a lump the size of an orange in it, and I just nodded, trying to keep a straight face.

We kept silent. I was hoping Priyanka would cry big time now.

'Well, things change. Life goes on and we move on to better things. It is like changing from PlayStation to X-box,' Vroom said.

I hate Vroom. Just when Priyanka was all mellow, Vroom's wise words brought her back to reality. She composed herself and changed the topic.

'How far away are we?' Priyanka said.

I looked at my watch.

'Damn, Vroom, it is past 4 a.m. How much further?'

'Around five kilometres from the call centre. I'm driving more slowly now. Do you want me to drive faster?'

'No,' we cried.

'We're going to be late. Bakshi will flip,' I said.

'I can take a shortcut,' Vroom said.

'Shortcut?' I said.

'Next left there's an untarred road. It was made for construction projects. It cuts through some fields and saves us about two kilometres.'

'Is the road lit up?' Esha said.

'No, but we have headlights. I've used it before. Let's take it,' Vroom said.

After a kilometre, he took a sharp left.

'Ouch,' Esha said, 'you didn't tell us this road would be so bumpy.'

'Just a few minutes,' Vroom said, 'actually the ground is wet today from yesterday's rain.'

We plunged on into the darkness, the headlights trying hard to show us the way. We passed fields and construction sites filled with cement, bricks and iron rods. In a few places there were deep holes as builders constructed the foundation for super-high-rise apartments. I think the whole of Delhi had decided to move to Gurgaon, and people were growing homes along with the crops.

'There, just one final cut-through and we'll be back on the highway,' Vroom said, taking a sharp right.

Suddenly the Qualis skidded and slid down an inclined path.

'Careful,' everyone shouted, holding onto anything they could find. The Qualis went off the road into a slushy downhill patch. Vroom desperately tried to control the steering, but the wheels wouldn't grip the ground. Like a drunk tramp, the Qualis rolled down into the site of a high-rise construction project.

Chapter 29

4.05 a.m.

THE SLOPE HAD FLATTENED OUT but the Qualis was still rolling forward, only slowing down when it hit a mesh of iron construction rods. Vroom braked hard, and the Qualis halted on the rods with a metallic clang, bounced twice and came to a stop.

'Damn!' Vroom said.

Everyone sat in stunned silence.

'Don't worry, guys,' Vroom said and started the ignition. The Qualis shook violently.

'Turn . . . off . . . the . . . ignition . . . Vroom . . .' I said. I peered under the Qualis. There was a floor of iron below us that was shaking.

Vroom's hands shook too as he turned off the engine. I think any remaining alcohol in his body had evaporated in fear.

'Where are we?' Esha said and opened the window. She looked out and screamed, 'Oh no!'

'What?' I said and looked out again. This time I looked around more carefully. What I saw was terrifying: we had landed in the foundation hole of a building, with a frame of exposed metal rods covering it. The foundation consisted of a pit that was maybe fifty-feet deep, with a frame of reinforced cement concrete rods across the opening. The rods were parallel to the Qualis and jutting out at the other end, and they were all that supported us. Every time we moved, the Qualis bounced, as the rods acted as springs. I could see fear in everyone's face, including Military Uncle's.

'We're hanging above a hole, supported only by tooth-picks. We're screwed,' Radhika said, summing up the situation for all of us.

'What are we going to do?' Esha said. The contagious panic in her voice made everyone nervous.

'Whatever you do, don't move,' Vroom said.

A few minutes passed where the only sound was the heavy breathing of six people.

'Should we call for help? The police? Fire brigade? Call centre?' Esha said as she took her mobile phone out of her bag.

Vroom nodded, his face naked with fear.

'Damn, no reception,' Esha said. 'Does anyone else have a mobile that works?'

Priyanka and Radhika's cell phones didn't work either, Military Uncle didn't have a mobile, so Vroom took out his phone.

'No network,' he said.

I took out my phone from my pocket and gave it to Esha.

'Your phone isn't working either, Shyam,' Esha said and placed it on the dashboard.

'So we can't reach anyone in the world?' Radhika said.

A rod snapped under us and the Qualis tilted a few degrees to the right. Radhika fell towards me; Vroom held the steering wheel tight to keep his balance. He froze in the driver's seat, unable to think of what else to do. Another rod snapped, and then another, like feeble twigs beneath us. The Qualis tilted around thirty degrees and came to a halt.

All of us were too scared to scream.

'Does anyone have any ideas?' Vroom said.

I closed my eyes for a second and visualized my death. My life could end, just like this, in oblivion. I wondered when and how people would find us. Maybe labourers the next day, or even after a couple of days.

SIX IRRESPONSIBLE DRUNKEN AGENTS FOUND DEAD would be the headline.

'Try to open the door, Vroom,' Military Uncle said.

Vroom opened his door, but the Qualis wobbled so he shut it immediately.

'Can't,' Vroom said. 'Messes up the balance. And what's the point? We can't step out, we'd fall right through.'

I turned around to look out of the rear window and noticed some bushes a few feet behind us.

'Move towards the left. No weight on the right. We have

to stay balanced until someone spots us in the morning,' Vroom said.

I checked my watch. It was only 4:14 a.m. The morning was three hours away. A lifetime. And people might turn up even later than that.

'Otherwise?' Esha said.

'Otherwise we die,' Vroom said.

We stayed quiet for a minute.

'Everyone dies one day,' I said, just to break the silence.

'Maybe it's simpler this way. Just end life rather than deal with it,' Vroom said.

I nodded. I was nervous and I was glad Vroom was making small talk.

'My main question is, what if no one finds us even after we die. What happens then?' Vroom said.

'The vultures will find us. They always do. I saw it on the Discovery Channel,' I said.

'See, that makes me uncomfortable. I don't like the idea of sharp beaks tearing my muscles, cracking my bones and ripping me to shreds. Plus, my body will smell like hell. I'd rather be burnt in a dignified manner and go up in that one last puff of smoke.'

'Can you guys stop this nonsense. At least be quiet,' Esha said and folded her arms.

Vroom smiled at her. Then he turned to me. 'I don't think Esha will smell too much. Her Calvin Klein perfume will keep her carcass fresh for days.'

Beneath us there were two sharp 'pings' as another two rods snapped.

'Oh no,' Priyanka said as we heard another ping just below her. A flicker of light appeared on the dashboard. My cell phone was vibrating. We sprang to attention.

'That's my phone,' I said.

It started ringing. Everyone's mouths hung open.

'How did it ring without a network?' Esha said, her voice nervous.

'Who is it?' Radhika said.

'Pick it up,' I said with my hand stretched out, unable to reach the dashboard and unwilling to move too much.

Esha lifted the phone. She looked at the screen and gasped.

'Who is it?' I said.

'Do you know someone called . . . God? It says . . . God calling,' Esha said.

Chapter 30

4.30 a.m.

Esha's fingers trembled as she pressed the button to take the call on speaker mode.

'Hi, everyone. Sorry to call so late,' a cheerful voice came from the phone.

'Er, who is it?' Esha said.

'It's God,' the voice said.

'God? God as in . . .' Radhika said as all of us looked at the brightly lit phone in fright.

'As in God. I noticed an unusual situation here, so I thought I'd just check on you guys.'

'Who is this? Is this a joke?' Vroom asked in a more confident voice.

'Why? Am I being funny?' the voice said.

I narrowed my eyes. Apart from the fact that I thought it unusual for God to use a cell phone, I had never considered my life important enough for God to call me.

'God doesn't normally call. Prove that you're God. Otherwise, you should get some help,' Vroom said.

'How do I prove I'm God? Do I make this cell phone float? Or do I create rain and lightning on demand? Or would you prefer a magic trick? A few special effects, maybe?' God said.

'Well, I don't know, but yeah, something like that,' Vroom said.

'So to impress you I have to break the very same laws of physics I created? I'm sorry, I'm not into that these days. And I have plenty of believers. I thought I could help, but I can hang up. See you then . . .' God said.

'No, no wait. Please help us . . . G . . . God,' Esha said and turned slightly so she could hold the cell phone between all of us.

Radhika put a finger on her lips to signal Vroom to be quiet.

'OK, I'll stay,' God said in a cheerful voice. 'Tell me, how's it going?'

'Help us get out. If a few more rods break we'll all die,' I said.

'Not that, tell me how it's going otherwise? How's life?' God said.

I'm very bad at tough, open-ended questions like that. I hate to admit the extent to which my life is screwed up.

'Well, right now we're trapped—' I said and God interrupted me.

'Don't worry, the Qualis isn't going anywhere. Just relax.'

251

I let out a deep sigh. Everyone was silent.

'So back to the question, how's life going? Do you want to start, Radhika?' God said.

'If you are God you must already know everything. Life is miserable,' Radhika said.

'Actually, I *do* know,' God said. 'I just want to find out how you feel about it.'

'I'll tell you how we feel. Life suc— sorry,' Vroom said, and checked himself, 'It's horrible. Like what have we done wrong? Why is our life in the pits, literally and figuratively? That pretty much sums it up for all of us, I think.'

We all made noises of agreement and God sighed.

'Let me ask you a question. How many phone calls do you take each day?' God said.

'A hundred, on busy days two hundred,' Vroom said.

'OK. Now do you know which is the most important call in the world?'

'No,' Vroom said and we all shook our heads.

'The inner call,' God said.

'The inner call?' everyone said in unison.

'Yes, the little voice inside that wants to talk to you, but you can only hear it when you are at peace, and even then it's hard to hear it. Because in modern life, the networks are too busy. The voice tells you what you really want. Do you know what I mean?'

'Sort of,' Priyanka said, her eyes darting away from the phone.

'That voice is mine,' God said.

'Really?' Esha said, her mouth wide open.

'Yes. And the voice is easy to ignore, because you are distracted or busy or just too comfortable in your life. Go on, ignore it – until you get tangled in your own web of comfort. And then when you reach a point like today, where life brings you to a dead end, there is nothing ahead but a dark hole.'

'You're making sense,' I conceded, more to myself.

'I know that voice. But it isn't subtle in me. Sometimes it shouts and bites me,' Vroom said.

'And what does the voice say, Vroom?' God said.

'That I should not have taken a job just for money. Call centres pay more, but only because the exchange rate is in the Americans' favour. They toss their loose change at us. It seems like a lot in rupees, but there are better jobs that pay less. Jobs that give me identity, make me learn or help my country. I justified it to myself by saying money is progress, but it's not true. Progress is building something that lasts,' Vroom said, sounding as if there was a lump in his throat. He pressed his face into his hands.

Esha put her hand on Vroom's shoulder.

'Come on, guys. This is getting far too sentimental. You can do a lot better than this. You are all capable people,' God said.

It was the first time someone had used the word 'capable' to describe me.

'We can?' I said.

'Of course. Listen, let me make a deal with you. I will save your lives tonight, but in return you must give me something. Close your eyes for three minutes. Think about what you really want and what you need to change in your life to achieve it. Then once you get out of here, *act* on those changes. Do as I say, and I will help you get out of this pit. Is that a deal?'

'Deal,' I said. Like you won't do a deal that saves you from death. Everyone nodded.

We closed our eyes and took a few deep breaths.

Man, I tell you, closing your eyes for three minutes and not thinking about the world is the hardest thing to do. I tried to concentrate, but all I could see was commotion. Priyanka, Bakshi, my promotion and Ganesh – my mind kept jumping from one topic to another.

'So, tell me,' God said after three minutes.

We opened our eyes. Everyone's faces seemed a lot calmer.

'Ready?' God said.

Everyone nodded their heads.

'Let's go around the Qualis one by one. Vroom, you first,' God said.

'I want to have a life with meaning, even if it means a life without Bed or daily trips to Pizza Hut. I need to leave the call centre for good. Calling is not my calling,' Vroom said.

I thought his last line was pretty clever, but it didn't seem like the right time to appreciate verbal tricks.

Priyanka spoke after Vroom. My ears were on alert.

'I want my mother to be happy. But I cannot kill myself for it. My mother needs to realize a family is a great support to have, but ultimately, she is responsible for her own happiness. My focus should be on my own life and what I want,' Priyanka said. I wished she had said my name somewhere in her answer, but no such luck. I think 90 per cent of Priyanka's brain is either occupied or controlled by her mother.

Military Uncle's turn came after Priyanka, and he spoke for longer than I had ever heard him speak.

'I want to be with my son and my grandson. I miss them all the time. Two years ago I was living with them, but my daughter-in-law did things I didn't like – she went to late-night parties and got a job when I wanted her to stay at home . . . I argued with them before moving out. But I was wrong. It's their life and I have no right to judge them with my outdated values. I need to get rid of my inflated ego and visit them in the US to talk it over.'

Radhika's turn came next. She was fighting back tears as she spoke. 'I want to be myself again, just as I was before I got married, when I lived with my parents. I want to divorce Anuj. I don't ever want to look at my mother-in-law's face again. To do this, I have to accept that I made a wrong decision when I married Anuj.'

Esha spoke after Radhika. 'I want my parents to love me again. I don't want to become a stupid model. I'm sure I can find a better use for my looks, if they are worth anything at all. Any career that makes you compromise your morals is not worth it.'

People now turned to look at me as I was the only one left to speak.

'Can I pass?' I said.

I was given an even harder stare. Sometimes you have no choice but to share your weirdest innermost thoughts with the world.

'OK. This will sound stupid, but I want to take a shot at my own business. I had this idea: if Vroom and I collaborate, we could set up a small web design company. That's all. It may never work, because most of the things I do never work, but then . . .'

'What else, Shyam?' God said, interrupting me.

'Uh, nothing,' I said.

'Shyam, you are not finished, you know that,' God said.

I guess you can't outsmart God and I was being forced to come to the point. I looked around and spoke again.

'And I want to be worthy of someone like Priyanka one day. Today I don't deserve her, and I accept that—'

'Shyam, I never said—' Priyanka said.

'Please, let me finish, Priyanka. It's about time people stop trampling all over me,' I said.

Priyanka looked at me and went silent. I could see she was in mild shock at my firmness.

I continued. 'But one day I'd like to be worthy of some-one like her, someone intelligent, witty, sensitive and fun, someone who can seamlessly merge friendship with love. And yes, one day I want to be successful, too.'

God stayed silent.

'God? Say something now that we've poured out our deepest secrets to you,' Esha said.

'I don't really have to say anything. I'm just amazed,

and delighted, at how well you have done. Knowing what you want is already a great start. Are you prepared to follow it through?'

Everyone nodded except me.

'Are you ready, Shyam?' God said.

I gave a small nod.

'Shyam, may I say something personal in front of your friends,' God said, 'because it's important for everyone else, too.'

'Sure,' I said. Yeah, use me as Exhibit I for 'how not to live your life'. At least I am of some use.

'You want to be successful, don't you?' God said.

'Yes,' I said.

'There are four things a person needs for success. I will tell you the two most obvious things first. One, a medium amount of intelligence, and two, a bit of imagination. Agreed?'

'Agreed,' everyone said.

'And all of you have those qualities,' God said.

'What are the third and fourth qualities?' Vroom said.

'The third is what Shyam has lost,' God said.

'What's that?' I said.

'Self-confidence. The third thing you need for success is self-confidence. But Shyam has lost it. He is a hundred per cent convinced he is good for nothing.'

I hung my head.

'You know how you became convinced?' God said.

'How?' I said.

'Because of Bakshi. A bad boss is like a disease of the

soul. If you have one for long enough you will become convinced something is wrong with you. Even when you know Bakshi is the real loser, you start doubting yourself, and that is when your confidence evaporates.'

God's words shook my insides like the vibrating Qualis had a few minutes earlier.

'God, I would like to get my confidence back,' I said.

'Good. Don't be scared and you will get it back, and then there'll be no stopping you.'

I felt the blood rush to my ears. My heart was beating hard and all I wanted was to be back at the call centre. Anger surged in me when I pictured Bakshi. I wanted to get even with the man who had killed a part of me, who had put everyone's job on the line, who had ruined the call centre.

'What's the fourth ingredient for success?' Vroom said.

'The fourth ingredient is the most painful. It is something all of you still need to learn. Because it is often the most important thing,' God said.

'What?' I said.

'Failure,' God said.

'But I thought you were talking about success,' Vroom said.

'Yes, but to be really successful, you must first face failure. You have to experience it, feel it, taste it, suffer it. Only then can you shine,' God said.

'Why?' Priyanka said. She was obviously focused on my character analysis, too. I tell you, Ganesh may have the Lexus, but she will never find a more interesting psycho case than me.

'Once you've tasted failure, you will have no more fear. You'll be able to take risks more easily, you will no longer want to snuggle in your comfort zone, you will be ready to fly. And success is about flying, not snuggling,' God said.

'Good point,' Priyanka said.

'So, here is a secret. Never be afraid of failure. If it has already come your way, it really means I would like to give you a proper chance later,' God said.

'Cool,' Priyanka said.

'Thank you,' God said.

'If only you had given as much to India as America,' Vroom said.

'Why, don't you like India?' God said.

'Of course. Just because India is poor doesn't mean you stop loving it. It belongs to me. But even so, America has so much more,' Vroom said.

'Well, don't be so high on America. Americans may have many things, but they are not the happiest people on earth by any stretch. Any country obsessed with war can't be happy,' God said.

'True,' Radhika said.

'And many of them have serious mental issues. Issues only call-centre agents know about. And you can use them to save your call centre tonight,' God said.

'The messed-up heads of Americans will save our call centre?' Vroom, Radhika and I spoke together.

'Yes. Consider their weak spots and you might win,' God said.

'Like what? They are fat, loud, thick and divorce all the time?' Esha said.

'There are others. Let me give you a clue. What exactly lies behind all this war sentiment?' God said.

'Fear. It's obvious, they are the most easily scared and paranoid people on earth,' I said.

'We'll scare them into calling us. Yes, that's how to retrieve our call volume,' Vroom said, his voice excited.

'Now you're thinking. In fact, you can figure out a way to get even with Bakshi too. Not completely fair and square, but I think you deserve to be able to bend a few of the rules,' God said, and I thought I heard a chuckle.

We all smiled.

'Really, do you think we could teach Bakshi a lesson?' I said.

'Sure, remember Bakshi is not your boss; your ultimate boss is me. And I am with you. So what are you afraid of?' God said.

'Excuse me, but you are not always there with us, otherwise how did we end up here?' Radhika said.

God sighed. 'I think you need to understand how my system works. You see, I have a contract with all human beings. You do your best, and every now and then I will come and give you a supporting push. But it has to start with you, otherwise how can I distinguish who most needs my help?'

'Good point,' Vroom said.

'So if I listen to my inner call and promise to do my best, will you be there for me?' I said.

'Absolutely. But I have to go now. Someone else is trying to reach me,' God said.

'Wait! Help us get out of this pit first,' Esha said.

'Oh yes, of course,' God said. 'OK, Vroom, you're balancing on a few rods now. There are two tricks to get out of such a situation.'

'What are they?'

'One, remember the reverse gear. And two, make friends with the rods – do not fight them. Use the rods as rail tracks and they will guide you out. Shake things around and you will fall right through.'

Vroom stuck his neck out of the window. 'But these steel construction rods are as thin as my fingers. How can we bunch them up?'

'Tie them,' God said.

'How?' Vroom said.

'Do I need to tell you everything?' God said.

'Dupatta. Use my dupatta,' Priyanka said.

'Here, I have this half-knitted scarf in my handbag,' Radhika said.

'I think you can take it from here. Bye now. Remember, I am inside you when you need me,' God said.

'Huh?' Vroom said and looked at the phone.

'Bye, God,' the girls said one after the other.

'Bye, everyone,' God said and disconnected the call. I waved the phone goodbye. Silence fell.

'What . . . was . . . that?' Priyanka said.

'I don't know. Can I have the dupattas, please,' Vroom said. 'Military Uncle, can you open the rear door and tie up the rods under the wheel. Tear up the dupatta if you want to.'

Priyanka flinched for a second at the last line, but that was the last we saw of her dupatta and Radhika's half-knitted scarf. Vroom and Military Uncle tied up the rods right under the wheel for the Qualis to do its ten-foot journey to firm ground. Several times they had to bend over and look deep into the pit. I was glad I wasn't the one doing it – I would have died just from the view.

'OK, people,' Vroom sat back on the seat, wiping his hands, 'hold tight.'

Vroom started the ignition and the Qualis vibrated as the rods below us started quivering again.

'Vroom . . . I am . . . sl . . . ipping,' Esha said, trying to grip the handle of the glove box.

In a nanosecond, Vroom put the Qualis in reverse and drove backwards. We all ducked down, partially so Vroom could see, but mostly in fear.

The Qualis shook as if it was motoring down a hill. But we didn't fall. My upper and lower jaws chattered so hard I thought a couple of teeth would break loose.

In six seconds, it was all over and we were out of the pit and on the slushy mud road again.

'It's over. I think I'm alive,' Vroom said with a grin of relief. He turned around, 'Are you still there?'

Chapter 31

4.40 a.m.

WE ALL RELEASED OUR BREATHS TOGETHER. The girls hugged, and Vroom reached out and backslapped me so hard I thought I'd broken my back.

He did a U-turn and drove back slowly in first gear until we reached the highway.

'We made it,' Esha said and wiped away her tears. Priyanka folded her hands and prayed a few times.

'I thought we were going to die,' Radhika said.

'What was that call?' Esha said.

'Something very strange – can we make a pact not to talk about it?' I said. Everyone nodded, as if I had said exactly what was on all their minds. It was true. The call felt so personal I didn't want to discuss it any more.

'Whatever it was, we're OK now. And we'll be back in the office soon,' Priyanka said.

'It's still only 4:40. We're just two kilometres away,' Vroom said. He soon regained his confidence and began driving at sixty kilometres an hour.

'I feel lucky to be alive, I don't care when we get there,' Esha said.

'I don't want to get back to find out about the layoffs. I'm leaving in any case,' Vroom said.

'You are?' Esha said.

'Yes, enough's enough,' Vroom said.

'What are you going to do?' Priyanka said.

'I don't know long-term – maybe get back into journalism. But as an immediate short-term goal, I'm going to try to save the call centre,' Vroom said.

'Hey, d'you want to open a web design company with me?' I said.

'With you?' Vroom said, looking back at me.

'I'm leaving, too,' I said.

'Really?' Priyanka's eyes popped open. She looked at me as if a seven-year-old had just announced his decision to climb Mount Everest.

'Yes, I came close to death in that pit. I could have died there without ever having taken a risk in my life. I am tired of soft, comfortable options. It's time to face the real world, even if it's harder and more painful. I'd rather fly and crash than just snuggle and sleep.'

Everyone nodded. I was taken aback; it seemed people were really listening to me for the first time.

'Plus, I've made one more promise to myself,' I said.

'What?' Vroom and Priyanka said together.

'I'm not going to work for an idiot any more, any-where. Even if it means less money. I could skip a meal a day and sleep hungry, but I can't spend my life working for a moron.'

'Not bad,' Vroom said, 'looks like our team leader-in-waiting has just wised up.'

'I don't know if I'm wise or not, but at least I've made a choice. We'll see what happens. For now I have a short-term goal, too.'

'Like what?' Vroom said, as he drove with utmost concentration.

'I have to take care of Bakshi too. Since we have nothing to lose, let's teach him a lesson,' I said.

Vroom screeched the Qualis to a halt and we all fell forward.

'Now what?' I said.

'Wait, I've just had a eureka moment. I have an idea for fixing Bakshi and the call centre at the same time,' Vroom said.

'What?'

'Aha, I like it,' Vroom said and smiled to himself.

'What, damn it?' I said.

He leaned back and whispered something in my ear.

'No way, I mean how?' I said.

'I'll tell you how when we get back. Let's meet in the WASG conference room,' he said and pressed the accelerator hard as we drove the final stretch to the centre. We entered the Connexions main gate at 4:45 a.m, passing Bakshi's car again.

'Shall we bump it? Should we give it a nasty dent?' I said to Vroom.

'The thought did cross my mind,' Vroom said and let out a sigh, 'but I love cars too much to hurt them. Don't worry, we'll deal with him inside.'

Vroom drove the Qualis into the parking lot. Our driver was sleeping in another vehicle, so we parked quietly next to him. We wanted to give him a few more hours of rest before he woke to find his mud-coated vehicle.

'People, let's go – 4:46,' Vroom said and jumped out of the car.

Back at our bay there was an A4-sized sheet stuck to my monitor with big bold letters scrawled on it.

'Check this out,' I said. It was Bakshi's writing.

WHERE IS EVERYONE? PLEASE CALL/REPORT TO MY OFFICE ASAP. WHERE ARE THE COPIES OF THE AGENDA FOR MY BOARD MEETING? WHAT HAPPENED TO THE PHOTOCOPIER? AND AGENT VICTOR'S MONITOR?

Vroom looked at the notice and laughed. 'Whatever. He'll get his answers. But first he'll answer us. Guys, conference room first,' Vroom said.

We filed inside the conference room and Vroom bolted the door.

'Guys, sorry to sound like an MBA type, but I think for the next few hours we have a three-point agenda to consider. One, to save this call centre, and two, to teach Bakshi a lesson. Agreed?'

'What's the third point?' Radhika said.

'That's between me and Shyam. It's private. OK, listen . . .'

And that is where Vroom revealed his plan. We jumped in our seats when we first heard it, but slowly Vroom convinced us. Between laughter and intense concentration, everyone joined in to refine the plan further. At 5.10 a.m., we concluded our meeting and left the WASG conference room.

'All set?' Vroom said.

'Of course,' we said.

'Good. Step 1: Bringing Bakshi out of his office,' Vroom said. 'Esha, are you ready?'

'Yes,' Esha said and winked at us.

She picked up the phone, dialled Bakshi's number and put on the voice of an older woman.

'Sir, this is Elina calling from the main bay. There's a call for you from Boston, I think,' Esha said in a dumb-but-conscientious secretarial tone.

'No, sir, I can't seem to transfer it . . . Sir, I've already tried, but the line doesn't seem to hold . . . Sir, I'm a new assistant here, so I'm still not sure how the phones work . . . Sir, sorry, but can you come down sir . . . Yes, sir,' Esha said and hung up the phone.

'Did it work?' I said.

'He's a total sucker for anything to do with Boston. He's coming right now. But he'll only be out for a few minutes, so let's rush.'

Chapter 32

5.15 a.m.

As planned, Bakshi's office was empty when we arrived.

Vroom went straight to Bakshi's computer and opened his email.

Radhika, Priyanka and I sat at his conference table.

'Hurry,' Radhika said, keeping one eye on the door.

'Just one more minute,' Vroom said as he typed furiously on Bakshi's keyboard.

I knew what we were doing was wrong, but somehow it wasn't associated with 'real, hard, painful guilt', as Esha had put it. In fact, it felt good. Once he'd finished, Vroom printed several copies on Bakshi's printer.

'Five copies,' he said, 'one for each of us. Fold it and keep it safe.'

I folded my copy and put it in my shirt pocket.

Bakshi came in twenty seconds later.

'I can't believe we have such outdated telephone systems,' Bakshi was talking to himself as he came into his office, then he noticed us at the conference table.

'There you all are. Where were you? And what happened to the photocopier and agent Victor's monitor?' Bakshi said. He wrapped his arms around his middle and looked at each of us in quick succession.

'Sit down for a second, will you, Bakshi?' Vroom said, patting a chair next to him.

'What?' Bakshi said, shocked at Vroom referring to him by his name. 'You should learn how to address seniors—'

'Whatever, Bakshi,' Vroom said and put his feet up on Bakshi's meeting table.

'Agent Victor, what did you say and what exactly do you think you are doing?' Bakshi said, still standing.

'Ahh,' Vroom said, 'this is so much more comfortable. Why don't people always sit like this?' Vroom crossed his skinny legs on the table.

'I can't believe you are misbehaving at a time when I have to recommend rightsizing—' Bakshi said as Vroom interrupted him again.

'You are mega fucked, Bakshi—' Vroom interrupted him.

'Excuse me? What did you just say, Agent Victor?'

'So you're not only dumb, but deaf, too. Didn't you hear him?' Esha said, trying hard to suppress a smile.

'What the hell is going on here?' Bakshi said and looked at me blankly, as if I was a renowned interpreter of nonsense.

Vroom pushed a printout towards Bakshi.

'What's this?' Bakshi said.

'Read it. They taught you how to read on your MBA course, didn't they?' Vroom said.

The email read as follows:

```
From: Subhash Bakshi
To: Esha Singh
Sent: 05.04 a.m.
Subject: Just one night


Dear Esha,
Don't be upset. My offer is very simple —
just spend one night with me. You make me
happy  — I'll protect you from the right-
sizing operation. My pleasure for your
security, I think it's a fair deal. And
who knows, you might even enjoy it, too.
Let me know your decision soon.
Your admirer,
Bakshi.
```

Bakshi's face turned white. His mouth opened five inches wide as he re-read the email several times.

'What is this? What the hell is this?' Bakshi said, his hands shaking as much as his voice. His mouth was open and vibrated as if it was battery operated.

'You tell us. It's an email from your inbox,' Vroom said.

'But I didn't write it,' Bakshi said, unable to hide a note of desperation in his voice, 'I did not write this.'

'Really?' Vroom said as he lit a cigarette. 'Now how can

you prove you didn't write it? Can you prove to the people in the Boston office that you didn't write it?'

'What are you talking about? How is this connected to Boston?' Bakshi said, his face spouting droplets of sweat through the oilfields.

'Let's see. What if we forward Boston a copy of this email? The same people who received a copy of the website manual, say. I'm sure they love employees who do, how did you put it? "fair deals",' I said.

'I did not write it,' Bakshi said, unable to think of a better line.

'Or we could send a copy to the police,' Vroom said as he blew a huge puff of smoke in Bakshi's face, 'and to some of my reporter friends. You want to be in the papers tomorrow, Bakshi? Here's your chance.' Vroom took out his phone, 'Oh wait, maybe I could even get you on TV.'

'TV?' Bakshi said.

'Yes, imagine the headline: CALL CENTRE BOSS ASKS GIRL FOR SEXUAL FAVOURS IN EXCHANGE FOR JOB. New Delhi TV could live on that for a week. Damn, I'd make a good journalist,' Vroom said and laughed.

'But what did I do?' Bakshi said and ran to his desk. He opened his email and checked the 'Sent Items' folder.

'Who wrote this?' Bakshi said as he saw the same email on his screen.

'You didn't?' Priyanka said as if in genuine confusion.

'Mr Bakshi, I held you in such high esteem. Today my faith in my role-model is shattered,' Esha said and put her hands to her face. She was good – I thought she should try for an acting career.

'I swear I didn't write this,' Bakshi said as he scrambled with his mouse and keyboard.

'Then who wrote it? Santa Claus? The tooth fairy?' Vroom shouted and stood up. 'Explain it to the police, journalists, and via video conference to our Boston office.'

'Hah! Look, I've deleted it,' Bakshi said with a smug smile as he released his computer mouse.

'Come on, Bakshi,' Vroom said with a sigh, 'it's still in your "Deleted Items folder".'

'Oh,' Bakshi said and jerked his mouse. A few clicks later he said, 'There, it's gone.'

Vroom smiled. 'One more tip for you, Bakshi. Go to your deleted items, select the tools menu and choose the "Recover Deleted Items" option. The mail will still be there,' Vroom said.

Bakshi's face showed panic again as he tried to follow Vroom's instructions. He clicked his mouse over and over again.

'Oh, stop it, Bakshi. The mail is in my inbox as well. And Vroom has many printouts,' Esha said.

'Huh?' Bakshi looked like a scared rabbit. 'You'll never get away with this. Esha, you know I didn't do it. You wear tight skirts and tops, but I only look at them from a distance. Even those jeans that show your waist, I only saw—'

'Stop right there, you sicko,' Esha said.

'You can't get away with this,' Bakshi said.

'We have five witnesses, Bakshi, and all of them will support Esha's testimony,' I said.

'Oh, and we have some other evidence as well. In Esha's drawer there is a packet full of cash, it has your fingerprints on it, in case we get that far,' Vroom said.

Bakshi's fingers trembled as if he was getting ready to play the drums.

'We also have a printout of your visits to pornographic websites,' Radhika said.

'You know it's not me, Esha. I'll be proven innocent,' Bakshi said, his voice sounding like a hapless beggar's. He looked as if he was about to cry.

'Maybe. But the amazing publicity will be enough to screw your career. Goodbye Boston,' I said and waved my hand to indicate farewell. Everyone else raised their hand and waved goodbye as well.

Bakshi looked at us in horror and sat down. His white face had now turned red, or rather purple, even though it was still as shiny as ever. I could see a nerve twitching on the side of his forehead and felt an urge to make him suffer more. I stood up and selected a thick management book from his bookshelf.

I went up to Bakshi and stood next to him.

'Why are you doing this to me? I'll be leaving you for ever to go to Boston,' Bakshi said.

'Boston?' I said. 'You don't deserve a posting to Bhatinda. You don't even deserve a job. In fact, one could argue you don't deserve to live. You're not just a bad boss, you're a parasite: to us, to this company, to this country. Damn you.'

I banged the management book hard on his head. Bakshi's head was hollow, and the impact made a big noise. God, it felt good. Few people in this world get to hit their boss, but those who do will tell you it's better than sex.

'What do you want? Do you want to destroy me?' Bakshi said, rubbing his head. 'I have a family and two kids. After a lot of effort my career is going fine. My wife wants to leave me anyway. Don't destroy me, I'm human too.'

I disagreed with Bakshi's last remark. I didn't think he was human at all.

'Destroying you is a good option,' Vroom said, 'but we have more worthwhile goals for now. I want to do a deal with you. We bury this issue and in return you do something for us.'

'What kind of thing?' Bakshi said.

'One, I want to have control of the call centre for the next two hours. I need to get on the tannoy,' said Vroom.

'The one management uses to make fire-drill announcements,' I said.

'Why? Will you announce this email?' Bakshi said.

'No, you moron. It's to save jobs at the call centre. Now, can I use the tannoy?'

'Yes. What else?'

'I want you to write out a resignation letter for Shyam and me. Layoffs or not, we are leaving Connexions.'

'Are you guys leaving right now?' the girls said.

'Yes. Shyam and I are going to start a small website design business. Right, Shyam?' Vroom said.

'Yes,' I said. Wow! I thought.

'Good. And this time, no one will take the credit for our websites except ourselves,' Vroom said and slapped Bakshi's face. Bakshi's face turned sixty degrees from the impact. He held his cheeks but remained silent, apart from one tiny, dry sob. His facial expression had a combination of 90 per cent pain and 10 per cent shame.

'May I?' I said.

'Be my guest,' Vroom said.

Slap! I gave Bakshi's face a good slap too and it swung sixty degrees in the other direction.

'So you'll write the resignation letter, OK?' Vroom said.

'OK,' Bakshi said, rubbing his cheek. 'But Esha will delete the email, right?'

'Wait. We're not finished. Our business will require start-up capital, so we need a severance package of six months' salary. Understand?' Vroom said.

'I can't do six months. It's unprecedented for agents,' Bakshi said.

'New Delhi TV or *Times of India*, you pick,' Vroom said as he took out his phone.

'Six months is possible. Good managers break precedents,' Bakshi said. I guess no amount of slaps could halt his jargon.

'Nice. Now the last thing, I want you to retract the right-sizing proposal. Arrange a call with Boston. Ask them to postpone the layoffs to try a new sales-driven recovery plan for Connexions.'

'I can't do that,' Bakshi said.

Vroom lifted his mobile phone and put it in front of Bakshi's face.

'I'll make sure all of India knows your name by tomorrow,' Vroom said. 'Listen, I don't care about this job, but there are agents with kids, families and responsibilities in life. You can't just fire them. They are people, not resources. Now, which news channel is your favourite?'

'Give me half an hour. I'll set up a call with Boston,' Bakshi said.

'Good. We'll bury the email. But make sure you get the hell out of this call centre, this city and this country as fast as you can. We need a new boss, a normal, decent, inspiring human being and not a slimy, bloodsucking goofball with a fancy degree.'

Bakshi nodded while continuously wiping the sweat from his face.

'Good. Anything else? Did you have something to ask me about my monitor?' Vroom said.

'Monitor? What monitor?' Bakshi said.

Chapter 33

5.15 a.m.

BAKSHI GAVE VROOM THE KEY to the broadcast room and then got straight on the phone to Boston to arrange a management meeting. I had never seen him work so efficiently.

Vroom went to the broadcast room and switched on the mikes while I went to the main computer bay to check for sound quality.

'Hello, everyone. May I have your attention, please? This is Vroom, from the strategic group.' Vroom's voice echoed through Connexions and all the agents looked up at the speakers while still talking to their customers.

'Sorry to bother you, but we have an emergency. This is about the layoffs. Can you please disconnect all your calls,' the speaker said.

Everyone heard the word layoffs and a thousand calls ended at the same time. New calls flashed, but no one picked them up. Vroom continued:

'Idiots have been managing this place up until now and it's because of their mistakes that more than a third of you will lose your jobs tonight. It doesn't seem fair to me, does it seem fair to you?'

There was no response.

'Come on, guys, I want to hear you. Do I have your support to save your jobs and this call centre?'

The agents all looked at each other, still in partial disbelief. There was a weak 'yes'.

'Louder, guys, all together. Do I have your support?' Vroom said.

'Yes!' a collective scream rocked Connexions.

I was standing at the corner of the main bay and all the agents had their eyes glued to the fire-drill speaker. Vroom continued, this time in a firmer voice.

'Thank you. My friends, don't you find it strange? The world's strongest and smartest people sitting here. An entire generation up all night, providing crutches for the white morons to run their lives. And why do we do this? So that we can buy stuff – junk food, coloured fizzy water, dumbass credit cards and overpriced shoes. They call it youth culture. Is this what they think youth is? Two generations ago, it was the young who made this country free – now that was something meaningful. But then what happened? We have been reduced to a high-spending demographic. The only youth power they care about is our spending power,' Vroom said, and even I was amazed at the attention the agents were giving him.

Vroom continued, 'Meanwhile bad bosses and stupid

Americans suck the life blood out of our country's most productive generation. But tonight we'll show them. And for that I need your support. Tell me, are you ready to work hard for the next two hours?'

'Yes!' a collective voice came back. The whole call centre vibrated as Vroom paused to take a breath.

'Good, then listen. This call centre will survive only if we can increase our call traffic, and my plan is to *scare* the Americans into calling us. Tell them that terrorists have hit America with a new computer virus that threatens to take their country down. The only way they can stay safe is to keep calling us to report their status. We'll do it like this: pull out every customer number you have and call them. I'll send you a call script on email in the next five minutes, but until then, dig out those numbers,' Vroom said.

Noise levels rose in the main bay as hundreds of localized conversations took place simultaneously. There was a frenzy as people printed off all the customer numbers on their database. Nobody was sure if the plan would work, but people were willing to try anything to avoid losing their jobs.

Vroom and I returned to our bay. He typed furiously on his computer and after a few minutes tapped on my shoulder.

'Check your email,' Vroom said and pointed to my screen.

I opened my inbox. Vroom had sent the same email to everyone in the call centre.

Subject: Operation Yankee Fear

Dear All,

Operation Yankee Fear's single aim is to increase the incoming call traffic in the Connexions call centre, capitalizing on Americans being the biggest cowards on the planet. Hopefully this will prevent the planned mass layoffs and help us buy more time to improve our call rates by implementing a marketing exercise to find new clients.

Operation Yankee Fear cannot succeed without your 100 per cent cooperation. So, please read the instructions below carefully and focus on making non-stop calls for the next two hours. When you call each customer, the key message you need to deliver is this:

1. Start with an apology for disturbing them on Thanksgiving Day.

2. State that 'evil forces' of the world have unleashed a computer virus that threatens to attack every computer in America. This way the evil forces will be able to monitor every American and eventually destroy their economy. Tell them that, according to your information, the virus has already hit their computer.

3. If asked what the 'evil forces' are, give vague explanations such as, 'forces that want to harm the US' or 'organizations that threaten freedom of speech and liberty' etc. Remember, the more vague you are, the greater the fear you will generate. Try to inject genuine panic into your voice.

4. In order to check whether the virus has hit them or not, ask them to carry out an MS Word test. Tell them to open an empty MS Word file, and type in =rand (200,99) and press enter. If a mass of text pops out, this signals that there is a virus located in their computer (Don't worry: the text WILL pop out — it's a proven bug in MS Word). After this, your customers will start shaking with fear.

5. Tell them you can save them from this virus as a) you are from India, and all Indians are good with computers, b) India has faced terrorism for years and c) they are valued clients and you believe in customer service.

6. However, if they want our help, they must keep calling the Connexions call centre every six hours. Even if nothing happens, they should just call to let

```
       us know things are OK. (The shorter
       the calls, the better as far as we're
       concerned).
7.     Once calls rise, I will speak to
       Boston about the sudden increase in
       traffic and recommend we postpone the
       layoffs for two months. After that, we
       can implement a revival strategy.
   Cheers,
   Varun @ WASG
```

Vroom grinned and winked at me as I finished reading the email.

'What's with the MS Word trick?' I said.

'Try it, open a Word file,' Vroom said.

I opened an empty Word document and typed in =rand (200,99).

As soon as I pressed Enter, two hundred pages of text popped out. It was spooky, and went something like this:

The quick brown fox jumps over the lazy dog. The quick brown fox jumps over the lazy dog. The quick brown fox jumps over the lazy dog. The quick brown fox jumps over the lazy dog. The quick brown fox jumps over the lazy dog. The quick brown fox jumps over the lazy dog. The quick brown fox jumps over the lazy dog. The quick brown fox jumps over the lazy dog. The quick brown fox jumps over the lazy dog. The quick brown fox jumps over the lazy dog. The quick brown fox jumps . . .

'This is unbelievable. What is it?' I asked.

'I told you. It's a bug in MS Word. Nothing is perfect. Now just wait and watch the fun,' Vroom said.

Vroom's email reached a thousand mailboxes and agents read it immediately.

Team leaders helped their agents by clarifying any doubts they had. Within minutes, agents were doing a job they knew only too well: calling people to deliver a message as fast as possible. I left my seat and passed by the main bay. I picked up random sentences from the telephone conversations.

'Hello, Mr Williams, sorry to disturb you on Thanksgiving. I am from Western Computers with an urgent message. America is under a virus attack,' one agent said.

'Yes, sir. According to our records your computer has been affected . . .' said another.

'Don't worry, sir. But, yes, it looks like the evil forces have targeted you,' an eighteen-year-old agent said. 'But we can save you.'

'Just keep calling us. Every four to six hours,' said one as she ended the call.

The more aggressive agents went a step further: 'And I want you to tell all your friends and relatives. Yes, they can call us too.'

Some customers panicked and needed reassurance: 'No

problem. We will save this country. The evil forces will never succeed.'

A thousand agents, four minutes to a call – we could do 30,000 calls in two hours. If they called us every six hours, we would have over 100,000 calls a day. Even if it only lasted a week, we would hit our targets for the next two months. Hopefully, with a new manager and extra sales effort, Connexions could be on its way to recovery, and for now no one would lose their job.

Vroom came looking for me in the main bay and we went back to the WASG. Vroom signalled me into the conference room.

'The response is amazing. We've only been calling for thirty minutes and traffic is up five times already,' Vroom said.

'Rocking, man,' I said. 'You make me feel confident about our web design company. But let's go back to the desk. Why've you called me here?'

'We have to discuss the third private agenda.'

'What's that?' I said.

'The third agenda is for you. Don't you want Priyanka back?'

Chapter 34

5.30 a.m.

'No, priyanka and i are over,' i said.

'Be honest, dude. You spoke to God and everything.'

I looked down. Vroom waited until I said something.

'It doesn't matter if I want to or not. Look at my competition. How am I going to succeed against Mr Perfect Match Ganesh?'

'See, that's the problem. We all think Ganesh is Mr Perfect, but nobody is perfect.'

'Yeah, right. A house with a pool, a car that costs more than ten years of my salary, freaking working for the world's top company – I don't see much imperfection in that.'

'Everyone has a flaw, dude. The trick is to find a flaw in Ganesh.'

'Well, how are we ever going to do that? And even if we find a flaw in him, what's the point? He's so good, Priyanka will still go for him,' I said.

'At least Priyanka will know she isn't making the perfect trade-off,' Vroom said.

I remained silent for two minutes. 'Yes, but how do we find Ganesh's flaw?' I said and looked at my watch. It was 5:30 a.m.

'There must be a way,' Vroom said.

'The shift is over soon and Priyanka will go home. What are you planning to do? Hire a detective in Seattle?' I said, my voice irritated.

'Don't give up, Shyam,' Vroom said and patted my shoulder.

'I'm trying to forget Priyanka, but if you search within me there is still pain. Don't make it worse, Vroom.'

'Wow, what drama. Search within me, there is pain,' Vroom said and laughed.

'Let's go back to the bay,' I said.

'Hey, wait a minute. You just said *search*.'

'Yes, search within me, there is still pain. Pretty cheesy, I know. Why?' I said.

'Search. That's what we can do. Google will be our detective. Let's do a search on his name and see what comes out. There may be a few surprises.'

'What? You want to do a search for Ganesh?'

'Yes, but we need his full name. Let's find out his college as well. I think he got his Masters in computers in the US,' he said and grabbed my shirt. 'Come on, let's go.'

'Where?' I said, even as I let myself get dragged along.

'To the WASG bay,' Vroom said.

Priyanka was busy on the phone, scaring Americans out of their wits. I think she can put on that voice of authority whenever she wants, and it's impossible not to believe her. It comes from her mother, I think. After she had ended a call Vroom spoke to her.

'Hey, Priyanka, quick question. My cousin also did a Masters in computers in the US. Which college did Ganesh go to?'

'Huh? Wisconsin, I think,' she said.

'Really. Let me email my cousin and ask him if it's the same one. What's Ganesh's full name by the way?'

'Gupta. Ganesh Gupta,' Priyanka said as she prepared to make another call.

'Oooh. Mrs Priyanka Gupta,' Esha said, putting on a smart voice and laughing. Priyanka poked her with her elbow. Priyanka's new name sent ripples of pain down my ribcage.

'Cool. Keep calling,' Vroom said and went back to his seat.

As Vroom's monitor was broken, he took control of my computer. He searched for the following terms on google.com:

```
ganesh gupta drunk Wisconsin
ganesh gupta fines Wisconsin
ganesh gupta girlfriend
```

Several links popped out, but there was nothing we could make much sense or use of. We hit upon Ganesh's list of classmates, and found out that he was in the Dean's list in Boston.

'Damn, what a boring guy. Let me try again,' Vroom said.

```
ganesh gupta fail
ganesh gupta party
ganesh gupta drugs
```

Nothing interesting emerged.

'Forget it, man. He was probably the head boy at school,' I said.

'You bet, one of those teacher's pet types,' Vroom said, letting out a frustrated breath. 'I give up. I'm sure if I type something like "ganesh gupta microsoft award" plenty of things will pop out, achiever that he is.'

More links popped out. We clicked through a few, and then we hit on one with his picture. It was Ganesh's online album.

'Damn, it is him, with his mates,' Vroom whispered and clicked on the link. 'Let's check out how ugly his friends are.'

The link opened to a webpage titled 'Microsoft Award party photos'. The party was at Ganesh's house. Ganesh had won some developer award at Microsoft and a couple of his friends had come to his house to celebrate.

'Look at the slideshow,' I said as Vroom selected the option. We looked up once to confirm the girls were still busy with their calls.

As the picture flicked onto the screen we saw a garden party full of Indian people. On the tables there was enough food to feed a small town. I saw Ganesh's house and the famous personal pool, which was no more than an oversized bathtub, if you ask me, even though Ganesh had made it sound like Olympic champions trained in it.

'Hey, I think we've found something. Check out our man,' Vroom said. He pointed to one of the photos in which Ganesh held a beer glass.

'What's the big deal?' I said. It was hardly scandalous to hold a glass of beer. Priyanka herself could knock back ten if they were free.

'Check out Ganesh's head,' Vroom said.

'What?' I said. I looked closer and then I saw it.

'Oh no,' I said and covered my mouth to keep my voice down.

Ganesh had a bald spot in the middle of his head. It was the size of a Happy Meal burger and had caught the camera's flashlight.

'Unbelie—' I said.

'Shhh!' Vroom said. 'Did you see that? He has perfect hair in the Statue of Liberty picture.'

'Are all his photos in this album like this?' I said.

'Yes, sir,' Vroom said and flicked through the slideshow. One boring picture after another followed, mainly of people with mouths and plates stuffed with food. Every picture had one thing in common, though, wherever Ganesh was, so was the shiny spot.

Vroom pushed his computer mouse away and reclined

on his chair with a proud expression, 'As I said, sir, no one is perfect. Apart from Google, of course.'

I looked at the screen and back at Vroom.

'So, now what?' I said.

'Now we invite the ladies for a viewing,' Vroom said and grinned.

'No, that's not right . . .' I said, but it was too late.

'Esha, Radhika, Priyanka. Do you want to see some more Ganesh pictures? Come here quickly,' Vroom said.

The girls dropped their phone calls and looked over at us. Esha and Radhika stood up.

'Where, where? Show us,' Esha said.

'What are you talking about?' Priyanka said and came over to our side.

'The power of the Internet. We found an online album. Come and see what your new house is like,' Vroom said. He kept quiet about the shiny spot so that the girls could see it for themselves. I saw the mixture of excitement and curiosity in Priyanka's face.

'Nice pad,' Esha said as she noticed the barbecue behind the pool, 'but where's Ganesh. Let me guess,' she said and touched the monitor with her finger. 'Here, this one, no. But wait, he's a baldie. Is he the elder brother?'

Priyanka and Radhika looked closer.

'No, that's Ganesh,' Priyanka said, her open mouth as round as the bald spot. I could sense that the wind had been knocked out of her sails.

'But I didn't notice the bald spot in the photo you showed us, Priyanka,' Esha said. Radhika squeezed

Esha's arm. Esha stopped talking and raised her eyebrows.

Priyanka came up closer to the screen and began flipping through the images. She didn't notice, but her hair was falling on my shoulders as she bent over. It felt nice.

But Priyanka wasn't feeling nice. She brought out the Statue of Liberty picture and we looked at it again. Ganesh had perfect hair.

'Maybe the guy in the online album is Ganesh's elder brother,' Radhika said.

'No. Ganesh doesn't have a brother. He only has one sister,' Priyanka said, her face distraught at the fact that he had deceived her like that. Such a tiny lie could lead to bigger lies.

There was silence for a few seconds.

'Well, it doesn't really matter much, eh? What's a bit of smooth skin between the true love of two souls?' Vroom said. I clamped my jaws shut to prevent a laugh escaping. 'Let's go back, people, enough fun. Don't forget to keep calling,' Vroom said.

Priyanka retraced her steps in slow motion. She went back to her seat and took out her mobile phone. She dialled a long number, probably long distance. This call was going to be fun – I only wished I could tap into it.

'Hello, Ganesh,' Priyanka said in a direct voice. 'Listen, I can't talk for long. I just want to check on something . . . yes, just one question . . . actually I was just surfing the Internet . . .' Priyanka said and got up from her seat. She moved to the corner of the room where I could no longer hear her.

I made a few calls and terrorized some more Americans. Priyanka returned after ten minutes and tossed her cell phone on the desk.

Esha jiggled her eyebrows up and down, as if to ask, 'What's up?'

'It *is* him in the online pictures,' Priyanka said. 'He didn't have much to say. He said his mother asked him to touch up his hair slightly in the Statue of Liberty snap as it would help in the arranged marriage market.'

'Oh no,' Esha wailed.

'He apologized several times saying he'd been against tampering with the picture, but had to agree when his mother insisted.'

'Can't he think for himself?' Esha said. 'That's not a good sign.'

'Oh god, what am I going to do?' Priyanka said.

'Did the apologies seem genuine?' Radhika said.

'Yes, I think so. He said he understood how I must feel and that he was ready to apologize in front of my family as well.'

'Well, then it's OK. What difference does it make? You don't really care about him being bald, do you?' Radhika said.

'Yeah, besides practically all men become bald in a few years anyway. It's not like you can do anything about it then,' Esha said.

'That's true,' Priyanka said in a mellow voice. I could see her relenting and turned to Vroom.

'Yeah, it doesn't matter. Just make sure he wears a cap

at the wedding – unless you want to touch up all the wedding pictures,' Vroom said and chuckled. Esha and I looked down to suppress our grins.

'Shut up, Vroom,' Radhika said.

'Sorry, I'm being mean. Honestly, it's no big deal, Priyanka. No one's perfect, we all know that, don't we? So, let's get back to our calls.'

Chapter 35

6.00 a.m.

FOR THE NEXT HALF HOUR we focused on one activity: making calls to save Connexions.

At 6:30 a.m. I went up to the main bay. Team leaders huddled around me as they gave me the news. The incoming calls had already shot up, even though we hadn't expected the big boost for another six hours. Despite their turkey dinners, Americans were scared out of their wits. Some had called us several times an hour.

Vroom and I went to Bakshi's office with some of the senior team leaders. He had arranged an urgent video conference call with the Boston office. Bakshi supported us as we presented the new call data, insights into the call traffic and potential new sources of revenue. After a twenty-minute video discussion, Boston agreed to a two-month reprieve before deciding on layoffs. They also agreed to evaluate the possibility of sending top team leaders on a short-term sales assignment to Boston.

However, the team leaders would have to present a clear plan over the next few weeks.

'How did we do it, man? I never thought it would work,' I asked Vroom as we came out of Bakshi's office.

'Promise Americans lots of dollars in the future, and they'll listen to you. It's only a two-month reprieve, but that's enough for now,' Vroom said.

Reassured that Connexions was safe, I returned to my desk while Vroom went outside to clean the Qualis before the driver woke up. I had told Vroom I wanted to slip away – no goodbyes, no hugs and no promises to meet, especially in front of Priyanka. Vroom agreed and said he would be ready outside with his bike at 6:50 a.m.

The girls stopped their calls at 6:45 a.m., just as our shift ended. Everyone began to log out so they could be in time for the Qualis, which would be waiting at the gate at 7:00 a.m.

'I'm so excited. Radhika is moving into my place,' Esha said as she switched off her monitor. She opened her handbag and started rearranging the contents.

'Really?' I said.

'Yes, I am,' Radhika said. 'And Military Uncle is going to recommend a lawyer friend. I need a good, tough divorce lawyer.'

'Don't you want to try and work it out?' Priyanka said as she collected the sweet boxes and placed them back in the bag.

'We'll see. I am in no mood to compromise. And I'm not going back to his house now, for sure. As of today, my mother-in-law will be making her own breakfast.'

'And after that, I'm taking Radhika to Chandigarh for the weekend,' Esha said and smiled.

Everyone was busy making plans. I excused myself on the pretext of going to the water cooler for a drink, so I could leave the office from there.

Chapter 36

6.47 a.m.

AT 6.47 A.M. I REACHED THE WATER COOLER and bent towards the tap to take my last drink at the call centre.

As I finished, I stood up to find Priyanka behind me.

'Hi,' she said. 'Leaving?'

'Oh, hi. Yes, I'm going back on Vroom's bike,' I said and wiped my mouth.

'I'll miss you,' she said, interrupting me.

'Huh? Where? In the Qualis?' I said.

'No, Shyam, I'll miss you in general. I'm sorry about the way things turned out.'

'Don't be sorry,' I said, shaking my fingers dry. 'It's more my fault than yours. I understand that. I acted like a loser.'

'Shyam, you know how Vroom said just because India is poor it doesn't mean you stop loving it?' Priyanka said.

'What?' I blinked at the change of topic. 'Oh yes. And I agree, it is our country after all.'

'Yes, we love India because it's ours. But do you know the other reason why we don't stop loving it?'

'Why?'

'Because it isn't completely India's fault that we are behind. Yes, some of our past leaders could have done things differently, but now we have the potential and we know it. And as Vroom says, one day we will show them.'

'Good point,' I said. I found it strange that she should talk about nationalism this early in the morning, not to mention at what was possibly our last moment together.

I nodded and started walking away from her. 'Anyway, I think Vroom will be waiting . . .' I said.

'Wait, I haven't finished,' she said.

'What?' I said and turned back to look at her.

'I applied the same logic to something else,' she said. 'I thought, this is the same as my Shyam, who may not be successful now, but it doesn't mean he doesn't have the potential, and it sure as hell doesn't mean I've stopped loving him.'

I stood there dumbstruck. I fumbled for words and finally spoke shakily:

'You know what, Priyanka? You say such great lines that even though I've tried to hate you all night, it's impossible. And I know I should hate you and that I should move on, because I can't offer you what Mr Microsoft can—'

'Ganesh,' she interrupted me.

'What?' I said.

'Ganesh is his name. Not Mr Microsoft,' she said.

'Yes, whatever,' I kept talking, without pausing to breathe.

'I can't offer you what Ganesh can. No way could I ever buy a Lexus. Maybe a Maruti 800 one day, but that's about it.'

She smiled.

'Really? An 800? With or without AC?' she said.

'Shut up. I'm trying to say something deep and you find it funny,' I said.

She laughed again, gently. I wiped a tear from my right eye and she raised her hand to wipe the tear from my left eye.

'Anyway, it's over between us, Priyanka, and I know it. I'll get over it soon. I know, I know,' I said, talking more to myself.

She waited until I had composed myself. I bent over to splash my face with water at the cooler.

'Anyway, where's your wedding going to be? Your mum will probably blow all her cash on a big gig,' I said, straightening up.

'In some five-star hotel, I'm sure. She'll be paying off loans for years, but she has to get a gold-plated stage that night. You'll come, won't you?'

'I don't know,' I said.

'What do you mean, you don't know? It'll be so strange if you aren't there.'

'I don't want to be there and feel sad. Anyway, what's so strange if I'm not there?'

'Well, it will be a little strange if the groom isn't there at his own wedding,' Priyanka said.

I froze as I heard those words, rewinding her last sentence three times in my head.

'What . . . what did you just say?' I said.

She pinched my cheek and imitated me: 'What . . . what did you just say?'

I stood there speechless.

'But don't think I'm going to let you go that easily. One day I want my 800 with AC,' she said and laughed.

'What?' I said.

'You heard me. I want to marry you, Shyam,' Priyanka said.

I thought I would jump for joy, but mostly I was shocked. And even though I wanted to hug, cry and laugh at the same time, a firm voice, like a guard inside me, asked, What's this all about? Hell, however miserable my life was, I didn't want pity.

'What are you saying, Priyanka? That you would choose me over Ganesh? Is this a sympathy decision?'

'Stop thinking about yourself. My life's biggest decision can't be a sympathy decision. I've thought about it. Ganesh is great, but . . .'

'But what?' I said.

'But the whole touching up of the photo bothers me. He's an achiever in his own right, so why did he have to lie?'

'So you're rejecting him because he's bald? My hair isn't reliable, either,' I said. It was true. Every time I took a shower the towel had more hair than me.

'No. I'm not rejecting him because he's bald. Most men go bald one day, it's horrible, I know,' she said and ruffled my hair. 'He might be fine in most ways,' she continued, 'but the point is, he lied. And for me that's a clue as to what sort of person he is. I don't want to spend my life with a person like that. In fact, I don't want to spend my life with a person I don't know very well beforehand. That's one part of my decision. The other is the big part.'

'What?' I said.

'I love you. Because you are the only person in the world I can be myself with. And because you are the only person who knows all my flaws and still loves me completely. I hope,' she said, with a quivering voice.

I didn't say anything.

'And even if the world says I'm cold, there is a part of me that's sentimental, irrational and romantic. Do I really care about money? Only because people tell me I should. Hell, I prefer truck-driver dhabhas over five-star hotels. Shyam, I know you and Mum say I am uncaring—'

'I never said that.' I interrupted, holding her shoulders.

'I'm sorry, Shyam. I've judged you so much. I'm such a bitch,' Priyanka said. She sniffed and her puckered nose looked cuter than ever.

'It's OK, Priyanka,' I said and wiped her tears.

'So that's it, Shyam. Deep inside, I am just a girl who wants to be with her favourite boy, because like you, this girl is a person who needs a lot of love.'

'Love? I need a lot of love?' I said.

'Of course you do. Everyone does. It's funny that we never say it. It's OK to scream, "I'm starving," in public if you are hungry; it's OK to make a fuss and say, "I'm so sleepy," if you are tired; but somehow we cannot say, "I need some more love." Why can't we say it, Shyam? It's just as basic a need.'

I looked at her. Whenever she delivers these deep, philosophical lines, I get horribly attracted to her. The guard inside reminded me to be firm.

'Priyanka?'

'Yes,' she said, still sniffling.

'I love you,' I said.

'I love you, too,' Priyanka said.

'Thanks. However, Priyanka, I can't marry you. Sorry to say this, but my answer to your mind-blowing proposal is no,' I said.

'What?' Priyanka said as her eyes opened wide in disbelief. The guard inside me was in full charge.

'I can't marry you. I'm a new person tonight, and this new person needs to make a new life and find new respect for himself. You chose Ganesh, and he's fine. You have an option for a new life and you don't really need me, so maybe it's better this way,' I said.

'I still love you, Shyam, and only you. Please don't do this,' she said, coming closer to me.

'Sorry,' I said and moved three steps backwards. 'I can't. I'm not your spare wheel. I appreciate you coming back, but I think I'm ready to move on.'

She just stood there and cried. My heart felt weak, but my head was strong.

'Bye, Priyanka,' I gingerly patted her shoulder and left.

Chapter 37

6.59 a.m.

'WHAT THE HELL KEPT YOU?' Vroom said, sitting on his bike at the main entrance. He showed his watch to me, it was 6:59 a.m.

'Sorry, man, Priyanka met me at the water cooler,' I said and sank onto the pillion seat.

'And?' Vroom said.

'Nothing. Just goodbye and all. Oh, and she wanted to get back together and marry me, she said. Can you believe it?'

Vroom turned to me.

'Really? What did you say?'

'I said no,' I said coolly.

'What?' Vroom said.

As we were talking, Radhika, Esha and Military Uncle came out of the main entrance into the wintry sunshine.

'Hi, you guys still here?' Radhika said.

'Shyam just said no to Priyanka. She wanted to marry him, but he said no.'

'What?' Radhika and Esha spoke in unison.

'Hey, guys, chill out. I did what I needed to do to get some respect in my life. Stop bothering me,' I said.

The Qualis arrived and the driver pressed the horn.

'We aren't bothering you – it's your life. Let's go, Esha,' Radhika said and gave me a dirty look. She turned to Esha as they walked to the Qualis.

'Where's Priyanka, madam? We are late,' the driver said.

'She's coming. She's on the phone to her mother. Ganesh's parents are going over for breakfast and her mother is making hot parathas,' Radhika said, loud enough for me to hear. The mention of parathas made me hungry, but I'd be the last person to be invited to their breakfast.

'Looks like their entire families are getting married to each other,' Vroom said. He lit a cigarette and took a few final puffs before beginning our ride back.

The driver started the Qualis. Esha and Radhika sat in the middle row, while Military Uncle sat behind.

Priyanka came dashing out of the main entrance, avoided me and went straight to the front seat. Then the driver turned the Qualis round so its rear end faced us.

As we began to move off, Military Uncle looked out from his window and said something. I could only lip read but I thought he said, 'You bloody idiot.'

Before I could react, the Qualis was gone.

Vroom stubbed out his cigarette.

'Oh no. I *am* a bloody idiot. I let her go,' I said.

'Uh-huh,' Vroom said as he wore his helmet.

'Is that a yes? You think I am a total idiot?'

'You are your best judge,' Vroom said as he dragged the bike with his feet.

'Vroom, what have I done? If she reaches home and has parathas with Ganesh's family, it is all over. I'm such a moron,' I said jumping up and down on my seat.

'Stop dancing around. I have to get going,' Vroom said as he placed his foot on the kick-pedal.

'Vroom, we have to catch the Qualis. Can you go fast enough?'

Vroom removed his helmet and laughed.

'Are you insulting me? Do you doubt that I can catch that wreck of a Qualis? I am so hurt, man.'

'Vroom, let's go. Please,' I said and pushed his shoulders.

'No. First you apologize for doubting my driving abilities.'

'I'm sorry, boss, I'm sorry,' I said and folded my hands. 'Now move, Schumacher.'

Vroom kick-started his bike, and in a few seconds we had zipped out of the call centre. The main road was getting busier as the morning progressed, but Vroom still managed a top speed of ninety. On the road into the city, we dodged cars, scooters, autos, school buses and news-paper hawkers.

Four minutes later, I noticed a white Qualis at a distant traffic signal.

'It must be that one,' I pointed out.

Just as Vroom moved ahead, a herd of goats decided to cross the road and fifty of them blocked our way.

'Damn, where did they come from?' I said.

'This urban jungle of Gurgaon was a village until recently; the goats are probably asking where did *we* come from,' Vroom said as he cracked his knuckles.

'Shut up and do something,' I said.

Vroom tried to move his bike, but bumped into a goat's horns. He considered taking the right side of the road where traffic flowed in the opposite direction, but it was full of trucks and we'd have been mowed down in seconds.

'There's only one option,' Vroom said and smiled at me through his helmet.

'Wha—' I said as Vroom lunged his bike up onto the road divider. 'Are you crazy?' I said.

'No, you're crazy to let her go,' Vroom said and started riding along the divider. The goats and drivers looked over at us in shock. Vroom dodged around the street lights until we'd passed the herd, and once we were back on the road he accelerated to a hundred. One minute later our bike was level with the Qualis at a red light. I got off and tapped the front window. Priyanka looked away, so I banged the glass with my palm.

She opened the window. 'What is it? We don't want to buy anything,' Priyanka said as if I was a roadside vendor.

'I'm an idiot,' I said.

'And?' Priyanka said.

Everyone in the Qualis rolled down their windows to look at me.

'I'm a moron. I'm stupid, insane and nuts. Please, I want us to be together again.'

'Oh really? What about the new man who needs respect?' Priyanka said.

'I didn't know what I was saying. What does one do with respect? I can't keep it in my pocket,' I said.

'So you want to keep me in your pocket?' Priyanka said.

'You're already in every pocket – of my life, my heart, my mind, my soul – please come back. Will you come back?' I said as the red light turned yellow.

'Hmm. Let's see . . .' Priyanka said.

'Priyanka, please answer fast.'

'I don't know. Let me think. Meet me at the next red light, OK? Let's go, Driver *ji*,' she said as the light turned green. The driver took off at full speed.

'What did she say?' Vroom said as I sat on the bike.

'She'll answer at the next red light. Let's go.'

There was a mini traffic jam at the next red light, so I got off the bike and ran past a few vehicles to reach the Qualis. I tapped the window again but Priyanka wasn't there.

'Where is she?' I asked the driver, who shrugged his shoulders at me.

I looked inside the Qualis. Radhika and Esha shrugged their shoulders, too; she wasn't in there.

Someone came up from behind and hugged me.

'I told you we didn't want to buy anything. Why are you bothering us?'

I turned around to look at Priyanka.

'I didn't know what I was saying at the water cooler,' I said.

'Shut up and hug me,' Priyanka said and opened her arms.

Our eyes met, and even though I wanted to say so much, our eyes did all the talking. I hugged her for a few seconds and then she kissed me. Our lips locked, and every passenger in the traffic jam looked on, enjoying the early morning spectacle. It was awkward to kiss in such a public setting, but I couldn't extract myself: after six months apart there was a lot of pent-up feeling. Vroom and everyone else from the Qualis surrounded us, and soon they began to clap and whistle, then all the vehicles on the road joined in, applauding with their horns. But I couldn't see them or hear them. All I could see was Priyanka, and all I could hear was my inner voice saying, 'Kiss her, kiss her and kiss her more.'

Chapter 38

WELL, GUYS, THAT'S HOW THAT NIGHT, and my story, ends. We couldn't know what, how or when things would happen, but that's what life's like: uncertain, screwed up at times, but still fun. However, let me tell you where we were one month after that night. Vroom and I started our website design company with the seed capital Bakshi had given us. We called it the Black Sheep Web Design Company. In a month, we had only managed to get one local order, but it helped us break even, or show a profit, depending on whether Vroom charged his cigarettes to the company or not. No international orders yet, but we shall see.

Esha gave up her modelling aspirations and continued to work at the call centre, but now she works for a non-governmental organization during the day. Her job is to fundraise from the corporate sector and I heard she's doing well. I guess male executives can't resist a hot woman asking for money for a good cause. Most of them are probably staring at her navel ring while they sign the cheque. Apart from that, Vroom's asked her out for a coffee on a semi-date – whatever that means – next week and I think she said yes.

Military Uncle got a visa for the US and went over to make amends with his son. He hasn't come back, so things must be working out. Radhika is fighting her divorce case with her husband and has moved in with Esha. She is also planning to visit her own parents for a while. Anuj has apologized, but Radhika is in no mood to relent yet.

Priyanka still works at Connexions, but in six months' time she plans to go to college for an accelerated one-year B.Ed. We decided that marriage is at least two years away. We meet often, but our first focus is her career. Her mother faked three heart attacks when Priyanka said no to Ganesh, but Priyanka yawned every single time until her mum gave up and closed the Ganesh file.

So it looks like things are working out. As for me as a person, I still feel the same for the most part. However, there is a difference. I used to feel I was a good-for-nothing non-achiever. But that's not true. After all, I helped save a lot of jobs at the call centre, I taught my boss a lesson, started my own company, was chosen over a big-catch Indian groom from California by a wonderful girl and now I've even written a whole book. This means that i) I can do whatever I really want, ii) God is always with me and iii) there is no such thing as a loser after all.

Epilogue

'Wow,' I SAID, 'SOME STORY THAT WAS.' She nodded, and took a sip of water from her bottle, holding it tight so it didn't spill in the moving train.

'Thank you,' I said, 'it made our night go by pretty quickly.'

I checked the time; it was close to 7 a.m. and our journey was almost over. Delhi was less than an hour away. The train was tearing through the night, and on the horizon I could see a streak of saffron light up the sky.

'So, did you like it?'

'Yes, it was fun. But it also made me think. I went through a similar phase to Shyam, at work and in my personal life. I wish I'd heard this story earlier – it might have made me do things differently, or at least would have made me feel less bad.'

'There you go. It's one of those rare stories that's fun but can help you as well. And that's why I am asking you to share it. Are you ready to turn it into a book?' she said, replacing the cap on the water bottle.

'I guess. It will take some time, though,' I said.

'Of course. And I will give you all the people's details. Feel free to contact them if you want. Through which character will you tell the story?'

'Shyam. Like I said, his story's a lot like mine. I can relate to him because I had similar problems – my own dark side.'

'Really? That's interesting,' she said. 'It's true, though, we all have a dark side – something we don't like, something that makes us angry and something we want to change about ourselves. The difference is how we choose to face it.'

I nodded. The train rocked in a soothing, gentle motion and we were silent until I spoke after a few minutes.

'Listen, sorry to say this, but there's one issue I think readers may have with this story.'

'What?'

'The conversation with God.'

She smiled.

'Where's the issue with that?' she said.

'Well, it's just that some people may not buy it. One has to present reality in a story. Readers always say, "Tell me what really happened." So in that context, how is God calling going to fit in?'

'Why? Don't you think that could happen?' she said, shifting in her seat. Her blanket moved, uncovering a book I hadn't noticed before.

'Well, I don't know. It obviously doesn't happen very often. I mean, things need to have a rational, scientific explanation.'

'Really? Does everything in life work that way?'

'I guess.'

'Well, let's see. You said you didn't know why, but you could really relate to Shyam. What's the scientific and rational explanation for that?'

I thought for a few moments, but I couldn't think of a suitable answer.

She saw me fidgeting and looked amused.

'Please try and understand,' I said. 'Calls from God don't happen often. How can I write about it?'

'OK, listen. I'm going to give you an alternative to God's phone call. A rational one, OK?' she said and put her bottle away.

'What alternative?' I said.

'Let's rewind a bit. So they drove into a pit and the Qualis was trapped, suspended by rods, right? Are you OK with that part?'

'Right. I can live with that,' I said.

'And then they felt the end was near. There was no hope in life, literally and figuratively. Agreed?'

'Agreed,' I said.

'OK,' she continued, 'so let's just say that at that moment Military Uncle spoke up saying, "I noticed you guys are in an unusual situation here, so I thought I should intervene and give you some advice."'

'That's exactly what God said,' I said.

'Correct. And from that point on, whatever God said, you can reword as if Military Uncle had said it – all the stuff about success, the inner call and all those other things.'

'Really? Is that what happened?' I said.

'No. I didn't say that. I just said you have the option to do that; so that everything appears more scientific, more rational. Do you understand my point?'

'Yes,' I said.

'So, you choose whichever version you want in the main story. It will, after all, be your story.'

I nodded.

'But can I ask you one question?'

'Sure,' I said.

'Which of the two is a better story?'

I thought for a second.

'The one with God in it,' I said.

'Just like life. Rational or not, life is better with God in it.'

I reflected on her words for a few minutes. She became silent and I looked at her face. She looked even lovelier in the light of dawn.

'Well, it looks like we're nearly in Delhi,' she said and looked out. There were no more fields, only the houses in Delhi's border villages.

'Yeah, the trip is over,' I said. 'Thanks for everything, er, let me guess, Esha, right?' I stood up to shake her hand.

'Esha? Why did you think I was her?'

'Because you're so good-looking.'

'Thanks.' She laughed. 'But sorry, I'm not Esha.'

'So? Priyanka?' I said.

'No.'

'Don't tell me, Radhika?'

'No, I'm not Radhika, either,' she said.

'Well then, who are you?'

She just smiled.

That's when it struck me. She was a girl, she knew the full story, but she wasn't Esha, Priyanka or Radhika. Which meant there was only one alternative left.

'So . . . that means . . . Oh my . . .' My whole body shook as I found it difficult to balance. Her face shone and our compartment was suddenly filled with bright sunlight.

I looked at her and she smiled. She had an open book next to her. It was the English translation of a holy text. My eyes focused on a few lines on the page that lay open:

Always think of Me, become My devotee, worship Me and offer your homage unto Me. Thus you will come to Me without fail. I promise you this because you are My very dear friend.

'What?' I said as I felt my head spin. Maybe my sleepless night was catching up on me. But she just smiled, raised her hand and placed it on my head.

'I just don't know what to say,' I said in the blinding light.

A sense of tiredness engulfed me and I closed my eyes.

When I opened them, the train had stopped and I knelt on the floor with my head down. The train was at Delhi station. The cacophony of porters, tea sellers and passengers rang in my ears. I slowly looked up at her seat, but she was gone.

'Sir, are you getting off on your own or do you need help?' A porter tapped my shoulder.

THE END

Acknowledgements

Just hang on a minute here, in case you're thinking this is just my book. It's never one person's book alone, and in my case, so many people supported me. In particular, I would like to thank:

Shinie Antony – for her scrutiny and standards when she gives me feedback. She is my mentor, guru and friend.

My call-centre cousins, sisters-in-law and friends – Ritika Sarin, Shweta Sarin, Akhil Sarin, Nikhil Sarin, Nithin and Jessica. Without you, this book would not exist. Thank you for helping me snoop around call centres at night, for providing information, stealing various training materials and arranging meetings with so many people.

One particular ex-boss. My life when I worked for him was living hell; it was probably the worst phase of my life. I used to wonder why it was happening to me. Now I know: without that experience I couldn't have written this book. Thank you, Mr Ex-boss, for making me suffer. On the same note, I want to thank all the women who rejected me – too many to name here. Without them I would not have known the pain of rejection.

My family – Anusha, Ishaan, Shyam, Ketan, Anand, Pia, Poonam, Rekha, Kalpana and Suri. My publishers Rupa & Co, an unpretentious, hardworking, high-quality and caring company that holds its own despite head-on competition with every other foreign publisher in town. Such companies make India proud. I specifically thank the people there who worked extra hard on my last book. Lastly, Mr Bill Gates and Microsoft for MS Word. I could not have written this without the software.

Q & A
Vikas Swarup

'THIS BRILLIANT STORY, AS COLOSSAL, VIBRANT AND CHAOTIC AS INDIA ITSELF . . . IS NOT TO BE MISSED'
Observer

How a penniless waiter from Mumbai became the biggest quiz-show winner in history . . .

Eighteen-year-old Ram Mohammad Thomas is in prison after answering twelve questions correctly on a TV quiz show to win one billion rupees. The producers have arrested him, convinced that he has cheated his way to victory. Twelve extraordinary events in street-kid Ram's life – how he was found in a dustbin by a priest; came to have three names; fooled a professional hitman; even fell in love – give him the crucial answers. In his warm-hearted tale lies all the comedy, tragedy, joy and pathos of modern India.

'A ROLLICKING READ AS WELL AS BEING A POLISHED, VARNISHED, FINISHED WORK OF IMPRESSIVE CRAFTSMANSHIP'
Hindustan Times

'*Q & A* IS A POIGNANT, FUNNY, RICH, BEAUTIFULLY WRITTEN NOVEL WITH AN UTTERLY ORIGINAL AND BRILLIANT STRUCTURE AT ITS HEART. A RARE JOY'
Meg Rosoff, author of *How I Live Now*

'SWARUP IS AN ACCOMPLISHED STORYTELLER'
Daily Mail

9780552772501

BLACK SWAN

A SELECTED LIST OF FINE WRITING
AVAILABLE FROM BLACK SWAN

77257 7	THE SUMMER PSYCHIC	Jessica Adams	£6.99
77115 5	BRICK LANE	Monica Ali	£7.99
99313 1	OF LOVE AND SHADOWS	Isabel Allende	£7.99
77243 7	CASE HISTORIES	Kate Atkinson	£7.99
77240 2	SAYONARA BAR	Susan Barker	£6.99
77269 0	THE FAMILY TREE	Carole Cadwalladr	£7.99
77358 1	THE PRINCE OF TIDES	Pat Conroy	£7.99
99954 7	SWIFT AS DESIRE	Laura Esquivel	£6.99
77182 1	THE TIGER BY THE RIVER	Ravi Shankar Etteth	£6.99
77285 2	RAKING THE ASHES	Anne Fine	£6.99
99847 8	WHAT WE DID ON OUR HOLIDAY	John Harding	£6.99
99848 6	CHOCOLAT	Joanne Harris	£6.99
77253 4	SKINNY DIP	Carl Hiaasen	£6.99
77109 0	THE FOURTH HAND	John Irving	£7.99
77216 X	EAT, DRINK AND BE MARRIED	Eve Makis	£6.99
77313 1	ONLY STRANGE PEOPLE GO TO CHURCH	Laura Marney	£6.99
99875 3	MAYBE THE MOON	Armistead Maupin	£7.99
99960 1	WHAT THE BODY REMEMBERS	Shauna Singh-Baldwin	£7.99
77250 X	Q & A	Vikas Swarup	£6.99
77310 8	HAVE LOVE WILL TRAVEL	Lucy Sweet	£6.99
99952 0	LIFE ISN'T ALL HA HA HEE HEE	Meera Syal	£6.99
77247 X	THE ROCK ORCHARD	Paula Wall	£6.99
99864 8	A DESERT IN BOHEMIA	Jill Paton Walsh	£6.99
77221 6	LONG GONE ANYBODY	Susannah Waters	£6.99
77309 3	A SAUCERFUL OF SECRETS	Jane Yardley	£6.99